The Trumpet Shall Sound

Also by Aline Templeton

Death is My Neighbour (Robert Hale, 1984)
Last Act of All (Constable, 1995)
Past Praying For (Constable, 1996)

THE TRUMPET SHALL SOUND

Aline Templeton

Constable · London

First published in Great Britain 1997 by Constable & Company Ltd
3 The Lanchesters, 162 Fulham Palace Road, London W6 9ER
Copyright © 1997 Aline Templeton
The right of Aline Templeton to be identified as the author
of this work has been asserted by her in accordance with
the Copyright, Designs and Patents Act 1988
ISBN 0 09 477590 7
Set in Palatino 10pt by SetSystems Ltd, Saffron Walden, Essex
Printed and bound in Great Britain by Hartnolls Ltd, Bodmin

A CIP catalogue record for this book
is available from the British Library

For JILL and ALASDAIR,
with my love and thanks
for countless kindnesses.

1

Smile, please.

Smile. Murmur polite inanities. Nod and wave to the people trying to catch your eye across the expanse of the Ramillies Concert Room. Smile again, in a parody of your usual charming vivacity, at the fat man whose tartan silk evening waistcoat is a valiant loser in the battle to contain the results of good living, and whose pudgy white hand has closed about your slim sun-browned arm. Smile, because he is a rich fat man who, if he chose, could come up with thousands of pounds in sponsorship for the orchestra, and if he will let smiles buy him, you must have more to spend. Smile, even if your head is aching and your nerves are so taut you could play them pizzicato.

Headaches and nerves, she had been brought up to believe, were self-indulgent. Penny Beaumont was a soldier's daughter, after all, an Army Brat: you learned early to be tough and bright and brave, whatever the cost. And if the cost was high – as it was tonight – you paid it uncomplainingly and smiled.

She thought she had forgotten what it felt like, this sense of impending disaster. Yet she had lived with it before, and it was as familiar as slipping your foot into an old pair of red dancing shoes which now gripped tight and wouldn't let go . . . But she mustn't think about that now.

She glanced about her. This was a beautiful room – the grand ballroom of the eighteenth-century house – with its painted ceiling of nymphs and shepherds in pastel shades and attitudes of rustic abandon, its satinwood carvings with their fluid, sensuous curves. The room itself was high and airy, but even so it was warm on this perfect July evening and the tall glass double doors giving on to the broad terrace had been thrown open.

Extricating herself gracefully from the clutch of Mammon, Penny wove her way towards cooler air through the milling interval crowd, reflected on three sides of the room in vast antique gilded mirrors.

These were of the period which to her suggested cotillions and quadrilles, and men with powdered hair strutting in gorgeous

7

brocades with their ladies in towering wigs and pannier dresses. Now there was an almost ghostly greyness in their depths, leaden and murky with age, pocked and pitted with blemishes like the liver spots on ancient hands.

She felt inexplicably disturbed tonight by that. It was an irrational reaction; the present scene was glittering enough, though men now were crow-sober in their dinner-suits, with only the occasional vivid tie or waistcoat or white tuxedo to hint at their peacock ancestry. But there was the pale gleam of women's bare shoulders, the sheen of satins and silks and the dazzle of their jewellery, and above, now as then, the sparkle from the prisms of the great chandeliers as they tinkled against each other in the movements of air with a tiny, fairy percussion inaudible above the rising bay of well-bred voices.

There wasn't a gilded chair in the place which wasn't graced by the rump of a gilded occupant. They might not all know much about music, but they all knew which was the man who did, and tonight Ramillies in Sussex was undoubtedly *the* place to be.

For the Sixth Hartington Festival, the Thursday opening Gala Concert at least was a spectacular success. Most of the audience would also have made sure of their seats for Jonah Dancey's performance, the closing event on Saturday night, but they wouldn't stick around for the string of lesser concerts, recitals and workshops in between. Anna Hartington couldn't give away tickets for those, and without three days of solid box-office, the Festival as a whole was going to be an expensive fiasco.

Anna herself, angular and severe in black, her mouse-brown hair confined in an unflattering French roll, was standing with an animated group while managing to create, Penny observed as she passed, a chilly psychic space about her. This was a natural talent. Penny, though a regular victim, could never work out how it was done.

Among the group she recognised a media baron and one of the minor royals; she caught the words 'extraordinarily impressive' and heard HRH murmur something regally complimentary about the Delius. As the promoter, organiser and financer of the whole Festival, Anna should have been thrilled by their evident delight tonight.

But then, it wasn't as simple as that, was it? It might be her Festival, but tonight wasn't her show.

As long as no one said too blatantly the wrong thing. There were

8

trails of metaphorical gunpowder everywhere tonight: one carelessly dropped inflammatory remark ... The headache that Penny wasn't prepared to acknowledge was getting worse, and she gained the outer air with some relief.

On the wide stone-flagged terrace beyond, urns on the parapet of the balustrade spilled pink geraniums. Beyond, at the bottom of the wide shallow steps, some of the famous white peacocks stalked about the lawns which rolled magnificently down to the long pond where the ornamental fountains were performing their own visual symphony in honour of the occasion.

The main house, its honey-coloured stone still warm in the afterglow of the fading light, was set at right angles, exquisite but disproportionately small in comparison with the grandeur of the ballroom wing. In the centre of the classic Queen Anne frontage a huge coat of arms was carved and incised beneath it 'Ramillies MDCCVI'.

'Penny, darling!' The woman who pounced to embrace her with air kisses on either cheek was repellently skeletal, in an outré black creation whose provenance one was clearly expected to recognise; she was further disfigured by diamonds ugly in their blatancy.

Penny sensed her own cream crêpe tunic and trousers being priced to the nearest 99p, but looking at her assailant took comfort in the reflection that whatever they said, you could after all be too rich and too thin.

'Isn't this a *triumph*?' the other continued, though whether this triumph were musical or merely social was not entirely clear. 'And this enchanting place, with those amazing peacocks! It's positively spooky how they always gather when there's a concert.'

'Spooky,' Penny echoed obligingly. You didn't disillusion the punters, even if it had more to do with scattered grain than intuition and you hated the birds anyway – ghostly creatures with snake heads, walking incongruously with the tortured delicacy of a butler with corns.

'It's just so perfect. I always say it seems impossible that Ramillies is only an hour from London.'

They always did say that, usually with some pride in this original thought. Penny resurrected her smile. No one would notice it was fraying around the edges.

'God bless Mr Bingham,' she said mechanically.

'Mr Bingham?' The woman looked blank.

Well, cheers! With unerring instinct she had managed to light on the one person in the place – probably in Britain, if not the world, the universe and space – who hadn't heard of Mr Bingham, hadn't read the story in every article about Ramillies and Eden Hartington, every *Hello*! feature. At the back of the blasted programme, come to that. Probably she couldn't read – or couldn't read anything except her bank-book. Penny could hardly bear it. Out it would all have to come again.

'That's the orchestra toast – "Mr Bingham, God bless him!" The man who built Ramillies.'

She waited hopefully for some sign of recognition, but the woman was looking at her with the mindless expectancy of an open-beaked fledgling.

She smothered a sigh. At least it was a set piece by now, which barely required conscious thought.

'It's a tragi-comedy, really; the death of a bourgeois dream. Successful merchant, not quite a gentleman; builds his expensive house and is comprehensively snubbed by the gentry. So, with a certain chutzpah, he calls it Ramillies after one of the Duke of Marlborough's victories and puts up the ducal arms to woo the nation's darling whose wife is best buddies with Queen Anne.

'The ballroom wing is where the Grand Ball was to be held when their Graces came, and he almost bankrupted himself in a sort of pathetic display of the trappings of social success.'

She felt her eyes irresistibly drawn to the other woman's diamonds, and averting them hastily, hurried on.

'They never came, of course. And anyway, Queen Anne and Duchess Sarah had a tiff, like the ordinary housewives they pretended to be, except that partly because of it Marlborough fell from power. And the gentry still snubbed Mr Bingham, only now they laughed at him as well, so there was never a Grand Ball after all.'

'Oh dear, poor vulgar little man! What happened to the house after that?'

Penny glanced back over her shoulder at the scene behind her, so elegant, so perfect. It was forbidding in its perfection, as if there could be no place within it for untidy enjoyment and love and laughter.

'It's had a rather sad history, in fact. No families with generations of children growing up here to love it – there have been too many owners for that. It ruined several – at least one killed himself – and after the war it sank into neglect and disrepair.

'But then there was the happy ending eventually, with darling Eden rescuing Ramillies from decay to be the perfect setting for his dream of a whole musical empire, and of course for this absolutely blissful festival. It seems – well, something of a hollow charade without him, doesn't it?'

Penny's smile was definitely unravelling now. 'Of course, I didn't know him.' She tried not to sound tart, but was aware that she had failed. 'Oh look,' she went on, with some relief, 'people are starting to drift back in. We'd better find our seats.'

She was thankful to sit down next to Anna who nodded, unsmiling, but said nothing; thankful at first that she could stop talking, stop making an effort, stop smiling – oh yes, yes, yes, stop smiling.

But when you had nothing to do except fold your hands, compose your features appropriately and listen to the music, you were at the mercy of your unquiet thoughts. Out they came, crawling and scrabbling and slithering from the dark corners of your mind to which you had banished them, and tonight you could not even sweep them away as imaginary with the broom of common sense.

Tonight she had seen the physical proof of the mental agony she had been obliged to witness but not permitted to share. The torn photograph, so nastily defaced: the baton . . . Her reaction to it, which she was trying so hard to ignore, was unpleasantly physical too.

Yet despite the flickering tongues of pain, like flashes of searing light darting through her head, and the foreboding which lay like a weight in the pit of her stomach, the music at last caught her up.

The great masses of sound were piling like thunderheads in a stormy sky, cloud upon towering cloud. She found that she was taking shallow breaths, as if the very air in the concert room had become oppressive.

Then, the electric shivering of the trumpets. They discharged the tension like lightning bolts striking the earth, once, again, and yet again until the final resolution, and afterwards, the almost shocking silence. When the applause came it was, she thought fancifully, like the pattering relief of rain, light at first then growing to the settled roar of the deluge.

The musicians, the cream of the Hartington Philharmonic Orchestra, lowered bows and set down instruments, shifting and shrugging to ease tired muscles. On the podium the conductor, a slim, immaculate figure in white tie and tails, turned to acknowledge the acclaim, the light from the chandelier overhead catching the sheen of sweat on his brow. He bowed deeply, face still set in lines of concentration, a lock of soft brown hair falling across his forehead as if by artistic calculation. He turned back, waving his players to their feet in a graceful, practised gesture.

Adam Beaumont. Tomorrow's maestro, consumed by his art. The new darling of the musical press. Her husband. For a moment all she could feel was an onrush of fierce pride.

Applauding along with the rest of the two hundred people, she studied this man she had been married to for two years now. Penny had given those years to supporting his genius and here was proof that her decision had been sound, whatever might have been her reasons for making it. She had contrived not even to think about these reasons for a long time now.

But tonight she was too worried and too much shaken for mental discipline. Tonight she was finding it impossible to forget that she had married Adam because – oh God, she should have buried the thought but it was too late now – because she couldn't have Dominic.

Dominic – shining, gifted, wicked Dominic – was dead, Dom who had been from the start too dear for her possession. He had always flown too near the sun and she had recognised transience, sensed doom and almost smelt the wax melting on his constructed wings. Perhaps it was the piquancy of foreboding which had dictated the strange exclusive intensity of their relationship; she had seen the death-spectre lurking in his face sometimes before the uppers had time to take effect when they were night-clubbing in London, and she had lived the exquisite agony of a knife-edge division between ecstasy and despair. If it hadn't been a random robbery and a bullet which finished him, it would have been something else, something even more ugly and cruel.

It was the golden, electric excitement he generated which was her own addiction; she had never needed drugs to get high. His company, and a couple of glasses of champagne when they could afford it, had taken her floating high above the workaday world. Like another pair of lovers they had mocked the warning of the midnight bell and she had been left – as somehow she had always known she must be – to discover that there was nothing left remarkable.

Like an addict, it had taken her a long time to recover, and like an addict she knew she could never expect to be wholly cured.

Adam had been wonderful then. He had been Dom's good friend, attracted and amused and appalled by him all at once, and his was the hand which had pulled her from the swamp of insane despair on to firmer emotional ground.

And eventually, she had come to love him. She loved him very much, because he was kind and clever and amusing and in his own way gilded (perhaps even more than Dom had been) by his extraordinary talent. The trouble was, she would never have considered reasons in the context of her crazy, all-consuming passion for Dominic, which even in sober recollection seemed like the sun to the farthing-candle of her warm, steadfast marriage.

So guilt stood always at her shoulder, and giving up her job in advertising to commit herself totally to Adam's needs was propitiation, a dowry of devotion she could feel she was bringing to their marriage. She had a generous heart as well as a proud spirit; this dedication was her private vow, as solemn as any she had made before the altar in the regimental chapel, dressed in cream silk and an heirloom Brussels veil, while her father in full dress uniform stood at her shoulder as if standing guarantor with a soldier's honour for her love and constancy.

There was certainly more than enough to keep her busy. Adam considered trivial everything except his music and her satisfaction came from seeing how dramatically he had flourished once freed from domestic cares. The importance of his genius was to her an article of faith: perfectly laundered shirts, travel arrangements, shrewdly calculated entertaining – she offered them all as reverently as plates of fruit laid before a Buddhist shrine.

With a shock of dismay, she saw with an onlooker's eye how thin he had become, gaunt almost, with the shadows under his cheekbones deeper than ever. If in her previous capacity she had been planning an advertising campaign for the Penny Beaumont Ministering Angel Service, she surely wouldn't be featuring him as the 'After' picture.

But whatever was wrong, it hadn't impaired his brilliance. In the seat in front, the *Musical Times* critic was applauding heartily, almost out of his seat in his enthusiasm. Almost, not quite: he wouldn't feel Adam deserved his standing ovation yet. That would come later, but it would never do to hail him maestro too early; you had to cover your back, award judicious praise and predict great things so that over the next year or so you could be proved right.

But there was no mistaking the audience reaction. Adam's début as conductor and musical director at the Hartington Festival had, indeed, been a triumph and following on the Middle East tour, and the bookings for the European tour in the autumn, and the rapidly rising sales of the Hartington Philharmonic recordings under his baton, Adam should be on the crest of a wave.

He wasn't. He was still unsmiling as he left the dais.

Since music was the only thing that mattered to him, what was it that could have gone so dreadfully wrong?

She had always known that when it came to his art, he travelled realms she could never hope to visit. Oh, she was very fond of music, naturally – but perhaps that said it all.

You would never say that Adam was fond of music. He was possessed by it, afflicted by it, even, like some awful disease for which there was no cure. Much of the time it didn't seem to make him happy. Sometimes he almost seemed to hate it.

'It's like Jacob and the Angel,' he had said to her once, in one of his rare attempts at explanation. 'Before it will yield up what you want, you have to wrestle with it almost to your own destruction.'

Then sometimes, when he had struggled to victory and felt the soul of the music in his grasp, she knew that he had fed on honeydew and drunk the milk of paradise, and recognised the state with searing envy, knowing that an angel with a fiery sword forever barred her own return.

But through him she still caught occasional glimpses of the glory. They had been a partnership, if an unequal one, in which he had taken her lovingly with him as far along the musical road as she was capable of going.

Then, a couple of weeks ago, he had gone on alone into some private hell he would not, or perhaps could not, discuss. He was coolly, courteously, implacably distant, and she didn't know what was wrong.

Anna was being difficult, of course. That was a bit like saying that apples were falling downwards out of trees today, and with her worries about the Festival she was indulging herself with a spell of unrelentingly impossible behaviour in every direction.

Anna was something of a specialist subject for Penny, who was a good listener, and her coffee pot seemed to act as a magnet for anyone at Ramillies wanting to let off steam, from Doreen Stone (who cleaned at Ramillies) to Adam himself. She knew of at least five people who could strangle the woman, smiling as they did

14

so, and she would go into court as a character witness for any of them.

Penny had tried to be charitable. 'She's just a woman who allowed her own life to be swallowed up in what she believed was her father's genius, and now even with a husband and a musical empire she feels she has nothing left,' she told Benedict Lousada, the lead trombone.

When he looked at her quizzically with his bright brown eyes and said, 'Well, you would know, wouldn't you?' she had been uncharacteristically short with him.

'That's entirely different. Adam's my husband, not my father, and being a conductor's wife and helping to promote the orchestra is a career every bit as rewarding as advertising. And anyway, Adam is – exceptional, whereas Eden, from all I've heard, was a charismatic, flamboyant conductor and a brilliant impresario, but not – not . . .'

'Profound,' Ben supplied. 'No, he wasn't profound, and Adam's something else, and you're in line for the first musical canonisation since St Cecilia. But his worst enemy couldn't accuse Eden of lacking style, and it was actually impossible to dislike the old bastard, somehow. Anna, on the other hand – ' And he had gone off again.

They had all learned to live with Anna's moods. The time would come when Adam would simply resign, but for the moment the Hartington Philharmonic was the perfect springboard. With the reputation he was building up, he would soon be getting invitations from other major orchestras – and they would pay him the sort of money he deserved instead of the pittance Anna allowed him. Not that he cared, but Penny sometimes thought wistfully that it would be nice not to worry about the dry-cleaning bills for his dress-suits.

Tonight was a step on the way, no doubt about that. The applause was still going on, unabated. Adam was returning to the podium, bowing, smiling now, a smile empty and meaningless as the grimace of the mouthpiece on a suit of armour, and Penny recognised chillingly that she knew as little as anyone else in this hall what were the thoughts behind that hollow smile.

At Penny's side Anna Hartington, clapping dutifully, shifted in her seat and gave a small, disapproving sniff.

'It's kind of them to feel they must give Adam so much encouragement,' she said, with an emphasis on the word 'kind' which indicated that it was spelt 'unnecessary'.

'Still, I'm glad they're prepared to be so indulgent. You've no idea how worried I was that it would prove little more than an insult to my father's memory.'

Bitch! Penny thought crisply, then bit her lip. The word danced before her eyes as she had seen it just before she came out, scrawled in savage red ink half a dozen times across one of the glossy publicity photographs of Anna herself, a photograph which had then been ripped in pieces and thrown down. But that was not the worst of it.

Four years before, Eden Hartington, in one of his characteristic charming gestures, had given Adam a baton, as one of the most promising of young conductors. This had been an important recognition, and Adam had treasured the gift – a pretty Victorian piece made of whalebone with an ebony handle secured by a silver band.

Now it lay on the floor of Adam's workroom, on top of the fragmented image of Anna's face, and it had been viciously snapped in two. She had stared at it, her skin creeping with a premonition she tried hard to convince herself was imagination. She had not felt like this since Dominic's death had brought her – in this one respect at least – relief.

When Penny arrived in the small concert hall created out of the old stables, the musicians, in their shirt-sleeves now, were packing away instruments and talking and laughing in that curious atmosphere which follows a successful concert, a mixture of relaxation and heightened excitement.

Adam too had taken off his tail-coat, loosened his white tie and wing-collar. He was laughing at something Ben Lousada had said.

'You were amazing,' Penny said, going over to give him a congratulatory hug. 'You were all amazing,' she added to Ben, including the other players in a generous sweep of her hand. 'I overheard HRH being very impressed. And Lady Beckwith's bosom was heaving so energetically with aesthetic excitement that I could hear the Beckwith pearls clattering.'

'A slight exaggeration, I feel sure,' Adam said, but he allowed himself to be amused and Penny's heart lifted. Perhaps, after all, she was over-dramatising. She knew all about pre-concert nerves, and he was bound to suffer more than usual before such a high-profile event. And the rest – well, even control-freaks like Adam had to throw temper tantrums sometimes, and she had let her imagination run crazy. She must remember she wasn't wild Penny Drayton-Smith any more, she was calm, sensible Penny Beaumont, the wife of a musician about to take his place on the world stage.

Then Anna came in. Without turning round, Penny could tell she was there by the sudden check in the hum of conversation, like the breath of an east wind chilling the air.

With her was Judy Freeman, her secretary and long-term friend, in a black jersey dress which clung unflatteringly to her rounded contours. Anna's husband Maurice Hicks was, as usual, a docile pace behind, and as they paused in the doorway in their sombre clothes they seemed somehow alien, threatening.

'Here comes the Mafia!' Penny heard the subversive comment of one young violinist while another, out of Anna's line of sight, took up his violin-case and swung it, machine-gun style. 'Duh-duh-duh-duh-duh!' he said, *sotto voce.*

The light went out of Adam's eyes and the shutters came down. The face he presented to Anna was politely blank.

Maurice, a mild and inoffensive man, said mildly, 'That was a very fine concert, Adam. Thank you.'

'Simply wonderful – wasn't it?' fluttered Judy in her tentative way.

Anna ignored them, much as one might ignore the meaningless buzz of a fly or the chirping of sparrows.

'Adam, I must speak to you about the seating for the orchestral part of Jonah Dancey's concert. I wasn't satisfied with your disposition of the sections tonight – I notice you've dropped the Hartington Variation with the violins and violas. You may have artistic discretion, but I'm sure Jonah, having performed under my father's baton, would be most unhappy at this departure. We must discuss it anyway.'

Adam said nothing, but his face was bleak and a muscle was jumping at the corner of his mouth.

'See me tomorrow at – when am I free. Judy?'

About them, people had fallen uncomfortably silent. Judy's soft round face flushed with the embarrassment of being brought into sudden prominence.

'Er – you've got a newspaper interview at nine o'clock. And you said to Jonah Dancey that you would check over the Lodge first thing, so he could arrive when he liked. We're waiting to hear from him when he's planning to get here – you'll want to be free to greet him.'

'His agent said they would probably lunch in London, so it shouldn't be till afternoon, but I'd rather have the Lodge off my mind. Half an hour for the reporter, maximum, and then the Lodge; I should certainly be finished there by ten. I'll see you here at quarter-past, Adam.'

'I can't give you long, I'm afraid.' His voice was icily controlled. 'I have a ten thirty rehearsal.'

'Quarter of an hour will be quite sufficient. We can look at the seating with the orchestra afterwards. And now I must get back to the reception. I take it you won't be long? HRH has very graciously expressed an interest in meeting you, and you can hardly appear like that.'

With a distasteful glance at his déshabille she swept out, followed by her meek entourage. After a prudent moment, a flautist derisively picked out the theme from *The Godfather* on the piccolo.

Penny felt her husband's humiliation as if the termagant lash of Anna's tongue had raised weals on her own flesh.

She put out her hand. 'Adam – ' but he had turned away blindly, shrugging on his tail-coat and heading for the cloakroom with his white tie in his hand.

Under Ben's sympathetic eye, Penny pulled herself together. The smile she pinned on was a little uncertain, but once she got out there with the paying public she would soon work it up to its usual wattage.

Penny left the reception ahead of her husband, hurrying back across the cobbled stable yard to their tiny house opposite the small concert hall. It was only two up, two down – a kitchen and sitting-room downstairs, a bedroom, bathroom and workroom for Adam created out of the old stables' loft-space – but it had a lot of character and Penny enjoyed the challenges of doll's-house living. She would have hated to live in the main house; it always seemed impersonal to her.

She had worked hard at her social duties tonight, but no one would miss her now and she could have supper ready for Adam when his up-market groupies could be persuaded to let him go.

Concert nights were always difficult. Adam refused to eat before-hand, then in the course of the evening gave himself the sort of workout most people perform wearing shorts and a singlet not white tie and tails. He would come back ravenous, but so high on adrenalin that it was difficult to eat and impossible to sleep.

Penny let herself in at the old half-door salvaged from one of the original horse-boxes, leaving the top half open to the velvety night air.

She had made the simple kitchen a pretty and welcoming room with old pine furniture and an eclectic collection of cheap and cheerful blue and white china. On the dresser stood a huge basket of flowers, picked from the bounty of the Ramillies gardens and dried last autumn.

Switching on the lamp that hung low over the small round table, she laid the places with care then fetched the platter she had made up that afternoon and left in the fridge along with a bottle of Australian Chardonnay. She had discovered that high-energy finger-food was best; Adam could be coaxed to nibble as he talked with slices of cheese and Continental sausage, bite-sized pastries or the big black kalamati olives which he loved, and the evening's tensions would gradually slip away.

Always before she had relished these intimate, peaceful, desultory conversations. They could go on far into the night, until the sound of the birds in the garden stirring from their sleep and the first pale streaks of dawn in the sky drove them to bed and drowsy love-making.

Tonight she had no appetite for it. Tonight she could only think longingly of soft pillows beneath her aching head and blessed oblivion.

What could they talk about, tonight? What sort of conversation could survive the crushing weight of thoughts they could not, or would not, share? It was their loving closeness – in every area except his music – that made their marriage work; if that went, she would be back in the mud and slime of loneliness and despair.

Perhaps if she kept everything absolutely normal, the cloud would pass. Perhaps if she could persuade Adam to sit down as usual and eat and talk, she could draw out the poison that was festering in his soul. Perhaps –

It was like the superstitious games you played as a child: if the blackbird doesn't fly away before I count to ten, Daddy won't be angry with me. If Adam eats a proper supper, this horrible apprehension will disappear. Oh, *grow up*, Penny Beaumont!

It was nearly midnight; surely they must all be going home soon.

She checked the table again, altered slightly the position of the blue jug full of summer flowers. A petal fell from an overblown pink rose, and she tidied it away. She had just lit the white candles in their blue glass holders when she heard Adam's footsteps on the cobbles outside.

As he appeared in the doorway, a trick of the light threw shadows on his face so that the brow and cheekbones were starkly accented and his eyes vanished into pools of darkness, like the eye-sockets of a skull.

A shiver seized Penny, but she said lightly, 'Darling! I thought you were never coming. What it is to be a star! How did you manage to escape from your fans without having your clothes torn off?'

Even to herself her voice sounded forced; too high, too bright.

His smile was dutiful, perfunctory. 'Sorry, Penny, I'm too tired for jokes. They were all very kind, I suppose. But all I really want is to get to bed.'

She should have smiled her acceptance and let him go. She knew that, but it was her anxiety that spoke.

'Oh, Adam, you know that's pointless! You'll just lie there, with everything going round and round in your head. And you haven't had anything to eat since lunch time.'

'I'm not hungry.'

'You never are, until you start eating. Look, it's all here . . . Have an olive, you know you like those – '

Please don't reject the food I have prepared for you, she was saying, but it was not his rejection of the food she was talking about.

His eyes went to the table, to the roses and the candles and the delicacies so temptingly displayed, and he sighed.

'Penny, you try too hard,' he said, more wearily than unkindly, and went out.

She heard his footsteps going up the short flight of stairs to the bedroom above. She dropped on to one of the waiting chairs, and sat, cold despite the heat of the night, as petals from the dying rose drifted down on to the despised feast on the table beside her.

2

At some level of consciousness Anna was aware that she was uncomfortable. Hot. Sticky. Tangled.

She was hot because she was running through sultry darkness, kicking out at creepers that snatched unseen at her bare pounding feet. Through arching trees above she caught a momentary glimpse of the moon, sickly pale.

She did not know what she was running from or running to, but a sense of urgency drove her on. In her arms, she was cradling something – a shape, a parcel – ill-defined but precious. She must protect it from ... whatever it was that menaced it. Something. Someone pursuing her, perhaps.

Ahead she could see a clearing, flooded by moonlight, and from it came the pure cold notes of a trumpet, shattering the heavy silence. The sound struck her like a blow, the cascade of notes like a douche of icy water, and she found herself shivering.

There were people among the trees; people moving almost at the periphery of her vision. Maurice, she thought, his face distorted by the flickering shadows to the image of a satyr. Judy, pale and staring, an unlikely nymph, with her round face sharpened to a foxy mask. Adam was there too, and Jonah, with hands out-stretched greedily, but she was not threatened by his attempted grasp.

She had reached the clearing now and the trumpet music was all about her, glittering and hard and passionless, the notes falling like hailstones on her naked shoulders, so that she shrank away.

A figure on the farther side, at the edge of the trees; that was the trumpeter, with the moonlight catching the bright metal of the instrument. It was all black and white and pearly, the trees and the sky and the silver notes, and the young man, gleaming in white from head to foot ...

A shroud. Shuddering, she saw the trumpet drop. The music ceased as he toppled back slowly; his face was revealed as he lay with sightless eyes staring up at the pallid moon.

And then it seemed that she turned in horror, away from the clearing and what lay there towards a light, glowing warm and

21

inviting in the distance. The burden she had carried suddenly was gone.

Aching with cold, she was drawn to this only promise of comfort, drawn down another arched, shadowy avenue. At the end of it, a golden corona encircled a little round gazebo, pillars under a dome ranged about a raised platform.

And he was there. With a lifting of her heart she ran towards him, her body weightless and her feet making no sound. It had all been a mistake, as she had known in her heart it must be.

He was a solid presence, sitting with his back to her on a low chair, and there was no mistaking the familiar head with its mane of white hair, the square shoulders.

She tried to call him. 'Papa!' But no voice would come and her steps had become ineffectual and slow, sinking into the soft ground and making no progress.

'Papa!' She tried again, with mounting desperation, but all around the smothering silence muffled her voice like black velvet.

And now he rose to go. He did not turn, stepping down from the light-bathed stage between the pillars at the back to be swallowed up in the impenetrable darkness of the wood beyond. She flung herself on the ground in an ecstasy of despair.

It was her own sobs that woke her. The curtains were closed but the room was not completely dark; she struggled to orientate herself as she sat up, blinking away the rags of the dream-mist that still clung about her and automatically wiping away the tears from her cheeks. It had been warm, but now she was bathed in sweat and chilly, as a breeze twitched the draperies at the open window.

In the twin bed opposite, Maurice slept neatly, as he did most things. His spectacles were primly folded away on his bedside table with their lenses uppermost so that they should not be scratched, beside the glass of water and the perennial book on some abstruse aspect of medieval music, and without their horn-rimmed frames his face looked much younger than his fifty years. He did not stir as she flung back her tangled sheet and got out of bed.

She cast a glance of irritation at his untroubled sleep, but hesitated. It was not that she had any scruples about waking him, but she was still shaken after her dream and not convinced that what she wanted was the cup of tea and the dutiful sympathy he would offer.

It was early morning, already growing light, and she crossed to the open window to look out. The greenish-pink backlighting of a summer dawn was throwing the trees into etched relief against the sky, and a light wind was ruffling the leaves. The glories of the Ramillies garden were still in heavy shadow, with only the silver foliage and pale blooms of the white border shimmering faintly. She could smell damp grass under heavy dew, and the perfume of the early yellow rose that climbed up the wall below.

It had been a long time since she dreamed of her father in this way. With her usual ruthless efficiency she had filled the aching cavity left by his death with the practical details of keeping his memory alive; the records, the biography, the scholarship fund, the archive, the Festival – above all the Festival. She clutched the thought to her like a talisman.

She was beginning to regain her composure, to feel more like herself again. Anna Hartington did not moon about gazing out of windows. She had better things to do.

Instinctively she reached for the properties which proclaimed that persona: the businesslike tailored dressing-gown in navy-blue silk which she girded about her spare form with a flourish, the gold man's watch from her bedside table to be buckled on by its wide crocodile-leather strap.

She glanced at the time. Half-past five! Well, she was awake now, and there were plenty of problems demanding her attention.

When she opened the bedroom door, Maurice sighed and turned over. It annoyed her, obscurely, that he was able to sleep through her unusual wakefulness, and she made no attempt to close the door gently.

The light from the east window illuminated her way across the gallery to the staircase, her slippered feet making little noise apart from the occasional creak from the wide oak floorboards.

It was a generous staircase, broad and with shallow treads, worn to a slight dip in the middle and highly polished. The square well of the hall was still in shadow, though the brass handles on the dark shape of the regency chest and the highly polished firedogs below the heavily carved chimney-piece gleamed brighter. In the days when money was no object Eden's interior designer had spared no effort or expense to achieve the grand country house look, to the point where you almost expected a ticket desk and stands with looped white cord.

Anna crossed the black and white tiles of the hall and the

vestibule then undid the bolts on the great double front doors and set them open. The sun was already coming up; on the lawns in front, three rabbits hopped away in alarm and a bird in the mulberry tree flew out with a noisy flurry, squawking its alarm.

As she so often did now, she went down the five steps on to the gravel turning-circle in front of the house where on a column in the middle stood the bust of her father, larger than life size, his fine aquiline profile turned so that he seemed to be looking out across his favourite view. She ran her fingers over the letters incised in the base: 'Eden Macaulay Hartington, musician. Born 1921.' She had never been able to bring herself to add the date of his death.

It was all very still, very peaceful now, apart from the birds singing in the trees and hedges around the garden. A faint mist veiled the meadow beyond the ha-ha, but the sun would soon burn that off.

Just so long as it stayed that way for the next two days. She cast a minatory glance at the sky in its profligate splendour, and with a sharp look at the blamelessly weed-free beds on either side of the front door, she once more climbed the steps, where urns with pink geraniums, like the ones on the ballroom terrace, flanked the front door. She noticed a faded bloom and stopped to nick it out.

She loved detail. It was rapidly taking on the character of an addiction; she used it to deaden the painful worries which, like spilled acid spreading, seemed increasingly to eat away at her comfort, her confidence, her self-esteem. High on the imperatives of organisation, she could escape the sense of failing her father which had soured her childhood and was returning once more. As keeper of the flame of his memory, she was afraid – very much afraid – of what else would be extinguished with it if that went out. Her whole life had been a quest for his approval and would be meaningless without it, even if it could be bestowed only from beyond the grave.

So she crammed her days with activity, and as she re-entered the house was thinking already of the tasks for the day ahead. A cup of tea first, then –

She paused at the door leading to the self-contained flat where Judy Freeman, her secretary-housekeeper, presumably lay in blameless slumber. If she woke her now, they could be well ahead with the paperwork by breakfast time.

It did not occur to her to wonder whether Judy would mind being wakened – poor Judy, as she called her, sometimes to her

24

face. She had every reason to be grateful for Hartington patronage, never having had what you could call a life of her own.

Anna pressed the buzzer by the door, waited for a few impatient moments, then pressed it again. She held it down for longer this time, until she heard the sounds of movement, and clumsy fumbling with the door.

Judy was clutching a pink-flowered wrapper round her, her fluffy fair hair tousled and her plump face puffy from sleep. Her brows were drawn together in a frown of confusion and anxiety, and for a disconcerting moment Anna was reminded of the face in her dream.

'Anna! What is it? Is something wrong?'

Anna laughed at her bewilderment. 'Wrong? Of course not! It's a lovely morning, I happened to wake up, and it just seemed foolish to waste the gift of some peaceful working time before the phone starts going as usual.

'But you look terrible! Off you go and stand under a shower. How long will it take you – half an hour? I'll go and have a cup of tea. Meet me in the kitchen at – say – quarter-past six?'

'All right. Yes. Fine.'

Judy was still speaking thickly, and Anna laughed again.

'My goodness, it's just as well we don't start work at this time every morning, isn't it?' she said heartily, heading for the kitchen as Judy, moving like a zombie, shut her door.

The kitchen was old-fashioned, with joiner-made cupboards and Formica work surfaces. Anna rarely cooked anything, and saw no need to spend money on it when Judy could manage perfectly well with the old gas cooker and the ancient Frigidaire. Maurice, who rather enjoyed turning his hand to cooking when Judy wasn't there, had insisted on a mixer and a microwave, but these were the only concessions to the second half of the twentieth century.

She switched on the electric kettle and brought over the old brown teapot to warm it, glancing impatiently at her watch. Ten to six. She didn't want to spend another twenty-five minutes alone, but Judy looked as if it would take her all her time to be ready to start work at six fifteen.

Anna was not by nature sensitive, and over the years had armoured herself against self-doubt, but this morning the panic and despair of her dream still lingered, like the mist on the meadow; with nothing to do except wait for the kettle to boil, she could not burn it off with comforting activity.

She had been ill-at-ease for some time now, but with practised skill had avoided any consideration of the wisdom of her actions. Now, with only her agitating thoughts for company, she found herself weakly wondering if, on this occasion, perhaps, it was possible that she might have gone too far?

That had been one of her father's phrases. 'Anna, you have Gone Too Far!' he would yell at her, his handsome, high-coloured face crimson and the photogenic mane of white hair tousled by his familiar gesture of irritation.

If you were wise, when the full force of a personality which habitually and effortlessly bullied anything up to seventy strong-willed musicians was turned upon you, you said, 'Yes, Papa,' as meekly as possible and got yourself out of the room.

But after that, he always put things right. Secure in his omnipotence, she had never had to live with the consequences of her behaviour, never had to apologise or patch up relationships. How she needed him now!

Maurice, of course, as she had always known, was useless. She had met him at a party given by the music publishers for whom he worked and had bulldozed him into marriage during a fit of pique when one of Eden's periodic amours had looked like turning into something more. It hadn't, and before long she was back with her father again, towing Maurice who seemed happy enough to abandon his career in exchange for being set up with a one-man business publishing books on rarefied aspects of medieval music, his only admitted passion.

Eden had been known to say trenchantly that it seemed to be against Maurice's principles to make a profit, but it was a price he and his daughter were prepared to pay for an accommodating husband who did not demur at Anna's retaining her father's surname.

Maurice fitted in with her life when he was needed and she left him otherwise to his own devices. She did not know if he had affairs; if he did, they were discreetly conducted. It had all suited Anna very well indeed.

But now, when she was beleaguered, what use was he? He seemed oblivious to the importance of her mission, indifferent to the lengthening list of problems she had encountered.

Even last year, there had been top performers begging to be included in the Festival programme; this year, those she chose to honour with an invitation had been capricious and she had been reduced to ruthless twisting of arms and calling in of favours.

Then there was Adam Beaumont, rapidly becoming a thorn in her flesh. She had chosen him because Eden had thought well of him, but now he had begun to make changes, play works by modern composers whom her father had despised, composers whom everyone knew were rubbish. And even if records by the Hartington Philharmonic were selling better than ever, her father's reputation wouldn't bail them out indefinitely. Indeed, it was amazing that the halo effect, which had to be the explanation for its continued success, had gone on for so long. And now Adam was being positively obstructive – aggressive, almost – about the sacrifices which must be made.

Even the domestic front was a headache, thanks to the absence of Doreen Stone, who had run the small army of cleaners needed at this time of year with such success in the past. She was totally taken up with that wastrel son of hers, a drug addict they were trying to rehabilitate – a waste of the country's money, if anything was. Anna had spelled out the consequences, of course, but all the stupid woman would say was that her son had to come first.

She sighed deeply. Judy had had to take on Doreen's job as well as her own, which meant Anna didn't have the support she was, in one of her favourite phrases, entitled to expect. So it was hardly surprising if, with so much on her mind, she might have done something which hadn't been – entirely wise. She shied away from the uglier name people might attach to it.

And speaking of Judy, it was high time she appeared. Anna had said quarter-past, and it was almost that now. In another couple of minutes she'd be late.

When Anna had left her, Judy closed the door of her flat and sagged against it for a moment, groaning.

What on earth time was it? The insistent buzzing of the doorbell had dragged her out of fathomless sleep, out of vivid dreams she could not now recall, but which still clouded her mind. She dug her knuckles into her eyes, like a sleepy child, then plodded obediently towards her tiny bathroom.

Her flat had been fashioned out of a series of cupboards and pantries 'below stairs', and, as someone had once said, if she went in for cat-swinging the poor beast would be unconscious before the first circuit was completed, but she was used to it now.

Through the open door of the bedroom she could see her rumpled bed with its frilly pink pillows looking warm and inviting. On the glass top of the chintz-draped table beside her bed, a rose-enamelled clock showed the time; a minute or two after quarter to six.

With returning awareness came rage. Bloody Anna! What right did she have to haul people out of bed at this hour to start another day which, if yesterday was anything to go by, would not finish until well after midnight? Perhaps Anna wasn't exhausted after merely throwing her weight around all day, but she might show a fraction of consideration for the slaves. Well, she might. In your dreams.

If she had any guts at all, she would walk out now, this minute, and leave Anna to run the show single-handed, the way she always claimed she did.

But then, she had never been brave, had she, she reflected with the easy self-contempt which had become a habit. She hadn't changed much from the timid thirteen-year-old orphan to whom Anna, dominant even at fourteen, had seemed the least of the terrifying evils of a girls' boarding school; because there was no one to love her, she believed herself unlovable. But she had no one to blame but herself for not striking out to make a real, risk-filled life instead of taking the easy option of working for nearly thirty years (could it possibly be as much as that?) for her best friend, whom she had never much liked.

Lately, though, things had changed, in more than one direction. Some were bad, like the atmosphere in Ramillies – last night, for instance, in the small hall it had been so hostile that she felt positively scared – and Anna's hysterical freneticism which, if she were prepared to be charitable, was the probable explanation for the early rising.

Other things, though, were good. Other things were very, very good, though she knew it was wrong and wicked to think that way. Oh yes, they were amazingly, ecstatically, fantastically good, and even if there could be no future, it had changed her for ever.

She had been prepared, drearily, to accept that her life was over when she hit forty, and that wasn't yesterday. How foolish and pathetic her attitude seemed now! She felt she was waking up from a lifelong sleep, revelling in sensations that before she had taught herself to believe existed only between the covers of the romances that she had bought and devoured secretly every month. Now these fictional passions – even as described in the heady *Beloved Sinner* which she had read four times – seemed tame compared to

28

the feelings she had not known she possessed, the great surging emotions which swept over you with the crash of Atlantic breakers, like hate and rage and jealousy.

And love. Her lips curved in a reminiscent smile as she turned on the shower and stepped under the hot, invigorating spray.

She had always been afraid of Anna, and now had greater reason. But things were changing, all sorts of things, and however frantic her reluctance, Anna would soon be forced to accept that she couldn't go on as if Eden's death had never happened. Judy ought to be sorry for her, but she wasn't.

With hindsight, Anna had been too calm when Eden died so dramatically of a heart attack as he was rehearsing the orchestra for a recording of Beethoven's Ninth. Her mourning had been brief, then she had thrown herself immediately into plans for the next Festival.

Judy herself had suffered shock with the falling from her firmament of that fixed star. For Anna it was a cataclysm. She had become her father's business manager and hostess at eighteen, after her mother's death; she had no life outside his.

Oh, but they had been such exciting years! Even if, like Judy, you were only an insignificant cog in the Hartington machine, it had been thrilling to be part of the orchestra's rise to fame, the move to Ramillies, that first pyrotechnic Festival.

But the mighty machine was running down now that Eden was no longer there to power it. The great names had come for him, and his musical acumen had filled out the programme with young players with a bright future. The competition for these slots, with their guarantee of prestige and press attention, was intense, and there had been four more very successful years – if you discounted that nasty business in the second summer. Even last year, nine months after his death, interest had still been running high and the Festival, under a guest conductor, had taken on the character almost of a memorial celebration of his life and work.

This year it was different.

Last year, after the final, emotional concert, she had dared to suggest to Anna that this might be a fitting moment to bring down the curtain on the Hartington Festival. It had been Eden's very personal creation; the suggestion that the Festival, too, should be laid to rest was prompted by vague images of tributes placed in Pharaohs' tombs, or the suttee of Hindu widows.

Judy had cowered under the onslaught.

'Are you out of your mind?' Anna had screamed, dark eyes flashing with the rage of unhealed loss. 'This is my father's monument, and you want to tear it down?

'How long would people remember him – the greatest conductor who ever lived? Look at the fuss they're making now over that Italian who hasn't the talent in his whole body that my father had in the tip of his little finger! His name, his music, his genius – without the Festival to keep his memory alive, all that would go. Is that what you want? Is it?'

Placatory as always, Judy stammered, 'No, Anna! No, no! How could you think such a thing? You know how I admired Eden – you know I've been with you every step of the way. It's just – well, I thought it might be hard for you to keep it up. He had such a reputation – so many contacts . . .'

'Of course he did. And that reputation will work for me now, and his contacts are my contacts too. I've lived with music all my life, and I know as much about it as anyone in the business.'

'I know you do.' Judy had soothed her. 'I'm sure you're right. The Festival must go on.'

But, Judy reflected as she reached for the shampoo, the real, unadmitted problem was that for all Anna's conscientiously acquired encyclopedic knowledge, she wasn't actually in the least musical. She could give you all the opus numbers, but she couldn't tell sharp from flat, never mind appreciate the finer points of interpretation.

Judy would never forget their school concerts. The March from *Scipio*, scraped out on the violin; *Für Elise* thumped on the piano; Mozart murdered on the clarinet; Anna took up instrument after instrument with an ardour which would, had the Fates been kinder, have propelled her to the top level of musical performance, only to abandon them after seeing the look of ill-concealed agony on her father's face.

As punchbag for her furious frustration, Judy was thankful when her friend abandoned all aspiration to performance and perfected instead the pretence of response to the music she heard. That, at least, was incapable of objective assessment, provided she read the right books and critics, and echoed her father.

But now Anna was out there on her own. It would be different if she'd consulted Adam, who was making a spectacular success out of everything he touched. And even if she wouldn't – which was perhaps, given her temperament, understandable – she could have

30

taken Maurice's advice, because he really was musical. But of course Anna never listened to him. The way Anna treated Maurice was –

Judy's lips tightened as she stepped out of the shower and began to towel her hair vigorously. She had spent too long in the bathroom. It would take her all her time to be dressed and in the kitchen by six fifteen, and Anna was a stickler for everyone else's punctuality.

3

Gary Stone opened the front door to the tiny house where he lived with his mother with infinite caution, wrinkling his nose at the familiar damp smell. It had been converted from storage cellars set into the wall of the kitchen yard at Ramillies, and the meagre windows cut into its frontage were permanently shadowed by the huge bulk of the ballroom wing.

He insinuated himself through the narrow gap which was all that was needed to allow him to pass; a stick-insect figure in a black T-shirt and distressed jeans bunched round his narrow waist by a studded belt. His head was shaved and on his neck a tattoo of a lightning bolt pierced by a black dagger was stark against the unhealthy pallor of his skin. Still, it was a well-shaped head, his dark eyes had the sort of eyelashes women buy in packets, and at least he was looking better than he had been a few weeks ago.

Gary paused in the hall to listen. A bicycle didn't have the speed or the style of the motor bike he really coveted, but the good part was it didn't rouse the neighbourhood when you came home. His mum had ears like a bat, and he didn't want her knowing he had been out all night. She'd barely let him out of her sight for the past six weeks, slept across the top of the stairs, more or less – well, it had been a bit heavy, and she'd been there for him, and he was grateful and all that, of course he was – but now she'd let up on him he didn't want the close-guard bit to start again. He had to rejoin the human race sometime, even she had to see that. It wasn't that he was scared of her, of course. He'd lay it on her straight when the time came, it was just – well, he didn't want to handle it right now.

He went into the dingy kitchen and switched on the electric kettle which was practically a museum piece. The green paint was blistered in places on the damp back wall, and he picked at it absently with one dirty fingernail as he waited for the water to boil. He wasn't hungry, but he could murder a cup of tea.

'Gary? Is that you, Gary?'

He groaned, but quietly. 'Yes. Mum, that's me. Who did you think it was – burglars come for your back numbers of *Cosmo*?'

'What sort of time do you call this?'

He heard her pattering barefoot down the narrow uncarpeted stairs and she came in, a small, plump figure in a lurid purple nightshirt, her improbably red hair standing up in spikes where she had lain on it and last night's mascara smudged round her eyes. Doreen Stone barely came up to his shoulder – and he was only five foot ten – but she could punch well above her weight and Gary was happier when she didn't.

He assumed an air of injured innocence which sat oddly with the silver rings through his ears and eyebrow and the glittering stud in the side of his nose.

'What're you getting on at me for? Just came down to make a cuppa, didn't I?'

'You lie the same way you breathe, Gary Stone.' Her voice, husky with nicotine and gin, was dispassionate. 'Been awake half the night, haven't I, working out what I was going to do to you when you got back.'

'Ought to be good, then,' he said cheekily. 'Going to put me over your knee, then, spank me for being a naughty boy?'

'Slap you round the chops, more like,' she retorted, but her eyes were anxiously scanning his face for tell-tale signs.

There is no indignation as powerful as the indignation of the delinquent wrongfully accused. And this time he was innocent – well, almost; you couldn't call a couple of drags on a joint drugs exactly, could you? – and he stared her down.

'Don't know what you're looking at me like that for. No wonder I get in trouble, if my own mum doesn't trust me. I told you, I'm clean! Would I be daft enough to go through all that again? Learned my lesson, OK?'

Doreen sighed. 'Oh, I'd like to believe you, don't think I wouldn't. I'd like to believe I was going to win the lottery next week and my next diet's going to give me a figure like Kate Moss.'

Gary was pouring strong tea into two mugs and she took one, sat

32

down at the kitchen table and took a cigarette from the pack which was lying there.

'Look,' she said, 'I gave up my job so I needn't let you out of my sight for the past six weeks. You know that.'

Not meeting her eyes, he mumbled something.

'Yeah, well, blackmail's an ugly word. But if you're planning on going down that road again, I'm ready to fight dirty.

'She's going to make me help over the next couple of days, but she's planning to kick us out of here the minute her stupid Festival is over. She'd have done it before, only I managed to string her along. Now she's going to sack me for spite. Anyway, we're out of here.'

She cast a disparaging look round at the stoneware sink with its wooden draining-board, the peeling Fablon on the work surfaces, and sighed. 'I know it's not much, Gary, but it was a roof over our heads, and now I'm back to square one.'

A slow painful flush mottled his face and his lips tightened. 'I could kill that snotty bitch.'

'That sort of talk won't help. Fair enough, in its way; house went with the job, and I wasn't doing the job. I'm only telling you this now because even if we're out in the street it was worth it to stop you dying in a cardboard box somewhere. But if you go back to it, like a dog to its vomit, it's all been for nothing. And apart from her it's been a good job, this.'

Her lip quivered, and she stubbed out the butt she had been puffing then lit up a second cigarette.

He squirmed uncomfortably. The rough side of his mother's tongue was in its way as reassuring as the rasping efforts of a cat grooming its kitten's fur. But he caught the glimpse of tears in her eyes and at this uncharacteristic and alarming sign of weakness he experienced a nasty moment of panic mingled with guilt.

Awkwardly he reached out to pat her work-worn hand.

'It wasn't like that, Mum, trust me. It was just a girl, that's all.'

'What sort of a girl? Where did you meet her?' Doreen was unappeased. There had been too many girls in the past – girls liked Gary – and all they ever did was cheer him on along the road to ruin.

'She's not some kind of slag, you know. She's cool – met her down the pub a couple of nights ago, first time you let me out on my own. She's got a job, she has.'

'A job?' Doreen's tired face brightened. 'A job she does for money? Well, that's a novelty!'

'Very funny, I don't think. She's clever – works for a newspaper. *And* she says doing drugs is for losers. You'd like her.'

'And whatever does she see in you?' His mother made the sharp comeback automatically, but some of the tension left her face. Girls who held down jobs – especially the kind where they expected you to do joined-up writing and read without moving your lips – had never before featured in Gary's life.

Perhaps they'd turned the corner. Perhaps she'd get another live-in job, with a decent house next time. Resident staff weren't two a penny, and Mr Hicks would give her a good reference even if Madam decided to put the knife in.

In spite of all the curved balls life had bowled her, she was a bone-deep optimist. She was singing 'Stand By Your Man' in her raunchy contralto as she went upstairs to coax the corroded showerhead in the bathroom to produce its customary trickle of hottish water.

Downstairs at the kitchen table with his second mug of tea, Gary sat scowling into space. A combination of guilt and impotence can be a powerful and dangerous cocktail.

The night after a concert the Beaumonts were in the habit of getting up late. With the Festival in progress, of course, the usual brunch in dressing-gowns at eleven o'clock was out of the question, but Penny had calculated they need not rise much before nine.

But Adam had hardly slept. Her own sleep had been very broken, and each time she surfaced she knew from his rigid stillness that he was awake too, lying turned away from her as if to exclude her from his thoughts. She was sure he was aware of her own wakefulness, but he did not speak even when at the blackest part of the night she softly murmured his name. After that she did not try again.

He grew restless at about half-past six and at seven, still without saying anything – though surely he didn't imagine she was asleep – got up as if he could bear it no longer and went into the bathroom.

She could hear the bath-taps running, and then the sound of the little transistor they kept in there, tuned to Radio Three. It was quarter to eight when he came back to the bedroom, looking very pale and with dark shadows under his eyes. But he was freshly shaven and she could smell the Floris Lime she had bought for him on her last trip to London.

'Did you manage to get any sleep at all?' she could not help asking him anxiously, but he said only, 'Oh, some, I suppose,' and went to the wardrobe at his side of the bed to fetch his clothes just as he always did, just as if nothing was wrong, or even different.

Penny got up and showered quickly, but when she came back to the bedroom he had gone. She could hear music through the wall from the sound-system in his workroom, turned up loud, and she recognised the orchestra's own highly acclaimed recording of Mahler's Ninth.

When she had dressed and tidied the room, she went out on to the pocket-handkerchief landing at the top of the stairs. The music was even louder here; with sudden decision she tapped on the door and not waiting for any response walked in.

Adam was sitting at his desk in front of the computer, where the screen in its rest position was silently showing a swirling pattern of exploding stars. He was not looking at it; he seemed to be staring out of the small Velux window above it, out at the cloudless blue sky and the gilded weathercock on its spire above the stable yard clock. There was no sign of the photograph or the snapped baton.

The Mahler was filling the room with music at a level that was almost brutal. Penny felt buffeted by the waves of sound as she crossed the room, picked up the remote control from the desk beside her husband and snapped it off. In the sudden silence she could feel her ears ringing.

'I'm just going downstairs to make breakfast,' she said, striving to appear cool, unemotional. 'If you don't want to tell me what's wrong, very well. I can't make you. I doubt if I've ever been able to make you do anything you didn't want to do. And just in case by any chance it interests you, what really hurts is that taking me into your confidence is one of the things you don't want to do.'

She swallowed hard and tipped her pointed chin in the air. 'But let's leave my personal feelings out of this. All I'm going to say is that if you go on starving yourself like this, you're going to collapse, and I fail to see how that can help anyone. Or punish anyone either, come to that, if that's what's at the bottom of it.'

He turned his head and looked at her at last. It was almost as if he was finding it difficult to bring her into clear focus, and when he spoke he sounded flat, as if all energy had been drained from him.

35

'Darling Pen, I'm sorry. I know I've been impossible to live with, but it's – I just can't . . .' His voice trailed away.

Then, with an obvious effort, he said, 'Look, I'll be down in two minutes. And I promise I'll eat – orange juice, toast, a nice cup of coffee. OK?' He produced the travesty of a smile.

He had made the suggestion as someone might offer an over-active child a plastic toy to distract it from the porcelain ornament it might smash. Penny felt patronised, and pride overcame her concern.

'Please don't force yourself to eat as a favour to me,' she said crisply. 'It will be there if you choose to come downstairs, but it's entirely up to you. You're a big boy now and I'm damn well not your keeper.'

She slammed the door and clattered down the stairs. Behind her, she heard the music start up again, as if in defiance, but a moment later it was turned off.

Down in the kitchen the sad remains of last night's supper were still on the table; she had had no heart to put them away, and now she felt cold anxiety seeping back, quenching her brief moment of rage.

For a moment tears prickled at the back of her eyes, but she blinked and sniffed them fiercely away. Whatever would the Colonel say?

It was a catch-phrase employed by Penny and her brother Neil in any moment of shaming weakness, its source one of their early schoolmistresses who, they were convinced, carried a torch for their impressively military father. The phrase was one she still used when she felt she must pull herself together, despite the fact that he had never seemed particularly satisfied with Penny even when she was as pulled together as the smocking on her Liberty party dress.

Grabbing a black plastic bag she briskly tipped in the wilting food and the tired flowers from the vase, and rammed it into the bin in the cupboard under the sink. She set open the top half of the back door, admitting a pool of sunshine. She determinedly pushed away the thought that the particular beauty of the morning seemed an almost calculated irony.

She boiled the kettle for coffee, spread the blue gingham cloth and set the table. She had just hacked a couple of slices from the brown wheaten loaf and put them in the toaster when she heard Adam's step on the stairs.

Immediately she busied herself afresh with preparations, fetching

36

butter from the fridge, wiping a sticky smear from the marmalade pot. She did not look up or speak when he opened the door.

Then she felt Adam put his arms round her waist and lay his face against her hair.

'I'm sorry, love.' He certainly sounded penitent enough. 'Believe me, I'm not doing this deliberately.'

She wanted to yield, to turn round into his embrace, but she steeled herself to stand passive within his grasp, staring straight ahead. There was a little brown spider crawling up the wall, she noticed inconsequentially.

'Doing what, Adam? I don't know what you're doing, or why you're doing it. I only know that I'm not prepared to let things go on like this any longer.'

In the long moment of silence that followed, the spider reached a crack up near the ceiling and disappeared into it. Then he gave a sigh, and she could feel it wrack his whole body.

'No,' he said, his voice low and ineffably sad. 'Well, they won't – go on like this, I mean. I had kept hoping I could do something, that I could find some way out. And God knows I've tried. I've thought of little else for days now, but it's no good. I'm helpless. There is simply nothing I can do.'

He dropped his arms from about her waist and going over to the table pulled out a chair and slumped into it, his legs outstretched and his head back against the wall.

Penny found she was shaking with nerves. Bad as uncertainty had been, she felt a deathly conviction that, after all, certainty would prove to be even worse.

The toast popped.

'Here you are,' she said. 'Eat that.'

Mechanically she put it on his plate, pressed the plunger in the coffee pot and filled the two cups.

Then she sat down in the chair opposite him and took a deep breath. 'Tell me about it,' she said.

Seated in the Hepplewhite chair behind the walnut desk in one corner of the Green Salon, Anna had regained her composure. She enjoyed using this room, particularly when she had to receive people; she wielded it, so to speak, with the same intimidating purpose as a mugger gently fingering the combat knife at his belt.

It was a room dauntingly perfect in its charmingly contrived domestic formality, used from time to time for small evening recitals. Behind the handsome Steinway, shrouded at the moment by a tailored dust cover to protect its rosewood case, the long windows looking out over the gardens in front were opulently draped in green damask with gold fringes; the same material featured on the walls above the oak panelling. In front of the creamy marble fireplace stood a vast arrangement of white flowers accented with sharp green foliage and on a pedestal at the far end of the room a Chinese vase held garden blooms in cream and shades of pink right through to deep crimson – evidence of Judy's artistic skills. Their rich heavy perfume spiced the air.

Eden Hartington's portrait above the fireplace dominated the room. It was the work of a famous painter, critically acclaimed as one of his finest pieces. He had caught Eden in a rare reflective mood and had suggested somehow – by the subtle droop of an eyelid, perhaps, or a line at the corner of the mouth – that here was a man who, though he had accomplished much, was perceptive enough to recognise, uneasily, that this 'much' was ultimately not quite enough.

Anna had never liked it, though Hartington himself had, which was why it still held pride of place. She would have preferred an image of Eden girt about with power, baton in hand, perhaps. She never defined her dislike, even to herself, but the heretical sugges-tion of uncertainty disturbed her. With her usual technique, she had trained herself not to see it even when she faced it across the room, as now.

Today, however, she was finding it extraordinarily difficult to put her foolish, early morning unease out of her mind. That niggling question – had she gone too far? – persisted, despite her employ-ment of the techniques which had always been successful before. She had worked hard with Judy in her poky, untidy office – it was a miracle that girl could ever find anything – until eight o'clock then she had breakfasted with Judy and Maurice, bathed and put on a black skirt with her favourite deep red linen jacket. She liked crimson; it was a confident colour.

But she still wasn't feeling confident, and what she needed now was something else to do. Picking up the file they had compiled for the day's programme, she set it neatly four-square in the middle of the immaculately tidy desk and picked up the schedule Judy had printed for her. She studied it briefly, then opening her file turned to the sheet headed 'Adam Beaumont'.

Taking her gold pen from the silver-gilt inkstand in front of her, she added a few more notes to her informal agenda for their meeting which she had dictated to Judy. She had no power to make him change musical policy, unfortunately, but it was her duty to Eden's public to see to it that ignoring her wishes was extremely uncomfortable.

The pretty French porcelain clock on the mantelpiece chimed melodiously and Anna looked up with a frown. That girl from the local paper – she should be here by now. She had allocated her precisely twenty-five minutes, which would leave her with five minutes to phone the caterers before she set off for the Lodge at nine thirty.

Of course, since she hadn't bothered to come on time, she could just be sent away again. In a happier world, these people knew their place as underlings who could be summoned with a finger and dismissed with a wave of the hand, but burning pride and high disdain must sadly yield to financial necessity, and the Festival needed every column inch it could get. Once, she wouldn't have contemplated bestowing her time on anyone below the rank of music correspondent to the quality nationals. Once, a regional rag wouldn't have had the impertinence to ask.

Anna got to her feet, feeling the unwelcome agitation come over her once more. She was staring bleakly out into the garden when the door opened at ten past nine.

From her angular height, Anna stared down incredulously at the child whom Judy was ushering in. It seemed impossible that she could be more than fourteen, this sharp-featured androgynous girl with crooked teeth, hair almost shaved to her head and a greyish complexion which spoke of poor nutrition and not enough fresh air. A set of ear-rings like staples marched down her ear and a stud glistened just below her lower lip with the effect of a pustule. Anna averted her eyes.

The creature might be small, but she was certainly not lacking in assurance. She tramped across the parquet floor and the Aubusson carpet in her workman's boots, her long rusty-black skirt and sagging grey T-shirt hanging on her insubstantial frame, and held out a hand which Anna felt, possibly unjustly, wasn't quite clean.

'I'm Liza Moxon, the *South East Express*.' Her voice was nasal; her accent had the hard edge of some industrial city.

Anna looked down at her, with the tightening of her lips which boded ill.

'How do you do?' she enunciated frigidly. 'You have kept me waiting for ten minutes, Miss Moxon, and – '

'Ms.' The word cut across sharply, like the buzzing of a hornet. 'I'm Ms Moxon. Or Liza, if you like. I'm not particular, except I don't answer to Miss.'

Judy, rooted to the spot in the doorway, gasped, but Anna frowned her away and she withdrew to her office leaving the door open, awaiting the explosion. Anna, displeased, could produce the sort of eruption that causes cold winters globally for the next three years.

But Anna didn't erupt. 'I, as you presumably know, am Anna Hartington,' she said, employing her distancing technique, which had once led Ben Lousada to claim that by comparison, the manner of the late Queen Mary was offensively familiar. 'You may call me Miss Hartington.'

The sharp grey eyes which had been assessing the room with a sort of professional malevolence, snapped back to her face.

'But you're not, are you? Miss Hartington? You're – ' she fished in her disreputable cloth bag for a spiral notebook and consulted it, 'Mrs Hicks, aren't you, by rights?'

Anna stiffened further. 'Hartington is the name I choose to use. In any case, this hardly seems relevant. My time is at a premium, so perhaps – '

'Not a very sexy name, Hicks, is it?' Having completed her survey of the room, the girl went to sit on a small tapestry-covered chair, apparently unimpressed by the grandeur of her surroundings and impervious to the deepening chill in the atmosphere.

'It's not something to which I have ever given any thought.' Fettered by the need for publicity, Anna could not afford to indulge herself by having this breath-takingly offensive creature removed. She allowed herself to say pointedly, 'Would you like us to sit down, or shall we just get this over as quickly as possible?'

From her perch the girl surveyed her thoughtfully, then disconcertingly scribbled something in her notebook.

The desire to set a solid barrier between them was subconscious, but Anna retreated behind the desk to open a drawer which could have been reached from the other side. She took out a neat pile of publicity brochures.

'I can only spare you another few minutes,' she said, attempting to remain in command of a conversation which was rapidly

40

spinning out of her control. 'Perhaps if I give you these, and some profiles of the soloists, it will save us both valuable time.'

She crossed the room and handed them to the girl, holding them by the furthermost corners as if afraid that by touching her some base contamination might result.

The reporter's thin lips flickered in what might almost have been a smile as she took the flimsies and flicked through them.

'Now, Jonah Dancey,' Anna continued. 'Of course, he is the star attraction of this year's Festival. Winner of six major international prizes – '

'You don't imagine I'm interested in this garbage, do you? I'm not the society editor, for chrissake!'

'I had hardly imagined you could be. In that case, perhaps you would be good enough to explain to me precisely what you think you are doing here, besides wasting my time?'

The girl got up. 'News,' she said tersely. 'That's all I'm interested in. The only thing that would drag me into this cruddy set-up is a good story. And there's a very good news story that no one's ever followed up about this Festival – the story about the unsolved killing.

'Whodunnit? That's what my readers want to know, and if I can find some of the answers for them, they're going to buy my paper, aren't they?'

Anna blanched, then blustered. 'I – I can't think what in the world you can be talking about.'

Liza Moxon sneered. 'Do me a favour! Forgotten, have you? Oh, I believe you. Not. A young man, good-looking, talented, setting out on a brilliant musical career and suddenly – whoops! There he is, dead, and somehow no one has ever bothered to work out why.'

Anna could not conceal her shock. 'But – but the police,' she stammered. 'They were satisfied that it was a break-in, a burglary that went badly wrong. He came back and surprised them, and they had a gun – '

'Yes, the police did say that, didn't they? I've read the reports too.' She laughed, a short ugly sound. 'But you see, that doesn't make a good story. What makes a good story is when there are lots of people like you – the fat-cats with the posh houses and the money and the flunkeys – all under suspicion of – '

She broke off. 'We-e-ell, got to be careful what I say, don't I?'

41

Anna's response was a natural reflex. 'This is entirely outrageous! Who is your editor? I warn you, I shall be phoning to complain.'

Moxon bared her little crooked teeth. 'Give you his number, shall I? His name's Emrys Clitheroe, and he's a fat slug. But he's a newsman, and if I bring him a scoop all the middle-class cows in the world screaming their heads off won't make a blind bit of difference.'

Anna was recovering. 'In that case,' she said silkily, 'I shall have to complain to your proprietor about you both. You will be surprised who I know. Would you care to give me his name? No? Oh well, it won't be hard to find out.'

She caught a flicker of alarm in the girl's eyes, and was swift to press home her advantage.

'You have hardly gone about your job in the best way to gain my co-operation. It seems to me that whoever is paying your wages should be told that you have a very great deal to learn, and that in my opinion you are most unlikely to learn it.

'And now you can get out of my house. I have the means to hand to have you thrown out unless you leave immediately.'

Moxon picked up her bag, stuffed in her pen and notebook and slung it over her shoulder.

'Try it,' she said. 'I'd get a real kick out of suing you. But you needn't get your knickers in a twist, I'm on my way. And I'm hardly dumb enough to believe you were about to dish the dirt if I said pretty please. Anyway, I've got plenty.'

She brushed past Anna on a wave of almost feral scent, something sweet and musky with a sharp sweaty tang.

Yielding to a playground impulse, Anna said, 'Perhaps you could manage to find a bath. It would make life so much pleasanter for anyone unfortunate enough to have to share a room with you.'

Liza Moxon was half-way through the door; she turned with an expression of such spite and venom that Anna physically recoiled.

'I wasn't planning to go easy on you anyway,' she snarled. 'But for that, you pay – in blood.'

Then she was gone, past a white-faced Judy peering from her office, her boots clattering on the black and white tiles of the hall.

Anna stared after her. Outside in the garden a peacock screamed its strange, unearthly cry, making her jump. Unconsciously, her hand went up to the collar of her deep red jacket and loosened it nervously. For some reason, the room seemed suddenly to have become unbearably hot.

42

4

When Adam stopped talking, a heavy silence fell.

Then Penny heard herself say, 'And with all that, you didn't feel you wanted to tell me?'

It was her sense of hurt and failure that spoke, and she could have bitten her tongue.

He winced, and she could read the thought: at a time like this, all the woman can think about is her own hurt feelings.

'No. No, sorry, darling,' she went on hastily. 'Forget I said that. It's the shock; it came out all wrong. I really meant, wouldn't it have helped to talk it over?'

'You do enough already,' he said tiredly. 'Sometimes I feel I'm a complete incompetent, relying on you for everything, and I simply didn't see the point in burdening you with this when there was nothing you could do about it anyway. I'm sorry if I did the wrong thing.'

'It doesn't matter now, honestly. But surely there's something – the Trustees – '

He shrugged. 'The Trustees are as furious as I am, but the way things were left there's nothing anyone can do, short of murdering the woman.'

His mirthless laugh indicated a joke, but Penny did not smile. His grey eyes were bleak, cold as a winter sea, giving no hint of the passion of rage and despair she knew he was feeling.

'It's my own fault,' he went on. 'When I was offered the job my head was in the clouds and artistic freedom was the only thing I made conditions about. So though it's politic to listen when Anna throws a fit of the vapours – she's the boss, after all – she can't sack me on artistic grounds. But at the time, may I be forgiven, I thought that money was only money, and as you know better than anyone, I've never been able to get myself worked up about it.'

He focused on her briefly. 'Sorry about that, love,' he said, putting his hand on hers.

Penny covered it gratefully with her own. 'We've done all right,' she said stoutly. 'And money isn't important, not really.'

His short laugh was bitter. 'You're talking petty cash. What Anna

43

has is financial control, and believe me, that's important. That gives her the power to bring everything to destruction in the pursuit of her ludicrous obsession. I'm – I'm desperate, Penny. Up against it.'

She felt again the sick lurch of panic. When he said destruction, it wasn't the collapse of a promising career he was talking about. His music wasn't his career, it was Adam himself, and Anna was destroying him as surely as if she were bringing down a sledge-hammer on his head.

And where would that leave them? What could she do with a husband whose mainspring was broken? There would be nothing left of Adam if you took his music away.

But that was foolish, defeatist thinking. Whatever would the Colonel say? Tilting her chin in her characteristic gesture she said stalwartly, 'Oh, surely – '

Just as she spoke, a figure passed in front of the little kitchen window and a head with a mop of tousled black hair appeared over the open half of the back door.

'The great man at breakfast! They've brought the papers – have you seen the reviews? I'm not sure if it's still OK for a mere first trombone to bum a cup of coffee?'

'Ben!' Penny's face brightened, as much with relief as anything else. She wasn't quite certain how she had been going to make the 'Oh, surely – ' sentence end in any cheerful or positive way. 'Come on in. Have you had breakfast, or do you want some?'

'We-ell, not exactly had breakfast. More sort of osmosed a mug of black Nescaff. Don't ask me why, but back there in the Players' Ghetto the only milk is always pale green with a blue furry layer on top.'

Penny poured him coffee and went to make more toast. Ben always seemed so terribly young, though he couldn't be much more than five years younger than herself. He was tall and energetic, with skin of that shade of creamy brown which suggests at least one exotic parent. He had only just joined the orchestra when Eden died, but now he was one of the best young trombonists in the country, the sort Anna should have been hiring to do recitals instead of dragging out and dusting down faded soloists of Eden Hartington's vintage.

Ben was full of the excellence of the reviews. Three of the quality nationals had given them space and he seemed to have memorised most of what they said, especially the bit about 'talented young Benedict Lousada in an impressive brass section'.

44

He was spreading butter thickly on his toast when at last Adam spoke, with an unconvincing attempt at lightness.

'I'm very grateful for such personal service on the reviews. Having a talking press-cutting service is an unexpected honour.'

Insouciant Ben might be, but he was not insensitive. His brows came together; he looked from one to the other with a frown.

'Oh, I was acting as message-boy really,' he explained. 'Jonah Dancey: Judy said to tell you he'd just phoned from London to say he and his agent should be here around three.' He paused, then said, 'I'm sorry, something's wrong, isn't it? I should have done my errand then gone, instead of barging in like this – ' He pushed his chair back, blundering to his feet.

'No, no, Ben, sit down,' Penny said automatically, but her eyes were on her husband.

There was a second's pause. Then, 'No, not at all, Ben,' Adam said. 'There's no need to go. I might as well tell you; I'll have to break the news to the orchestra at the half-past ten rehearsal. The European tour is off.'

'Off?' Ben stared at him in blank incomprehension. 'But surely – we have confirmed bookings all the way, don't we? And you said the ticket sales were spectacular!'

'We do, and they are. But we're going to have to withdraw – cancel the whole thing.'

'Withdraw? Adam, have you flipped? That's suicide – the end of the orchestra! You'll never work again! Nobody, but nobody *withdraws* from the Musikverein and the Concertgebouw – '

Adam's voice was very quiet, very flat. 'Do you think I don't know that? I've been pulling every string I can think of, but it's no use. The trouble is, getting the tour under way involves a considerable initial outlay – '

'Well, sure it does! That's hardly news, is it?' Ben spoke hotly, then flushed. 'Sorry, that was out of line. But why the problem, suddenly?'

'There isn't any money. It's all being swallowed up by this damned Festival. And before you say it, yes, I know we'll make a serious profit on the tour in the long run. But the bank has put its foot down; no more borrowing unless she kills the Festival. Which Anna won't consider.

'And again before you ask no, I have no financial or executive control over what she does. She is at liberty to go to hell in a handbasket, and take us all with her.'

45

His pallor had increased and he got to his feet. 'I'm sorry, I really can't talk about it any more at the moment. Will you excuse me?'

He went out of the back door. They watched in silence for a moment as he crossed the yard and disappeared from view. Then Penny's dark blue eyes met Ben's brown ones in wordless dismay.

Ben found his voice. 'Oh Jeez, I knew things were iffy – *maestoso* rather than *allegro vivace*, to coin a phrase. But this – '

'Is it – is it truly the end of his career, Ben?'

'Oh, get real! Of course not.' The pat reassurance tripped off his tongue, but seeing that she was not convinced he qualified it. 'Well, perhaps not, might be nearer it. He's, like, a b-i-g talent. But it's take-your-last-bow time for the orchestra – the Hartington Phil ain't never gonna work no more. We'll all be out of a job, and whatever anyone says, he'll carry the can.'

Fiddling with the knife on her plate, Penny said, 'I simply can't think what he's going to do now. He's got to see Anna in three-quarters of an hour to have his ear bent, and in the circumstances I don't know how he'll take it.'

'Perhaps he'll freak out. When someone as controlled as Adam loses it, they usually lose it good. She just might think again if someone put the frighteners on her.'

Penny shuddered. She didn't want to think of a snapped baton and a mutilated photograph; she hurried on.

'But what I don't understand is why people didn't want to come this year. They always did before.'

Ben considered. 'It's the first time I've been invited here to join the elect, but I did know someone who was here in the glory days, and what he said was what made me want to join the orchestra in the first place. As far as I can make out, Eden just simply threw brilliant bashes; it was a case of be there or be square and the Festival was one huge up-market rave. But Anna thinks no one will notice if she cuts corners.

'She could get hungry young musicians – like yours truly – but she doesn't know the right ones. So she's got has-beens, who are overcharging because she was desperate. And it must have cost her serious, but serious money to get flavour-of-the-month Jonah Dancey – that's probably what finally brought the roof in.'

'But she had to have a star if there was to be any Festival at all. Jonah's concert and the Gala last night are the only sell-outs.'

Ben sighed. 'True. No one's going to turn out for the drongoes,

46

that's for sure. So – what do you reckon? Where do we all go from here?'

Penny shrugged. 'From what I can make out, she's going to have trouble raising the wages for this year's Festival unless she renounces her ego-trip-by-proxy.'

Ben's lips tightened, his eyes hardened, and suddenly he looked a man not a boy, and an angry man at that. 'She really is one Grade A selfish cow, that woman. You'd think there must be some way of stopping her.'

'Well, if you think of it don't keep it to yourself, will you?'

He went, leaving her hopelessly surveying the table, yet again, with its debris of uneaten toast and cooling coffee, and trying not to hear the tiny, insidious whispers of warning inside her head.

Anna was feeling upset and even a little shaky when she left the house just after half-past nine to walk the half-mile to the Lodge, which stood in its own pretty grounds at the entrance to the main drive from the road.

She had carried out her threat of phoning the editor of the *South East Express* and to her fury the man, who seemed to be some sort of Welsh Bible fanatic, had laughed at her complaint.

He had said something about putting down the mighty, by which he seemed to mean her, then added, 'Great is the truth, and it shall prevail, as it says in the Good Book. Surely you're not afraid of the truth, Miss Hartington?'

'I have never,' she responded haughtily if disingenuously, 'been afraid of anything in my life.'

'Then you're a very foolish woman, isn't it?' he had said, and put the phone down on her.

Judy was even now, she trusted, tracking down the name of the proprietor, but the thought of a fresh picking-over of Dominic Leigh's death was another worry to add to her growing list.

The grounds, at least, were looking wonderful. Atkinson the head groundsman and his band of temporary helpers had done well, and everything was trim and tidy – apart from the figure she now spotted, stretched out on the front lawn. It was an insult to the landscape.

It looked like some sort of shambolic scarecrow toppled from its pole, but she recognised, with a sense of outrage, Doreen Stone's son, the drug addict.

'Excuse me!' Having been a lacerated victim of the press, there was some satisfaction in a bully's swagger. 'You! Stone! What exactly do you think you're doing?'

The youth raised himself on one elbow, squinting up at her in the sunshine.

'I think I'm sunbathing, aren't I?'

His tone was impertinent; she was further outraged.

'You have no right to be on the front lawns at all. It's quite enough having to tolerate your presence here – not that I'm planning to do that for much longer – but I don't expect to have to spend my time warning you away from the public areas.'

'Not good enough to breathe the same air, is that it?' Gary, angry in his turn, got up and was advancing belligerently when he heard his mother's agitated voice.

'Gary! Gary! Come here at once,' she called, as if he were seven years old again. 'I'm sorry, Miss Hartington. He didn't mean to be a nuisance. He's just coming inside.'

Anna stared with autocratic insolence at the boy who, contenting himself with a contemptuous sneer, slouched off.

'See he does, Mrs Stone. I'm too busy to want to waste my time calling the police, and I'm sure you don't want to have him in more trouble.'

She marched off down the drive leaving the other woman looking after her, her face carefully expressionless.

The little house, when she reached it, looked like an illustration for an 'English Idylls' calendar on this glorious morning. It was a classic lodge cottage, built of the same warm stone as the main house and deeply gabled, with a garden given privacy by shrubs all round and shade by an ancient over-arching chestnut tree. Its flowerbeds were planted out cottage-garden style with lupins and hollyhocks and old-fashioned roses, and a tiny rustic summerhouse occupied the south-facing corner of the lawn. There was something almost unsettling about such implacable tranquillity, as if the history of two centuries of birth and death, love and rage, passion and violence had been smothered by a relentless, imperturbable serenity.

Anna, however, was untroubled by any such reflection. She let herself in through the white wicker gate and after a critical look at the flawless garden detached the house key from its labelled ring in the keycase she always carried in her handbag and let herself into the cottage, leaving the door open to the summer air.

It was charming inside as well as out, with two small bedrooms and a larger sitting-room with four deep-set windows overlooking the garden, framed at this time of year by the tall hollyhocks and a climbing rose. Outside Festival week, it brought in a very useful income from holiday lets.

The sitting-room was pleasantly cool after the heat. She looked with some resentment at the baby grand piano set in one corner which had been brought across from the small concert hall in the stables. After his meeting last week to finalise the contract details with Dancey and his agent Larry Marcini, Adam had had to sign an agreement that a Steinway would be to hand for practice whenever the Muse dictated.

It was all part of Marcini's commercial logic; big stars are demanding: my client is demanding: therefore my client is a big star. In philosophical terms, that was a syllogism with an undistributed middle, but he didn't seem any more bothered by that than he was by the undistributed middle which bulged repellently over his trouser belt. He was a formidable negotiator, as Anna knew to her cost.

It had been an irritation to have to pander to Jonah; it seemed almost an insult to the whole tone of the Hartington Festival. If anyone had tried that sort of preciosity on Eden, he would have roared with laughter.

'Just jog across to the stables when the humour is on you, dear boy! The exercise will do you good – musicians spend too much time sitting on their fat backsides anyway.' She could almost hear him saying it, and Dancey, or whoever the temperamental artiste happened to be, would have laughed with him and agreed. But it wasn't like that now.

It wasn't just for this year, that was the problem. Despite the frightening cost, if Jonah was a yearly fixture, if she could get him to associate himself firmly with the Festival, it might, just might be saved. So should he demand to have everyone lined up and standing on their heads while they sang the Soldiers' Chorus from *Faust*, she would have to see to it.

She wasn't finding it easy, though, after all the years of giving orders and having them obeyed without question. She wasn't finding anything easy.

But it didn't help to stand around feeling sorry for herself. She went briskly to check the bedrooms, opening the window in the larger one which felt rather stuffy, then going through to the compact kitchen to make sure that Judy had carried out her instructions to put a welcoming bottle of champagne (non-vintage, of course) in the fridge. Bread, milk, butter, coffee, sugar and eggs; everything seemed to be in order.

Judy had done a vase of flowers for the sitting-room yesterday which she had left in the cool of the kitchen for Anna to set in place today. She filled a small plastic jug with water and topped it up, then lifted it carefully to carry it through.

It was all very peaceful. Outside the window she could hear a bumble bee buzzing heavily as it blundered among the lupins. Somewhere in the distance a dog barked, and the open front door creaked a little as it swung in a gentle draught. She set the vase down on the elegant Edwardian pedestal.

Anna suffered no premonition, experienced no sense that she was no longer alone in the house. She did not hear the door behind her edge a fraction wider open, or see the evil, snub-nosed muzzle of the old-fashioned pistol appear.

It was very nearly quarter to one when Judy came scurrying into the kitchen. Her round rosy face was unbecomingly flushed and tendrils of her fine fair hair were sticking sweatily to her forehead. She flung open the fridge door and grabbed up butter, cheese and pâté, sighing gratefully as the blast of chill air greeted her.

It would have been so much easier if they could eat with everyone else during the Festival. Despite the limited budget there were crisp fresh salads with cold meats and strawberries and cream for lunch – perfect on such a hot day. Judy had complimented the caterers, thinking what a treat it would be to sit down to a meal someone else had prepared for her.

But Anna didn't want to socialise with the hired help, as she saw them. They didn't like her much at the best of times and today the tension in the air had been positively oppressive. Even Judy had been greeted with black looks, so perhaps Anna was wise to insist on her normal domestic routine with meals on the table in the usual place at the usual time. Prepared by Judy, of course.

When the kitchen door opened behind her, Judy was just making a pot of coffee. Everything was, by some miracle, ready for Anna to sit down and eat, but it was Maurice who appeared. Judy looked round and smiled, a little tentatively.

He was a man of compact build and little more than medium

height, fractionally shorter than his wife. He was darkish and slimmish, of unmemorable appearance apart from the heavy horn-rimmed spectacles. The collar points of his blue cotton shirt were crisp, his grey flannels sharply creased. In the absence of Mrs Stone – whose way with the smoothing iron was so dashing as to be positively debonair – he had taken on his own and Anna's ironing, and the results were a marked improvement.

Maurice looked round the kitchen. 'No Anna?'

Judy looked at her watch. 'Five to one. According to her schedule she'll be here at one o'clock.'

'Five minutes' peace, then,' he said.

'Oh, Maurice!' She held out her arms and came across the room to him, holding up her face like a child to be kissed.

When he released her, it was to smile at her flushed face. 'You look all hot and bothered. Has it been a difficult morning?'

She pushed the sticky hair back from her forehead. 'It's just that hurrying in weather like this is so uncomfortable. Though everyone seems in a nasty mood today, have you noticed?'

He shook his head. 'I've been inside all morning, keeping out of the way. Amazingly enough, I haven't laid eyes on Anna since she went off to the Lodge. I even got a chance to start reading Professor Achron's manuscript – you remember I mentioned it, fascinating stuff on the history of Jewish music, starting with the disappearance of instrumental music in synagogues after the Diaspora . . .'

He talked on. His theme was not new, but love can lend interest to any tale, however often told, and Judy listened in dreamy contentment.

It was incredible to think that for so long she had seen Maurice as a puppet purchased by Anna and given life only by her manipulation. But then, of course, she herself had been Anna's rag-doll, dragged along as often as not by one leg with her head bumping in the gutter. Until three months ago.

The third of April. That date was written on her heart.

Anna – back from a difficult visit to the accountants in London. She – keeping well out of the way, gulping her latest romance (*Dangerous Desire*) in her tiny sitting-room whose wall adjoined Anna's much grander one. Maurice – his voice greeting his wife. Then Anna's voice, rising in temper.

Arguing? Surely not. Maurice was so docile, the orchestra had a rhyme about him, of which the only printable line was 'Anna had a little lamb.'

If they were, she didn't want to know. She switched on her television to muffle the sound (was there really a mass audience for documentaries on satanist encounter groups?), and went back to *Dangerous Desire*. It was only five minutes later – those five minutes which she now thought of as the last five minutes of her old life – that she heard a door slam, and above her head the stamping of feet going up the staircase. Anna. Maurice didn't stamp.

Then her own doorbell ringing. Anna, presumably, so had Maurice been stamping after all? Perhaps, she remembered thinking in a happy confusion of metaphors, the worm had not only turned nasty but had lost its temper and bitten her on the ankle.

But not Anna, Maurice – face aflame and with a deeper red mark on one cheek.

She, gasping foolish questions. He, apologetic, incoherent, contradictory; asking her to listen then supplying her refusal till, greatly daring, she actually laid her hand over his mouth and drew him into the little sitting-room, with the incongruous stridency from the television set ('nonetheless, it is *our right* . . .') until she snapped it off, and they were together in the silence.

It had poured out, confused justification and misery, like a dam whose breaching has loosened the silt and detritus of years. She had let him talk, until he began to apologise. And then she said, 'No.'

Such a simple word – only two letters – to have such enormous consequences. Because when she said it, he really looked at her, and she had looked at him, as if they were staring straight into each other's souls, just like Simon and Perdita in *Eternity and Beyond*.

'You too,' he had said softly. She would never forget the way he said it. 'You too,' and took her hand. It was the most romantic moment of her life.

And then, it seemed, they went speeding across bridges which burst into flame behind them.

It hadn't been a trivial row. Anna was planning on closing down Aubade, his publishing company; he had been so good, so honourable about that. But the Festival, she said, must continue, even if the orchestra was disbanded and Ramillies sold.

Not the best way, he had pointed out, to enshrine Eden's memory and she had raved, screamed, called names.

She could still picture how he had sat opposite her, in the little

52

pink Dralon buttoned chair, bowing his head in shame, shading his brow with his hands.

A eunuch, Anna had called him. He had found it hard to frame the word.

And then his own confession.

'I'm not a fool; I've always known she and Eden despised me. But somehow, this . . . I heard myself saying to her, "It's a pity you balked at incest. It's the only thing that would satisfy you."' Anna had slapped him, and fled.

Judy didn't blame him. She had sometimes thought it herself, in a mental whisper, of course.

And that was where it had all begun. They had so many things in common, she discovered happily; they were, she mused with the incredulous bliss of first love, almost uncannily two of a kind.

It had not been easy to find time together in the goldfish bowl that was Ramillies, though there had been a few precious nights when Anna had been away. But to Judy, beloved for the first time in her life, these crumbs of romance were a banquet; she feasted on their snatched moments, and dreamed intoxicating dreams.

With a start, she became aware of the passage of time.

'Good gracious, is that quarter-past one? Whatever's happened to Anna? It's not like her to run behind schedule on a day like this.'

Maurice tore himself away from Professor Achron's assessment of the influence of local folk-music on synagogal cantillation.

'How odd,' he said slowly. 'What was she doing after she'd given the cottage her seal of approval?'

'Handbagging Adam, I think, but her timetable's on her desk. I'll check.'

She came back a few minutes later with the printed sheet.

'Here we are. 10.15, Adam, then 10.30 checking the orchestral seating for the Dancey concert. 11.00, Simon Byrd's cello master class – we've got all of three paying customers for that, at the last count, so she was going to swell the numbers. She was coming back to the office after that, but by then I was with the caterers so I wouldn't have seen her anyway. She didn't pick up the phone messages, though, so it doesn't look as if she's been back at all.'

'I'll ring Adam.'

After a brief conversation, he put down the phone looking puzzled.

'Adam hasn't seen her. He was a bit short, but as far as I can make out she wasn't at the orchestra rehearsal, and the meeting didn't happen either.'

Judy was surprised. 'But she wouldn't have missed that! She was looking forward to it. It was quite clear – mainly from things she didn't say – that it was going to be her revenge because Adam did far too well last night. The reviews were the last straw. After that she kept adding little pinpricks to what she was going to say as she thought of them.'

An awkward silence fell. Then Maurice said, in a tone so casual that it screamed unease, 'I think I might just pop down to the cottage. In case she's fallen and twisted her ankle, or anything. You could shout your head off there and no one would hear you.'

Judy's response, too, sounded elaborately unconcerned. 'Yes, why not? I'll come down with you, shall I? Just in case.'

5

Clutching her story, Liza Moxon tapped on the door of the tobacco-haunted box that was Emrys Clitheroe's lair and went in.

Clitheroe overflowed, in body and spirit, not only his chair but the whole tiny room. He slouched over a desk swamped by a tidal wave of paper in a suit that seemed organically moulded to the contours of a form at once flabby and reptilian in the fluidity of its movements. His head turned on his curiously stringy neck and the lizard eyes flickered in her direction.

He was notoriously unpredictable, more or less as policy, and like all his staff Liza was nervous in his presence. There were sins you could commit just by breathing in this office, and much depended on whether Welsh chapel or hard-headed Yorkshire heredity were in the ascendant that day.

'Miss Hartington,' she said tentatively. 'Did she phone you?'

He picked up the cigarette burning in the huge ashtray on his desk and took a drag as he looked at her through narrowed eyes.

'Miss Hartington. Ah, yes. "A continual dropping on a rainy day and a contentious woman are alike," isn't it, Liza?' He snapped his fingers impatiently for the story.

Well, at least that was an indication. A Welsh day today, all biblical quotations and 'look yous', so everyone would be watching their language and burying the saucy pix. Sales figures must be up; they would be heavily reminded this was a family paper until the next dip, when Yorkshire would appear uppermost and he'd be demanding one of the local beauty queens strutting her stuff on page three with a turn of obscene phrase that would win even a compositor's admiration.

She handed it over. 'Just flying a kite,' she said, gnawing the edge of her nail as he read through it. The Hartington cow couldn't have threatened him with Lord Smethurst or she'd have heard all about it. Smethurst, the proprietor, was a self-made millionaire who seldom interfered but when he did, interfered to such purpose that Clitheroe always went ballistic. He would junk a good story out-of-hand to keep him off his back, so she surely wasn't going to warn him.

He was a man given to snap decisions; she had never known him hesitate so long over a piece.

He looked up at last, flicking the paper with a long yellowed fingernail. 'Evidence?'

Liza shrugged. 'Just someone I talked to about it, and the news files. Makes a good story, I reckoned.'

'Mmmm.' He scanned it again. 'It does, but ... My nose – ' he tapped that organ – 'tells me it's dodgy. Something you're not telling me?'

Liza managed not to gasp as the pale eyes beneath their leathery lids flickered up to her face. Superstitiously she crossed her fingers behind her back and met his gaze.

'Don't know what you mean,' she said.

The shrewd eyes narrowed further. 'Well now,' he said and with a darting movement shoved the paper in his hand straight on to the old-fashioned, murderous spike which he kept like a weapon at the side of his desk. He smiled a saurian smile.

'Bad luck, Liza. But then, that's life, *cariad*, isn't it?'

Oh, very Welsh. Very patronising too. Liza, dropping her eyes to veil the rage in them, was not the first *South East Express* reporter to find herself eyeing the spike with a wild temptation. She bit her lip as he went on.

'As I said to the grand lady herself, "Great is the truth, and it shall prevail." But as someone else said,' the singsong voice was silky now, 'what is truth? And that's what I like to know before I put something in my paper.'

55

Then the Welsh accent died and the voice became harsh and unforgiving. 'My reporters don't lie to me, not if they want to stay in a job. Now get back to your desk and get on with what you're paid to do, girl. And since you did this on the firm's time, you'll be working late tonight to make up.'

There was no wise reply. She left, shutting the door respectfully behind her, then went to turn the air blue in the subs' department.

The grounds were deserted as Judy drove Maurice the short distance down to the Lodge in one of the three Ramillies cars kept for common use. They were both tense; she tried to lighten the atmosphere.

'It's silly, really, isn't it, to be worried? Anna's probably got involved with some problem, hasn't realised the time . . .'

Maurice did not immediately reply. Then he said, 'It's just – oh, I don't know. I expect I'm being fanciful, with all this hot weather, but it's seemed to me these last few days that Ramillies is like a tinder-dry forest, that only needs the merest spark to set off some massive conflagration.'

She couldn't think of anything to say to that.

When they reached it the Lodge, in its hedge-sheltered seclusion, looked perfectly normal. On the side nearest the drive, a window stood open, floral curtains moving gently on a waft of air. The front door, when they tried it, was locked just as it should have been.

'Well, she's clearly not here or the door wouldn't be locked,' Judy said. 'Wherever can she have got to?'

Maurice shrugged, then walked round through the gap in the hedge at the side. Judy followed him; the garden and the little summerhouse were empty and peaceful in the noonday sun, and they walked round the house in the aimless manner of people who are not sure what to do next. Somewhere in the grounds a peacock began its jackass braying.

'Everything *seems* in order,' Maurice said. 'Do you suppose she's been here at all?'

'The window was open,' Judy pointed out. 'But then, perhaps I didn't close it. Yesterday was so hot, I had all the windows open when I was working here, and with all I had to think about I could have forgotten my head and never noticed.'

They were just turning away when she said suddenly, 'Oh, I know! I left a vase in the kitchen, because it was the coolest place.

Anna was going to put it on the table in the sitting-room today. Shall I – '

But Maurice, ahead of her, went back round to the sitting-room windows and stepping across the narrow flowerbed peered through one of them, cupping his hands round his eyes to get a better view.

He looked for too long, stood too still. Then he took a step back, awkwardly, and staggered offbalance.

'Maurice? Whatever – ' She went towards the window, but he prevented her.

'No, Judy. No, don't look. It's Anna – she's lying on the floor in there. I'm going round to climb in that window.'

He did not tell her what he had seen; he did not need to. Judy grabbed his arm as he set off, pulling him back.

'Don't,' she said. 'We must go and get someone, fetch a key – '

He demurred. 'But what if we could do something – help – ' But he did not believe it himself. 'Well, perhaps you're right. You go back, find Atkinson or someone, and I'll stay here.'

She forced him to look at her. 'She's dead, isn't she? Anna's dead.'

He broke from her grip, turning aside to put up a hand to cover his eyes. 'I – I think so. Oh God, yes, I think she's dead.'

'Then we don't take any chances,' she said fiercely. 'You don't go in alone to find the body, you don't stay here alone. The husband's always the first suspect, and if they find out about us – '

His features sharpened into anxiety and he said harshly, 'Us? They mustn't! How could they?'

'People can always find things out if they try hard enough.' She was impatient. 'Come on; someone may have seen us coming down. We mustn't be any longer than necessary, in case it looks suspicious.'

Atkinson was an old countryman, a Korean veteran who had lived long enough to have seen most things. At the door to the Lodge he put a restraining hand on Maurice's arm.

'Now, sir, just you wait here. No call for you to go upsetting yourself more than need be.'

Maurice shook him off with a fretful gesture. 'I'll be all right. Just open the door. If you can. The key may still be in the lock on the inside.'

But it wasn't. Atkinson fitted the spare key Judy had fetched for him in the lock without difficulty and they disappeared inside.

Time seemed to stand still. Up at the main house, the ripple of rumour was spreading fast, and a small crowd was beginning to gather, as more people came hurrying down the drive. Judy, light-headed with heat and tension, stood a little apart, speaking to no one.

When they came out at last, Atkinson was supporting Maurice who was moving like an old man. The gardener helped him to a low seat outside the front door, and he slumped into it then bent forward with his head in his hands. Atkinson himself was looking shaken and pale under his weathered complexion.

'But what's *happened*?' Judy heard a shrill voice cry, and realised it was her own.

'Some bastard's shot the poor lady,' Atkinson said, and sat down heavily beside the other man. 'Right through the head.'

'I'll tell you the trouble with him. He's past his sell-by date, that's his problem.'

It was early afternoon and the CID office in the police head-quarters at Fotheringham was quiet, with three of its five desks empty. Haunted by the ghosts of a thousand dead cigarettes, the room was hot and stuffy.

Diane Braithwaite, sitting at her desk with the file she was attempting to study erected in front of her in a manner as pointed as a barbed wire fence, groaned inwardly. She had tried to project a lack of interest so intense that he would be forced to shut up. Dream on! The man was impervious.

Abandoning the struggle she lowered her barricade, though that meant that she had to look at Brian Jenks, with his puffy cheeks and little piggy eyes and short blunt nose, and that silly scrubby moustache like a ginger kitchen scourer attached to his upper lip. Diane had contrived so far to have very little to do with the new detective constable – a former car salesman who was a recent recruit – but that little had suggested that finding the mind's construction in the face wasn't as tricky as they would have you believe.

It was seriously depressing. As she had said to another woman officer in the pub last week, just after Jenks had arrived, 'If it looks like a pig and talks like a pig, why let it join the force and undo years of painstaking PR?'

58

He was warming to his theme now. 'You got to let the dog see the rabbit, that's the point. Here we are, heading for the twenty-first century, and Peckham's idea of white-hot technology is the internal combustion engine.' He sniggered at his own wit.

'But joking apart, young talent needs to have its head, not a dead hand on the tiller.'

Diane eyed him dangerously. She was not tall, but she was squarely and solidly built. The fact that she was blonde from choice and believed in lipstick had led more than one rookie to take liberties which the strength of her uncompromising jawline should have warned him were unwise.

'Young talent,' she said slowly. 'That would be you, I take it, constable?'

Gratified by his success in gaining her reluctant attention, he came over to perch on the corner of her desk, his beefy thigh bulging in green polyester trousers. In the heat, sweat patches were appearing under the arms of his short-sleeved shirt and his powerful neck with its incipient roll of fat was glistening.

'Well, naturally, *sergeant*.' He managed to make the word sound suggestive. 'Young talent, that's me in a nutshell. You haven't really had the pleasure of getting to know me yet, have you? Bit of luck the others are out this afternoon. Gives us a chance to cosy up a bit.'

Diane closed her eyes briefly in weariness. Not that it was a problem; her father had been RSM to one of the more macho regiments, and from the age of six it had been her birthday treat to drill a troop of battle-hardened commandos. She had had better men than Jenks for breakfast on the way to her stripes.

But just sometimes she wondered if it was worth it, constantly finding yourself with the battle you had fought and won to be fought all over again. Surely her reputation as a tough, bright, able officer should have spared her the task of educating this lower form of life? But then, he had probably seen that reputation as a challenge. Once more, with feeling.

She smiled a steely smile. 'What a good idea. So – something tells me you're not much impressed with DS Peckham?'

'And you are?' His expression was knowing as his gaze flickered unpleasantly over her, lingering at the open neck of her cream linen tailored shirt.

Well, actually, she wasn't. Jack Peckham was within a year of retirement and his aim in life was to see that nothing rocked the boat until he could grab his pension and take the gangway to shore.

But then there were reasons for that. This last quiet posting was a transfer from the cutting edge in Manchester where he had spent most of his police career, after the bullet which had left him with a permanently damaged shoulder had missed his lung by a hair's breadth. You wouldn't go out looking for the action after that.

'He's a very experienced policeman,' she said coldly. And, she thought but didn't say, he's smart enough to make good promotions. His sergeants – including herself – were all sound officers, and his detective inspector, Will Canning, was on course for great things.

'That's official-speak for lost his touch, is it?' He smiled, raising a short upper lip to show nicotine-stained teeth. 'Well, their judgement does tend to go when they reach a certain age, doesn't it?'

He took out a cigarette from the pack in his top pocket, lit it and drew on it, exhaling the smoke unpleasantly close to her face. 'Especially when there's a pretty girl involved. Plenty of good lads to choose from here, I should have thought – wonder what made him pick you, *sergeant*?'

Coolly she surveyed him; the leering expression, the cocksure posturing of the natural bully. She could report him, of course, and blight his career before it began. She could give him a tongue-lashing, for which she had a talent that was justly famous. But this seemed to call for more direct action.

Lying in the pen-tray on her desk was a small, needle-sharp letter-opener, souvenir of a holiday in Spain. In one swift, decisive movement she swept it up and jabbed it neatly the merest fraction of an inch into the fleshiest part of that bulging thigh.

It did not even tear the cloth, but he rose like a rocket with a bellow of shock and pain and an obscenity.

'Christ, you bitch, what did you do that for?'

She set it down again and smiled at him sweetly. 'To show you who's boss, Jenks. And you can add "ma'am" when you're calling me a bitch. Let's not forget the little courtesies.

'Did none of the lads warn you that I bite? Oh, they really are too bad. They rather enjoy watching the fall-out, that's the trouble. They like to think I'm the toughest woman on the strength, though I'm a pussycat when I get my own way.

'Of course, it's assault, isn't it? But naturally I would register a formal complaint about sexual harassment, and tart it up a bit with insubordination and gross disloyalty. Wouldn't look good on a new DC's file; find yourself back on the beat, I shouldn't wonder.'

Braithwaite's bright blue eyes glinted like quartz. 'And of course, all the lads would think it was a helluva good laugh. It's the way I tell 'em.'

Brian Jenks stood bemused, regarding her with an expression of animal bewilderment and rubbing his thigh.

'I don't believe this,' he said at last.

'You'd better believe it, Jenks. But now I've made my point – you should forgive the pun – I'll make a pact with you. I'll forget this whole thing if you will. Provided, that is, you start treating me as just another superior officer who will have a great deal to say about your future in the CID. If you have one.

'And now, constable, get back to your desk, get on with your work and stop wasting my time.'

His face burning with impotent rage he turned slowly, then was brought up short by a parade-ground bark.

'Say "Yes, ma'am" when I give you an order.'

His neck muscles bulged as he clenched his jaw, but he mumbled the formula without looking round, went back to his desk and apparently became engrossed in paperwork. The atmosphere was toxic with hostility, but if that was the price she had to pay, so be it. She had done her fair share of seething helplessly, and now it was his turn. Part of the learning process.

It was about quarter of an hour later that Peckham himself opened the door. He was a white-haired man of slight build, not tall for a policeman of his vintage, and he had the drawn, wearied look of someone who suffers constant pain.

But he wasn't stupid. Sensing the tension in the room, he looked sharply from Diane to the studiously bent head of DC Jenks, then back to Diane again.

She met his look blandly.

'Good afternoon, sir.'

'Afternoon, sergeant, Jenks.'

Brian, his colour still heightened, muttered something in reply.

Peckham registered but did not confront the problem, saying only, 'Job for you, Diane. A call's just in that I want you to check out. Ramillies – you know the music place?'

'Yes, of course. What's happened?'

61

'Fatality. We haven't any details, but it seems to be Hartington's daughter.'

'Anna Hartington?' Diane was startled. Ramillies and its owner had a high profile locally. 'Is it an accident?'

'Definitely dead, it seems, but nothing else has come through yet. Take someone with you and get over there. I'll phone Canning if need be, but I don't want to drag him from his day off if she's tripped down a flight of stairs and broken her neck. And I needn't remind you, Diane, need I? Party manners. People like that can make trouble.'

There was a muffled snort from Jenks and Peckham turned. His eyes, under the heavy lids, were still sharp and there was an edge to his voice as he said, 'You'd better go along with Braithwaite. It's about time she got you house-trained.'

Not precisely what she would have chosen at this juncture. Diane did not look at Brian Jenks as she grabbed her bag from the desk and followed her boss from the room, but he was hard on her heels.

As they walked through the car-park, Diane scrabbled in her bag for her car-key. To her annoyance, it did not immediately come to hand. Her capacious shoulder-bag served as filing-cabinet, vanity case and even wardrobe; she had to grope among lipsticks, note-books, old receipts and the spare pair of tights she always carried, sensing rather than seeing her companion's sneer.

Provocatively, he dangled his own keys. 'Why don't we just take my car, *ma'am*? I've got the key right here.'

Successful at last, Diane said coolly, 'So have I. And I always drive myself.'

She was a good driver, and she liked the sense of control. She had suffered too often from men who seemed to feel that taking corners too fast was some sort of proof of virility, and she really didn't want to go through that routine again.

Jenks got in with an ill grace, every angle of his body expressing rigid resentment. With an impatient sideways glance at him, Diane drove off.

It was a pity this had been forced on them. He needed time to lick his wounds, and it would be better if they could have kept out of each other's way for a day or two. But there was no room for personal feuds in a police team, so he would just have to learn to be professional.

'How much do you know about Ramillies, Brian?'

She had spoken exactly as she would to anyone else, but he responded sulkily.

'Never heard of it.'

'In that case, I'd better fill you in on the set-up before we get there.'

She gave him a brisk summary of what she knew about the late Eden Hartington's empire, but he was unresponsive. She wondered in exasperation if he was even listening; she almost expected him to put his fingers in his ears like a naughty child. Bearing grudges wasn't her style, but he was definitely pushing his luck. Still, they hadn't far to go and when they arrived there would be other things to think about.

The approach to Ramillies was still magnificent, even after three centuries had transformed the toll-road which ran past its gates into a modern highway. A stand of broad-leaved trees obstructed any distant prospect so that on rounding a corner the golden elegance of the house in all the glory of its grounds and gardens burst upon the eye as if by theatrical contrivance. It was magnificent, without doubt, Diane acknowledged, but the sort of place you would hate to live in because you would know you were always falling short of its standards.

Surprised out of his sullenness, Brian exclaimed, 'Strewth! Must take wads of the folding stuff to keep this going.'

It was the obvious remark, but Diane said thoughtfully, 'Yes, you're right there,' and filed it away for future consideration if that should prove to be necessary.

As they turned into the drive, it was immediately clear that what had happened had not taken place at the big house but here at this dinky little lodge cottage, just beside the road.

The patrol car was there, beside another car and a Land Rover parked haphazardly, as if their drivers had simply abandoned them. Half a dozen people clustered at the gate turned their heads as the car drove in, and on their faces Diane could read not only shock but a sort of horrified unease.

Not a fall downstairs, then. Probably not even suicide. Her stomach lurched.

She had served her time with Traffic and inevitably had seen the ugliest forms of death in the intimate entanglement of machinery and human flesh. She had been called to burning homes, and seen the charred and unrecognisable bodies taken out. Then there had been the kids dead from their own folly, because they believed they were immortal and the rules didn't apply. But working here in this pleasant, prosperous corner of the English countryside she had never seen death inflicted with callous calculation by another's hand.

One of the uniformed men was at the patrol car, talking urgently into his radio telephone. He broke off when he saw them and hurried across. He was pale and in a state of obvious anxiety, but there was a sense of something more, a sort of queasy excitement, which made the situation as clear to her as if the word had been written across his forehead. Murder.

6

Liza Moxon was sitting sulkily at her computer terminal. Afternoon torpor had descended on the main newspaper office; a couple of other reporters were gossiping casually, but apart from that the only sound was the fast, ill-tempered rattling of Liza's keyboard.

She was typing up an article from her hieroglyphic notes ('Councillor Ashford (Con) expressed himself surprised and disappointed at the wild and totally unfounded allegations made by Councillor Stitt (Lab) . . .') but her mind was far from the tribal strife of Danby Town Council.

Don't get mad, get even, was one of her maxims, and her eyes narrowed thinking of Clitheroe. She'd underestimated him: she'd have to be sharper when she needed to lie to him in future.

When the phone on her desk rang, she finished her sentence before picking it up.

It was Clitheroe's secretary, Mrs Babington, a middle-aged lady who didn't seem to have a Christian name and who was of such excessive gentility it was hard to believe she could tolerate his coarseness for ten minutes, far less the twenty-two years she had clocked up in his service.

'Liza, dear, I wonder if you could possibly just pop into Mr Clitheroe's office? He's anxious to have a little word with you. I'm sure you're busy, but if you could spare the time he'd be awfully grateful.'

'Get my ass in there, I suppose you mean,' Liza said offensively, putting the phone down.

There was nothing to stop Emrys from opening the door of his office there in the corner of the big room and just bawling, apart from the fact that he'd have to get off his spreading butt to do it. It bugged her, too, that he'd phoned his secretary to phone her instead of doing it direct; that was another little power-play.

Well, she was in no hurry to make it to the next in the Clitheroe series of lectures on newspaper ethics. She rounded off the adventures of Councillor Ashford and his merry chums and pressed 'Save' before she got to her feet, just as the door of Mrs Babington's tiny glass cubicle opened and her agitated rabbity face peeped out.

Her expression cleared as she saw Liza making her way across the room. 'Oh, I'm so glad to see you're on your way, dear. He was getting just a little fretful.'

As bad as that? Oops. Liza straightened her slight shoulders as she knocked on the door and went in.

He said, 'What the hell kept you?' but his voice was surprisingly mild and there was just a hint of Yorkshire. Usually for one of his set pieces he chose Welsh.

'I've got a job for you.'

Her quick eyes noticed that on the desk in front of him was her piece on Ramillies, the one he had spiked. It had been resurrected, clearly, its torn edges smoothed carefully together, and her heart lifted in triumph. *Yes!*

'Oh, don't you go getting carried away, lass. I'm holding this meantime; I haven't changed my mind – yet. But one of my snouts in the police force says there's been a bit of bother up at Ramillies this morning. It's not confirmed, but he thinks someone's shot the Hartington woman.'

Her eyes rounded in surprise and speculation and her body positively quivered, like a whippet on a leash at the sight of a hare. '*Shot* her?'

It never crossed her mind that there might be conventional noises to make. She had an almost freakish lack of humanity which would make her a relentless newshound, but there was distaste in Clitheroe's face as he looked at her.

'Wasn't you, was it? OK, OK, that was a joke. I hope. Now, I want you over there. Quietly; don't make a fuss, don't tell anybody. Pick up whatever you can, and if it's good enough I'll give you a by-line on the front page. And I want it quick. We won't scoop it, of course, but if your piece is sharp enough I might manage to flog it on to one of the nationals.'

She fixed him with a gaze like a gimlet and stood her ground. 'What's in it for me?'

He bellowed then. 'No job's what's in it for you, if you're not out of here in ten seconds.'

Then, as she turned to slouch out, he added, 'If they buy it, maybe a bonus. Small. If it's good enough.'

She swung round to favour him with her narrow, uneven smile.

'Trust me,' she said. 'I've got an inside track.'

With a brave show of confidence, Diane led the way into the little house. She could have done with one of the usual team at her back, ready to exchange a supportive groan or grimace of unease. Instead she had Jenks, watching beadily, no doubt, for any sign of feminine weakness.

As they went into the little hall she recognised, with a pang of revulsion, the sweetish, remembered smell of blood on the hot still air and switched automatically to breathing through her mouth. The other man from the patrol car, a sergeant whom she did not know, was hovering by the open sitting-room door, though he had been wise enough to stay outside.

'Through here,' he said. 'No one's been in, except the two who found her – the husband and the gardener. I've got them waiting in the garden.'

'Good, good,' she said absently, bracing herself. Behind her Jenks blundered clumsily into the door and she snapped, without turning round, 'For heaven's sake, Brian, don't touch anything.'

It was exactly the sort of room you would expect it to be. You saw pictures of them in magazines all the time, usually labelled 'charming', which was code for pricey and upper-class; she found them seriously depressing, herself. Anaemic glazed cotton curtains; plain linen chair covers piped in cream like an iced cake; twee china displayed in a recess; a couple of insipid floral prints on the walls. The baby grand piano – probably some sort of culture-statement – took up too much space for the size of the room.

In its curve, on the expensive beige carpet there was a crumpled sprawl of limbs. Good patent shoes on the feet, she noticed first automatically, black skirt and a dark red jacket (poor Anna's 'confident colour'). Nearby, a mahogany pedestal had toppled over and the urn of flowers which had presumably been set on it had spilled water, flowers and greenery, and then rolled unharmed to the corner of the room.

Anna Hartington had grabbed at it, perhaps, in the instant when the shot took her, in the staggering step which would be all she had time to take before the nerve messages stopped from her shattered brain. She wouldn't, in the time-honoured phrase, have known a thing about it.

She had finished up on her side. The small entry wound was just visible in the back of her dark head; the exit wound, at an odd angle – ricocheting down off bone, presumably – had been much more destructive. There was blood and splintered bone and . . .

Diane had the excuse of tracing the trajectory of the spent bullet to allow her to look away. She saw it at once, buried in the wainscot where the wood had split on impact. But the experts would deal with that.

Beside the pitiable, broken creature on the floor, amid the strewn flowers, there lay a ballpoint pen, yellow, with a black top. It was commonplace enough; there were millions like it, and that very fact made its appearance in these circumstances the more macabre.

'Not yours, is it?' Diane asked the sergeant, pointing.

'Haven't been further than the doorway till now.'

'Looks as if it fell out of the pocket of someone bending over the body. Could have been one of the two who found her – or maybe she was holding it for some reason when she was killed. But maybe, just maybe – '

It was strange how detached she felt from the horror of it all. Her mind was racing as she scanned the room, trying to make sure she didn't miss anything; she had a job to do, and that made all the difference. In the other cases of sudden death she had encountered, it had been the sense of helplessness which had driven her to private tears when duty was over.

Finishing her rapid survey, she recollected belatedly the silent man at her side and said, 'Anything you can see that I've missed, Brian? The SOCOs will be here soon, of course – oh, for goodness' sake, man, if you're going to faint, get out! *Don't* do it in here!'

The sergeant leaped forward to catch Brian Jenks, whose face had taken on the same hue as the tasteful celadon green wash on the walls. Mercifully, he caught him before he collapsed on to the body; every contact, as they said, left a trace, and, Diane thought with exasperation as she followed them out, the contact which Jenks's solid thirteen stones was set to make with the scene of the crime could have wiped out any amount of forensic evidence.

He did not actually pass out, though his knees were buckling drunkenly as the older policeman supported him into the hall.

'Get him outside and shove his head between his knees, will you, sarge?' Diane said crisply. 'Just try to keep him from grabbing on to walls and surfaces as you go. I'll have a quick look round inside.'

She was aware from his sideways look that the sergeant thought her harsh; she heard him say, 'Never mind, lad, it could happen to anyone,' as she turned back.

Men! Diane thought savagely, as she cautiously prodded open doors with the top of a pen and looked at the pristine bedrooms, noting automatically the curtains blowing open in the draught from one open window – could the assailant have come in that way? She peered at the ledge, which didn't tell her anything, but made a note in case the SOCOs missed it.

Men all talked tough, and were merciless in any situation where you showed your softer side. But just try being tough when they couldn't hack it – and women, after all, have famously stronger stomachs than men – and you were a hard unpleasant bitch. Well, she'd tried to get that message across to Jenks already this afternoon.

But it wasn't professional, was it? She checked out the bathroom, untouched as far as she could tell, and tried to ignore the inconvenient thought.

She had treated him differently because she didn't like him. She would have protected any other new DC, made sure he was prepared beforehand, and found something for him to do that would have removed him promptly from the horrors.

This time, she had won hands down in the macho stakes, but she had humiliated him twice today, once publicly, and his resentment at his loss of face would be a festering impediment to working together. So she had boobed – but why did he have to be such a stupid bastard in the first place?

And what was worse, she was letting herself be distracted from the job in hand – the ultimate sin. Resolutely she put it from her mind and went on to the kitchen.

A woman's handbag, expensive soft black leather, lay on the table, and there was a plastic jug on the stainless steel surface by the sink. A dribble in the bottom of the jug showed that it had been used, perhaps to top up the water in the vase. She made a note of that too.

There was a window to the garden above the sink; a movement out there caught her eye, and she bent a little to look out.

There were four people there: a tallish young man with light brown hair with a grey linen jacket slung over his shoulder, a white shirt and light trousers, standing in earnest conversation with an older man in workman's clothes, and two others sitting together on a rustic seat shaded by the venerable chestnut tree.

The man was leaning forward, hands clasped and elbows on his knees, his head lowered so that all Diane could see was the dark line of his spectacles below neatly parted hair. The woman at his side in a solicitous attitude was plump and rounded, with wispy fair hair and the kind of face which may in youth have a sort of boneless prettiness which crumples in middle-age, like a pink tea-rose past its prime.

Her hand was on his shoulder in a gesture that was almost maternal as she bent her head to speak to him. But something about the angle of their bodies caught Diane's attention, and she eyed them shrewdly. So often in domestic cases the obvious solution was the right one, and as she moved away the old, foolish joke about the Bible came into her head: it starts with a man and a woman in a garden and ends in Revelations.

Outside, they told her that DI Canning was on his way. That was a relief; he'd been involved in two or three successful murder investigations with an inner city force before coming to Fotheringham. In that case, she should go for tidying up and organising rather than trying to be creative.

Brian Jenks, still pale but upright now, was standing talking to the sergeant.

'Feeling better, Brian?' As a sop to her conscience, she added, 'I'm sorry about that. In the heat of the moment I forgot that you probably haven't had much experience of that sort of thing.'

'None at all, as it happens.' His tone was self-pitying, and the sergeant was looking reproachful.

Stuff them both. She'd tried, hadn't she? She said brightly, 'Had to meet it sometime, then. Now get round to the garden and take details from the people there. DI Canning will tell us what statements he wants later. I'll sift through this lot.'

69

She jerked her head to the group, larger now, at the gate.

There was a slight, scruffy-looking girl with a notebook asking questions, and Diane's heart sank. That was all they needed – the press in attendance already.

She went forward and the girl, noticing her immediately, abandoned her current prey mid-sentence and came over, flashing a card.

'Press,' she said briefly. 'Are you in charge here? What can you tell me about the situation inside?'

'Not a lot,' Diane said, taking the card. 'Ms Moxon, is it? Right. Well, as you can see, we're pretty busy just now. We'll be making a press statement as soon as we can. And now, if you don't mind – '

'Not good enough.' The flat grey eyes surveyed her contemptuously. 'You can't kiss me off like that, copper.'

Diane was irritated and amused at the same time. 'No? Well, naturally, we're always anxious to help the *South East Express*. But you see, it cuts both ways. You be a good girl, Ms Moxon, and go with the officer here – ' she had signalled to the constable – 'and I promise I won't make it my business to see that all the nationals get the info before you do. All right?'

Diane did not wait to see the death-stare, though she could feel it boring into her spine. She could, however, hear her saying to the constable, 'OK, OK, so I'm on my way. But even the bitch-goddess can't stop me going to see one of my friends who lives here, up near the house.'

Out of the corner of her eye she saw the odd, childlike figure in the long skirt and heavy boots set off up the drive as she got out her notebook and set to work among the people at the gate.

'And your name, sir, if you don't mind?'

Routine. The backbone of every investigation, whether you were talking about the nicking of a packet of fags from a corner store or the brutal murder of a rich and powerful woman.

The wait in the garden seemed interminable – interminable and very strange. There was coming and going, cars arriving, people holding earnest conversations, but for all it appeared to concern them, Maurice and Judy might have been invisible, existing in another dimension.

Above them the leaves of the old chestnut tree rustled and

twisted in the light breeze, casting a dappled shade. Unseen birds sang and chirruped, and for minutes together Judy watched a butterfly sun itself with such meticulous attention that she could have drawn the pattern on its wings.

There was nothing else to do, except repeat in her head like a mantra the words she had so carefully calculated she must say. Words were their friends and their enemies too; they could trap them in a web of suspicion, or set them free to – but she would not, no, she must not think of that, or God would surely punish them.

She had said nothing to Maurice for some time now, though before that she had tried to find comforting things to say which might make the agony of waiting more bearable. But from the moment of finding Anna's body, he had withdrawn completely, and now, despite the fact that she could reach out and touch his dear, familiar hand – though she mustn't – he seemed very far away.

Perhaps that was best. It left her to concentrate on the role she herself must play. She was a woman who had lost her oldest friend and her employer, that was all. She was involved, of course – and seriously upset, naturally – but at one remove. She closed her eyes the better to concentrate on the portrayal of that character: shock, a few tears (though not too many), coupled with a determination to be practical for everyone else's sake . . . Rather like Janina Mayfield in *The Hand of Destiny* . . .

When she opened her eyes again, there was a podgy man with reddish hair coming towards them across the grass. He had a disagreeable, almost porcine face, and he was carrying a notebook. With a surge of fright Judy recognised the first of the inquisitors.

But it was with something of the relief of the performer when the curtain rises at last that she jumped to her feet saying warningly, 'Maurice!' to alert him to the man's approach.

Maurice looked up, shaking his head as if to clear it. With Judy fluttering round, Adam came across to help him up. Taking his proffered arm, Maurice seemed grateful for the support.

The policeman was flashing a badge. 'DC Jenks,' he said, then, 'Right, now – '

Maurice squared his shoulders, as if the onslaught against which he was bracing himself were a physical one.

'Your name first, sir, if you wouldn't mind . . .'

It was in a curious way disappointing, an anticlimax. He took

71

their full names, ages and addresses, inscribing all the information in his notebook carefully, then moving on to Adam Beaumont and Atkinson, who had come across from the other side of the garden.

Then something made her turn. In the gap in the hedge leading to the front garden a young woman was standing, She was neatly dressed in a cream tailored blouse and beige slacks, but she looked – Judy groped for the word – hard-bitten, that was it. A tough cookie, in the dated phrase, with that bright lipstick and the blonde hair which did not quite match her skin tone. Even at this distance, Judy could see that her eyes were bright blue and their laser gaze was directed upon Maurice and herself. She felt, superstitiously, that they could search the dark recesses of your soul and read the light-loathing secrets you kept hidden there. She took an instinctive step sideways to distance herself from Maurice, then saw that this had been noted too.

Suddenly, Judy was afraid. She was so afraid that the tears she had decided she must be seen to shed sprang to her eyes unbidden.

7

Penny had taken herself off for a walk after lunch. She couldn't bear it any longer with Adam upstairs in his study with the door shut, pacing to and fro like a caged panther.

He had done quite a bit of tail-lashing at lunch too; he was almost monosyllabic, and twitched when she asked him if he'd seen Anna. No, was the answer, but he didn't explain whether she had changed her mind, something else had cropped up, or he himself had decided to cock two fingers and not turn up to be lectured, since she'd killed his career anyway.

He had dutifully eaten the pasta salad she had put in front of him, but more as if he were doing it for the sake of peace than from any real appetite.

She had spent so much time lately feeling sick with dread that it was almost a relief to be able to feel straightforwardly exasperated. It was a hideous situation, but hiding under the bedclothes wasn't going to help.

Surely it couldn't end like this? Anna would have to see reason before the whole thing fell apart. Or Maurice would put his foot down. Though perhaps it was more likely that a brigade of flying pigs would swoop down and carry Anna off.

Oh, Adam might be right that there was nothing more to be done. Perhaps he was simply mourning an inevitability, and she should respect his grief. But even so . . .

She could never bear to saunter so despite the heat she was striding along at a good pace, skirting the house and garden and heading for one of the shady wooded walks round the back. The last thing she wanted was to meet any of the orchestra, with them all in a state of fury and frantic anxiety. The artistic temperament lent itself to drama, and she had had enough of that for the moment, thank you very much.

Penny paused, looking back at the vista towards the house. Considering the turmoil which she knew was raging within its walls, it was unnerving that it could all look so incredibly peaceful and beautiful; three of the white peacocks were pecking about, occasionally pausing to strike an Attitude in the manner of a nineteenth-century Beauty. Great houses, she thought fancifully, have chilly souls; secure in their enduring splendour they diminish human experience to nothing more than a passing show.

As she stood, a group of three or four people came into view round the side of the house and she could see from their gestures that they were in a state of considerable agitation. Oh lord! she didn't have to ask what *that* was about. She turned swiftly into the dappled shelter of the trees and went on.

The exercise was satisfying and helped to work off her bad mood. It was quarter-past two when she turned to come back, feeling that she ought to go and support Simon Byrd's cello recital. His master class this morning had bombed, and Judy said they'd only sold ten seats for this afternoon. Even if a few more turned up at the door, an extra body would count so an extra body ought to go, even if it had little expectation of enjoying itself. He had chosen a programme consisting mainly of pieces 'from the Moffat collection', whatever that might mean. Lesser-known hits of the eighteenth century, they seemed to be, which was hardly going to pull the punters.

When she got back to the small concert hall, the stable yard was deserted. Oh dear, she thought. Not that she had expected they would be queuing up.

The hall could hold about seventy, but thirty seats had been set up in a circle near the stage. There were perhaps fourteen in the audience, who had dotted themselves about instead of filling in the front rows, which somehow seemed to accentuate the number of empty seats. They were quite a lively lot, though; where two or three were sitting together there were low-voiced, animated conversations instead of the preparatory hush which concert-goers normally observe to show how terribly, terribly serious they are about the treat in store.

There was only one person sitting in the front row, right in the middle. She was an elderly lady, sporting a striking emerald-green toque. It was hard to say what else she was wearing, since there were so many layers; flowered chiffon, printed voile, a yellow linen jacket and two or three gauzy scarves in different pastel shades. Penny felt drawn to her immediately.

The face which turned to greet her in the happy expectation of company was raddled, the skin sagging in folds with a network of wrinkles like the craquelure of an old oil painting. It was impossible to tell whether or not she had been good-looking, but the faded eyes still held an almost girlish sparkle and the thin lips, defiantly exaggerated to their youthful outline by a coating of fuchsia, curved in a smile of great warmth and charm.

'Are you going to sit with me, dear? How lovely. I arrived far too early, you know. I always do, these days, because I was never blessed with a sense of time and now I'm getting a bit ga-ga it's worse than ever. I kept finding I'd missed whatever it was completely, which was a mite discouraging. So now I arrive hours too soon and have nothing to do but run through the old memories, and the trouble is now that it's like a film you've seen too many times before; you've got all the good lines by heart and there are no unexpected twists to the plot.

'And then when people start coming in they do this awfully English thing of sitting as far away from everybody else as possible. Do you suppose it's a race memory of the Black Death?'

Enchanted, Penny burst out laughing – attracting, she noted with amusement, censorious stares from the rest of the audience. 'I've certainly remarked the phenomenon, but hadn't considered that explanation. Have you been here before?'

'Been here before?' Her laugh was a rather engaging cackle. 'I've been to just about every concert here, my duck, since the whole thing started. Such luck: I never expected to have real music right on my doorstep. I'm a Londoner, you see, but when I married my darling Bert we had to come down here. He'd had a rotten war, poor old sweetheart, and he couldn't take the noise and bustle. Bought a nice little pub down in the village here, in Cambourne – the Hart and Trumpet, known as the Tart and Strumpet to one and all. Do you know it?'

It was the nearest pub, the orchestra's local, brewery-owned with maroon flock wallpaper and fake Victorian mirrors. Penny nodded.

'Tarted it up, right enough, haven't they?' She cackled again. 'Used to be a good honest English pub. Ruined it, of course, but then they gave me a fancy price for it six years ago when I sold it to them after my lovely Bert died.

'I still go in, of course – well, it's a habit, and I get to know all the boys and girls from here. But I miss the old days with the horse-brasses and the open fire and me on the old honky-tonk piano.'

She stretched out her hands with their fragile, wrinkled skin and the knobbly joints of arthritis. They cracked painfully.

'Wouldn't think it, would you, my darling, but I could play anything once. I was répétiteur to some of the greats in my time.'

Penny was interested. 'So did you know some of the people who came to perform here?'

'Oh, bless you, yes. Knew most of them before they were anybody – darling Eden, of course – what a fraud the man was, God rest his soul! But charming, charming . . . When Ramillies came on the market, I told him about it, you know. And Jonah Dancey; got to know him right at the start when he was only beginning to make his mark before he went off to America and then got himself famous. Lovely boy. All of them lovely boys. And girls. I used to come to the parties here – '

Her voice trailed off wistfully, and Penny cut in, 'Then we must get you to come again. I'm Penny Beaumont, the conductor's wife – '

The old woman turned to study her with renewed interest. 'Young Adam's wife – are you, indeed! Well, he's certainly setting the Thames alight, isn't he? I saw Toscanini conduct, and I've never seen anyone since I thought might be able to touch him, until now. You should be proud of him.'

'Yes, I am.' Penny swallowed, then went on quickly. 'But there's a party after Jonah's recital – you must come to that. Tell me your name.'

'Letty, darling, Letty Wells. Short for Lettice.'

'Lettuce?' Penny looked startled, and Letty emitted another shrill chuckle.

'It was fashionable in the Twenties, my love. Not the frilly green stuff with no taste. It's the good old English form of the Latin for "joy" – Laetitia – and thank the lord they weren't inspired to call me that, or I'd have gone through life known as Titty, wouldn't I?'

'But look, here comes poor old Simon now. Let's give him a lovely clap.'

The soloist seemed, Penny thought, oddly on edge. He was a stout, stolid-looking man on the wrong side of middle-age who looked more like a banker than a musician, but he was making nervous mistakes she would not have expected.

They applauded dutifully after the first suite, then settled back for the sonata which seemed very long and composed of an excessive number of movements. Penny, counting them off surreptitiously on her fingers, got the impression that even Simon didn't have his heart in it, which was too bad; even if it wasn't much of an audience, he owed them a professional performance.

He left the stage for the interval with unseemly haste, but his place was immediately taken by Chris Medway who played double-bass in the orchestra and also helped Adam with management. He was looking pale and very ill-at-ease. Penny looked up at him enquiringly, but he started speaking without meeting her eye.

'Ladies and gentlemen. Some of you may have been aware as you came in that there was a – a problem – ' he swallowed nervously – 'at the lodge cottage.

'It has just been officially confirmed to me, and I am extremely sorry to have to tell you that Anna Hartington has been killed. Well, murdered, actually. In these circumstances – well, to be quite honest with you, I don't know quite what we should do. Simon's prepared to finish the programme, but as you could probably see he's a bit upset; he's known Anna a long time. And perhaps we should abandon it anyway, I don't know if it would be right to go on – '

There was a murmur of shocked agreement. He thanked them awkwardly, then left the stage mopping his brow. After a moment's pause, people began getting to their feet, collecting belongings, and hushed conversations started between strangers united by the horror of events.

The colour drained from Penny's cheeks. Cassandra's curse, she thought wildly. I could feel disaster coming but I couldn't stop it. Just like Dom, all over again.

There was a sickly waft of perfume as Letty fished out a lace-edged handkerchief to dab at the tears that were gathering in her old eyes.

'So that's another one,' she said wretchedly. 'Just like my darling naughty Dominic.'

You could not help wondering, Diane reflected drily, how someone so universally admired and respected could get herself murdered at all.

DI Canning had arrived; he was inside now awating for the SOCOs who should not be long now. He had brought DS Simcox and DC Lane with him, and had detailed them all to start taking preliminary statements.

Diane had spoken to Adam Beaumont ('a woman of amazing energy and dedication'), Bill Atkinson ('poor lady, poor lady, she didn't deserve a thing like that should happen to her') and Judy Freeman ('she was my best friend, my oldest friend. I can't imagine – ' sob – 'life without her').

Only the husband had said nothing. 'Poor Maurice,' Judy Freeman had offered. 'You can see he's in shock. They were such a *devoted* couple, you see.'

DS Braithwaite wrote that down too, without comment.

She was in the back garden when she became aware of a disturbance: a man's voice loudly raised in some sort of argument. She excused herself to Atkinson, who was just finishing his statement, and went round to the front.

For once, Jenks actually looked pleased to see her. He was defending the gate as if it were the pass at Roncesvalles, with himself an unlikely Roland, against the determined onslaught of a short man in a loud silk shirt. The belt buckled round his cream linen trousers, roughly where a waist might be postulated, supported an impressive belly; he had a bald dome to his head with a frill of long dark curls round the back and his arms, rather more lavishly endowed with hair, were strong and muscular. Jenks, perspiring more than ever, was losing the battle to keep the gate shut.

'Just what do you think you are doing, *sir*?' Diane's glacial tone would have congealed boiling oil, and the man, startled, desisted.

Breathing heavily, Brian said, 'I've told him he can't come in, sarge, but – '

'Whad'ya mean, we can't come in?' The voice was not American, but had the mid-Atlantic whine affected sometimes by media personalities and frequently by wannabees. 'Look, I can see you're having a bit of local difficulty here, but if you let me in to talk to the bossman instead of the menials,' his look disparaged them both, 'maybe we can straighten it out.'

United in astonishment, the two police officers stared at him.

He tried again, with elaborate patience. 'Look, I'll spell it out for you. I've got *Jonah Dancey* sitting back there in the car.' He waited for reaction, but getting none shook his head in resignation and continued.

'I should have figured that wouldn't mean anything to you. OK, we've got a piece of paper that says he stays here for the concert – the b-i-g concert, you know? And what I have to sort out is a) what the hell is all this about and b) what do you propose I do with J.D. in the meantime?'

Diane drew breath, almost ready to tell him in graphic detail precisely what he could do with 'J.D.', but before she could speak there was a parting of the crowd, and a tall man came through.

She didn't know him – presumably this was Jonah Dancey, whoever he might be – but he certainly had presence. It wasn't just his height, though he must be over six feet, and he wasn't exactly good-looking; his face was square, his features irregular and his hair a nondescript brown. But he seemed, somehow, more substantial than the people round about. He was casually dressed in a blue-striped short-sleeved shirt and light trousers with a blazer round his shoulders, and somehow you could tell that it would cost a couple of your wage-packets to look as casual as that.

He was clearly concerned. 'What on earth's going on?' he asked, reaching the impasse at the gate.

The short man turned towards him. 'You think I haven't asked, J.D.? Tell me, I said, lay it on the line, but these dodos – '

'Watch it, Larry. The act is all very well, but you're in danger of losing the place. These are real police, and if they're here at all it's a real problem.'

He looked from Jenks to Braithwaite and without hesitation addressed himself to her. 'I do apologise. I'm Jonah Dancey and this is my – over-enthusiastic – agent, Larry Marcini. He's obviously told you that this is where I was expecting to stay?'

'Well, you can forget that, for a start,' Jenks snarled, smarting from his humiliation.

'Whad'ya mean, forget it?' Larry was more than ready for him.

'Cool it, Larry – '

'Now, let's take this calmly – '

Diane and Dancey spoke together; he gestured to her to proceed but as she shook her head went on with a faint smile, 'Right. Larry, don't speak till you're spoken to. Now, officer, are you in a position to tell me what's happened?'

Daring Jenks, with a fierce glance, to open his mouth, Diane said, 'Well, to a certain extent, sir. I think you'd better both come through.'

She opened the gate for them, Larry smirking triumphantly at Brian as he passed. She led them round to the back garden, then said, 'I'm afraid there is a very serious problem. Anna Hartington is dead.'

'Dead?' Larry yelped.

'Dead?' Jonah's jaw dropped. 'Dead? Anna? But – but Anna was – indestructible! What happened?'

'I am not at liberty to say.' Diane took refuge in the formula. 'But the police consider the circumstances to be very suspicious indeed.'

He stared at her blankly. Larry had gone very quiet.

'Are you – are you trying to say she's been – murdered?'

Eloquently, Diane did not reply.

'But this – this is awful! I can't believe it. I've known Anna for years – years!' He swallowed hard, turned aside. He took out a handkerchief to mop his brow.

It was only then he noticed the others, huddled together in an earnest group with their backs turned.

'Adam! Maurice!'

Beaumont reached him first, his drawn face brightening a little. 'Lord, Jonah, am I glad to see you!'

Maurice followed more slowly, but they both converged on Jonah as if his physical presence were in itself a reassurance. Jonah put an arm round the shoulders of both men, and after the initial greeting they stood close together, talking quietly.

Diane could appreciate their feelings. There was something about the man – the width of shoulder, perhaps, or his strong square powerful hands – that suggested reliability.

Marcini, who had not moved, was looking subdued. 'Hey, look,

I'm sorry about that. I didn't realise – poor bloody Anna! Of all the things!'

Jenks seemed to be preparing to get in a good kick while his adversary was down and Diane, noting with some relief that the scene of crime officers had arrived, said swiftly, 'Brian, that's the SOCOs. Could you direct them, please?

'Now, Mr – Marcini, is it? Perhaps you could explain to me what your position is?'

Larry scratched his stomach thoughtfully with both hands.

'Right. I'm a musical agent – hey, now I'm being modest. *The* musical agent. J.D.'s my client and he's a b-i-g star. Right now we're in negotiations with the BBC to have him front an autumn series on the love-lives of the all-time greatest composers and how it affected what they wrote, that's how big he is. He's performing here tomorrow night, so today I lunch him in town – San Lorenzo, and you wouldn't believe who was there lunching together – and come down to see him settled in. I want to check the arrangements, see he has his piano all right, that sorta thing. Sorta thing I do all the time for J.D.

'This is where we fixed for him to stay. They were moving in a Steinway for him – that's his big condition. Partly because they sponsor him, and partly he's conscientious, you know? Something isn't right, he gotta get it right, right then. It's the Rubetskoi method – you never heard of Rubetskoi?'

He gave her a pitying look and went on, 'J.D.'s teacher. Only the greatest in the world. But now you're going to tell me he can't stay here, right?'

'Right.'

'So that leaves us with b-i-g problems. Sure, the man can live in a hotel. But how many hotels do you know have a Steinway he can play in the middle of the night, if that's what it takes to be his sort of perfect for the concert?'

'If there is a concert.'

Diane had thought Larry looked shocked at the news of Anna's death; she realised now that he had registered only mild surprise.

He staggered backwards. 'No – no *concert*? You're kidding me – say you're kidding me! He's prepared a whole programme, all the biggest names are coming – '

'It's not up to us, sir. We're only concerned with the actual scene of the crime. But there might be a general feeling that it was inappropriate.'

'Inappropriate? What kind of word is that? J.D.! J.D.! Come here, and get this straightened out.'

Judy had joined the three men to fling her arms round Dancey's neck; now she was standing between him and Adam, her arms linked with both; the vulnerable individuals seemed to be forming a tight, impregnable circle against the world. At his agent's voice Jonah turned.

'What about the concert, J.D.?' Larry wailed.

'Oh God, the concert. I'd forgotten all about it.'

'Perhaps,' Adam said stiffly, 'it ought simply to be cancelled. As a mark of respect.'

Marcini groaned theatrically, and Jonah shot him a warning look. 'This is no time to start thinking about your commission, my friend. I'm happy to scrub the whole thing. I don't want anyone to think there's a lack of respect for Anna. Mind you – ' He stopped. 'Perhaps I shouldn't say this. But I wonder if pulling the plug is what Anna would have wanted? We're on sacred ground here – Eden's Festival was more important than anything else. We were all just cogs to turn the great wheel, as far as she was concerned.

'Anyway, does anyone know who has the authority to decide?'

'I do,' said Maurice, and taken aback by the crisp decisiveness of the statement, Diane eyed him sharply.

At once, Judy was at his elbow. 'Maurice, you're in shock,' she said, with the faintest admonitory edge to her voice. 'Jonah, you can't expect Maurice to make important decisions when he's obviously not fit to do it. He must get back up to the house, lie down – '

Maurice continued as if she hadn't spoken.

'You're quite right, Jonah. Anna would have died for the sake of the Festival.' He seemed oblivious to what he had just said. 'I'm going to cancel the String Quartet concert this evening. We've sold very few tickets, and anyone coming now would come for the wrong reasons. But tomorrow's different. She would trust me to see it to a fitting conclusion. Make it a really grand finale, Jonah, for her and for the last Hartington Festival.'

At those final words, Diane sensed a reaction within the group: a relaxation, at least one person letting out a sigh, as it might be, of relief. She wasn't quite quick enough to see who it was before Larry was exclaiming triumphantly, 'Well, thank God for a sensible man. It would be a tragedy, J.D., if you couldn't do this gig.'

81

Dancey winced. 'Do you ever think before you open your mouth, Larry? In this context, "rather a pity" is what you mean,' he was saying, when DC Lane appeared round the corner of the house.

'Young lady here, sarge. Says she wants to speak to Mr Beaumont.'

'Oh – that will be Penny,' Adam said. 'I couldn't find her to tell her myself. Can I go to her now, or can you let her through?'

'If you like.' Diane nodded to the policeman to bring her. She could hardly say 'the more the merrier' in these circumstances, but it was undeniably useful to watch these initial reactions.

The slim fair woman wearing a pink blouse and blue denim skirt had been crying, but it hadn't diminished her fine-boned prettiness. When Beaumont went over to her, the tears started again as he took her in his arms, but it was only for a moment that she gave way. She pulled herself together with a visible effort as Dancey, who had been watching sympathetically, came over. Her face brightened; she went to him naturally as a child with her arms out to be hugged.

Diane knew that face. She would have known the girl anywhere.

She was the reason Diane had blonde hair, when in her heart of hearts she knew that brightening her natural mouse-colour would have been more becoming. It was because of her that Diane had acquired the habit of relentless exercise in a fruitless effort to refine her stocky frame to leggy elegance. She had been the galling embodiment of everything Diane had wanted to be: popular, pretty, confident and charming even as a tomboy ten-year-old.

Diane's dad had been Regimental Sergeant Major, but Penny Drayton-Smith had been the Colonel's daughter. Diane had hated her then, and, as she watched Penny react to the situation with instinctive grace, she hated her still.

8

The sound of a scream, a harsh, painful, strangled scream, ripped through the gathering dusk outside the long windows. Then there was another, and another, before a chilling silence fell.

Jonah Dancey leapt to his feet, his face blanching. 'What in heaven's name was that?'

Judy Freeman's giggle was a foolish, inappropriate sound. 'It's only the peacocks, Jonah. You remember – Eden's peacocks.'

It seemed to take a moment for the sense of what she had said to penetrate, then he collapsed back into his chair with his hand to his chest as if to still a racing heart.

'Eden's peacocks,' he said slowly. 'Of course. Stupid of me. I'd forgotten. "Now droops the milk-white peacock like a ghost" – there always was something faintly uncanny about them, wasn't there?' He took a gulp from the glass of brandy on the little pie-crust table by his chair, and managed a half-smile. 'Sorry. But that cry – I suppose I'm just a bit on edge, and . . .'

His voice trailed into silence. Maurice, in the blue velvet spoon-back chair by the window, had not reacted, staring straight ahead as if studying with grave attention an invisible shadow-show passing before his eyes. Judy sighed, looking at him across the room with naked yearning.

They were in what had always been called Anna's sitting-room; what, Judy found herself wondering inconsequentially, would they call it now? It was smaller than the other public rooms, a pretty morning-room, perhaps, for some previous lady of the house, though Anna had never made it in any sense her own, content to have it impersonally furnished by Eden's designer with antique pieces on an appropriately delicate scale and restful, understated fabrics.

None of the room's present occupants, however, were in any mood to appreciate the professional harmony of their surroundings. The atmosphere, once they had eaten the sandwiches sent over from the kitchen and drunk the coffee, became increasingly sombre, so that Judy had gone round switching on the lamps long before the encroaching darkness warranted it. Conversation was awkward and desultory; Maurice had barely spoken at all for the last half-hour.

After Jonah's outburst, Judy looked at her watch. 'Quarter to ten. Goodness,' she said meaninglessly.

She was worn out with emotion and the strain of smoothing the ruffled feathers of patrons who had been told bluntly by police at the gate that tonight's concert had been cancelled, and she did wish Jonah would take himself off and leave them together – go to bed, or go and practise on his blasted Steinway. There had been enough fuss about it, after all.

That agent of his had somehow managed to winkle out the

information that there was one in the Green Salon, so then of course she had no alternative but to say, with feigned enthusiasm, that *of course* Jonah must stay here rather than go to a hotel. But it would have made such a difference, if she and Maurice could just have been on their own tonight.

Not that they would have – her mind shied away from completing the thought, as if someone might overhear, but she could have stopped him bottling everything up the way he was obviously doing. Perhaps they might even have allowed themselves to make a tentative, very tentative, plan or two about the future; her heart gave a little skip, before she recalled the dragons in their path. Involuntarily, her eyes turned to the window from which could be seen the arc-lights from the cottage and a single blue light still flashing, and her heart again missed a beat, though for a different reason this time.

As if he had read her thought, Jonah got to his feet. 'I think I might go through to the Green Salon and practise for a bit, if it wouldn't disturb anyone.'

'Of *course* not,' said Judy, her enthusiasm this time genuine. 'Of course not, Jonah! Hearing you play – well, that would be a real treat, wouldn't it, Maurice?'

She knew that she was fluttering, overdoing the response. She had never been very skilled in subtlety; her feelings always seemed to come through, like the greasy stain on a wall when you try to mask it with fresh wallpaper. She could tell from Jonah's carefully polite expression that he had guessed their secret, knew what was in her mind.

Unexpectedly, Maurice spoke. 'Don't go yet, Jonah. There are one or two things – if you wouldn't mind, Judy?'

For a second she did not understand, then her face turned an ugly, mottled purple in humiliated comprehension. All the time she had been willing Jonah to leave them alone together, she had been sure that Maurice, too, was waiting for him to go. But in fact he had been waiting, perhaps with equal impatience, for her to remember her position as the hired help and clear off.

She jumped up, mumbling something incoherent, and rushed from the room, stumbling over a low beadwork stool in her haste to get out before tears of anguish and mortification overcame her.

*

84

'Oh dear,' Maurice said inadequately. As the door closed behind her, he put his head in his hands and groaned. 'I think I find myself in something of a predicament.'

'That's one way of putting it.' Jonah's tone was dry. 'You always were a bit of a dog, under that mild exterior, but – how can I put this – *Judy*?'

He groaned again. 'I know, I know. But she was extraordinarily sympathetic and understanding, and somehow I – I just lost my head. You simply cannot conceive of what my life has been since Eden died, Jonah. I used to have some freedom, some personal space, and there was always the excuse of a conference somewhere or an author to meet in London when this place got too much. But since then, Anna's been treating me like her poodle, walking to heel and allowed out only on a leash. That makes me sound hopelessly inadequate, I know, but – well, you know what Anna was.'

'Yes, of course I know what Anna was. We all know what Anna was. What Anna was is what Anna always has been. It still doesn't explain why somebody should suddenly decide it's a good enough reason to kill her.'

'That's one of the things I need to talk to you about. I'll be the principal suspect, won't I? The husband always is, especially if they discover he's got – got – '

'A bit on the side?' Jonah suggested, unhelpfully.

'I wouldn't have put it like that, but I suppose they will. And if you think that Judy can maintain any form of concealment, it's an optimism I don't share. What can I do to convince them that this isn't some sort of *crime passionnel*?'

Jonah shrugged non-commitally, saying nothing, and Maurice continued. 'The thing is, there must be a dozen other people with a better motive. Anna was determined to keep the Festival going till she broke the bank, you know – winding her arms round the pillars and pulling until the temple fell in, to punish everyone for being alive after the glory was departed.'

Jonah's gaze sharpened. 'Well, it's no surprise to hear there are problems. There's been a lot of gossip, and she certainly piled on the pressure to make sure I would come; Larry wasn't keen, but she played the gratitude card – you know, I owed it to Eden because he saw my potential even before I went to Rubetskoi, and so on. But I hadn't realised it was as bad as that.'

'Worse,' Maurice said tersely. 'Cancelled tour, problems with paying the wages … I tell you, every musician in the place was ready to use the nearest blunt musical instrument on her.' His tone was almost flippant.

'But it wasn't a blunt instrument, was it?' Jonah did not sound sympathetic. 'It wasn't done in the heat of the moment. And if you'll forgive my being blunt in my turn Maurice, you don't sound precisely distraught about the death of your wife.'

Behind the horn-rimmed spectacles, Maurice's eyes fell. 'Oh dear,' he said again. 'I suppose I do sound inexcusably callous. You haven't been here to see how Eden's death affected her. Before that – oh, I'm not going to claim we had a marriage made in heaven, but in its peculiar way it suited our idiosyncrasies efficiently enough. Afterwards – well, a woman who is powerful and unstable and a monomaniac … Strictly betweeen ourselves, Jonah, my main problem is disguising an overwhelming sense of relief.'

He looked up, but the other man's face was in shadow. 'Was it you who killed her, Maurice?' The question was almost casual.

'No!' Maurice shot upright in his chair with the first signs of real animation he had shown all evening. 'Good God, Jonah, you know me better than that! I have problems with blood sports and killing wasps. And if you consider Judy out there, with the matrimonial noose at the ready to slip over my head the second a decent interval has elapsed, don't you think I would have taken the precaution of dowsing the fire before I stepped out of the frying pan?

'But …' he hesitated. 'There was another thing. There was a reporter here today. You may have noticed her, a scruffy-looking child, ratty face – '

'The one who was forcing her card on everyone and told me that if I had any "inside dirt", as she engagingly termed it, she'd make it worth my while to spill it?'

Maurice nodded. 'That's her. She came to interview Anna this morning, and afterwards Anna seemed seriously upset. She'd been caught cold, of course, thinking it was the usual publicity stuff, and in fact the wretched creature has been grubbing around and is trying to resurrect that unfortunate business with Dominic Leigh.'

'*Dom*?' Jonah's exclamation held both shock and astonishment. 'What can have set her on to that? But it was years ago, and the police said – '

'Well, of course they did. An interrupted burglary – and if it wasn't that – ' Maurice shifted uncomfortably – 'you know as well as I do that Dom was mixed up in some fairly unsavoury stuff.'

'We all knew that.' Jonah sighed. 'But he'd have grown past it, Maurice, given time. He had such a dazzling talent, and he was almost there. He'd have got such a buzz from making it big he wouldn't have needed to find his kicks elsewhere.'

'If you say so.' Maurice was more sceptical. 'You knew him better than I did, I suppose. But do you – do you think there could be any connection? It seems so – bizarre.' He shuddered suddenly, then added, his voice unsteady, 'But then, it's all – bizarre, isn't it?'

'Yes, Maurice, old son, it is.' For the first time, Jonah sounded supportive. He considered for a moment, then said, 'I can't say I see it, myself. It was all so long ago.'

'They never solved it though.'

'That's certainly true. Well, perhaps . . . But considering the dismal statistics for catching house-breakers it doesn't really prove anything.'

'And if they were – more than that, they'd be good at covering their traces, wouldn't they?'

'One would imagine so, but since neither of us moves in those circles we can't usefully speculate, can we?'

With sudden decision, Jonah got to his feet. 'Go to bed, Maurice,' he said. 'You're shivering, and it's a warm night. You think you're taking this calmly, but actually you're in shock and it's going to hit you later. Take up another brandy with you and get some sleep.'

'I've got to put in a bit of practice – there's a phrase that's bothering me – but I promise I'll keep the soft pedal down.'

Maurice rose obediently. The cracks in his composure were beginning to appear, and a muscle in his face had begun to twitch. 'Make it a lullaby, will you?' he said. But as he turned to go, his eyes went to the lights at the bottom of the drive. 'Have they – taken her away, Jonah?'

'I expect so.'

'God rest her soul.'

He was walking like an old man as he left the room.

Emrys Clitheroe rarely waited to see his newspaper come off the presses. He was content to see the *South East Express* to bed, then get off home to his wife and a late supper of steak and kidney pudding or a nice bit of Welsh lamb. She knew what he liked, his Myra; they had been childhood sweethearts and she still thought that saying 'Perhaps' to him instead of 'Yes, Emrys' constituted a violent argument.

Tonight, however, he'd instructed Myra to get off to bed and leave his plate by the microwave. He settled back into his squalid office, comfortable as a second skin, screwing up his lizard's eyes against the drifting smoke from the perpetual fag stuck to his bottom lip. Tonight he was going to see the first proof of the front page he had been waiting for all his professional life.

All the nationals would be running the murder and the police statement, naturally; inside page stuff, so far, despite the up-market social angle. And he'd screwed a good deal out of one of the tabloids for Liza's punchy on-the-spot report.

But he still had his scoop. He switched on the answering machine by his telephone with a malicious grin; by tomorrow morning it would be loaded with messages from the big boys (the ones who usually couldn't remember his name but who would now be calling him 'Emrys, old sport' and inviting him for a drink) scrabbling frantically for pay-dirt. The police too, more than likely. He'd eat Myra's Sunday chapel hat if there was a flatfoot sharp enough to have come up with the connection by now.

This neck of the woods wasn't exactly Chicago, after all, or even Glasgow. Shooting the place up wasn't something the locals did on a Saturday night when there was nothing on the telly. Yet this was the second person connected with Ramillies who'd been shot.

The bullet that had killed Dominic Leigh had come from the sort of gun your grandad brought back from World War II. And Liza, ferrety little Liza, who had the gift of being invisible when she wanted to be, had hung around eavesdropping, probably from her broomstick. Along with a few other choice little titbits, she had heard a detective mention the bullet Ballistics had been examining.

'Chummy must have robbed a museum to get that one,' he had said.

Which was enough to make the link to let him run the story nobody else had, which elevated the case from a one-off crime – possibly even an open-and-shut domestic – to a Mystery, with the promise of further revelations to come. He'd let her write it; it was a masterpiece of innuendo, and he hadn't grudged her a generous by-line. Phrases like 'it could be said' and 'sources suggest' laced the disparate facts together without once going over the legal score. She was a natural, and he wouldn't keep her long; at this rate, probably not much longer than the end of next week.

He knew she was still in the office, waiting to savour the heady moment when the physical proof of her first major triumph was put into her hands. Anyone else in the same situation he'd have called in to join him in a celebratory scotch. But Liza Moxon . . .

Though he prided himself on being a hard-nosed newsman, and though he'd never had a hack like her, he would watch her sneer her way off his paper without regret. She was destined for the cutting edge, for the newsworld where the qualifications for reaching the top were to have no scruples, no shame and no heart.

Well, like the man said in Ecclesiasticus, all wickedness is but little to the wickedness of a woman. She'd cream the lot of them.

It had started as a business meeting. There were details to put in place for next day: the orchestra's statement for the Press, the cancellation of the party after the concert, the tribute at the beginning and the minute's silence. Chris Medway, the assistant manager, and Jancis Jackson, the leader of the orchestra, had come, and later Ben Lousada had arrived looking for Chris with a query about dates for the next London rehearsals.

The tiny sitting-room of Adam and Penny's cottage was crowded even before Adam called up the stairs to Penny who had been keeping out of the way, that the business was over and they were all having a drink.

Penny was happy enough to be asked to join them. Up there by herself in the little bedroom under the eaves she had been doing her best to find occupation that would banish thought, jumping when the peacocks screamed though heaven knew she should be used to them by now.

She wasn't exactly mourning Anna. It would have been the height of hypocrisy to pretend that she had liked the woman or would miss her overbearing presence. But this death could not help but carry the echoes of another death, as a sea shell whispers the thunder of the ocean. She needed no reminding of the power of the undertow which dragged you down with the black waters of despair closing over your head.

She had tried reading, but though her eyes travelled obediently across the page, the meaning escaped. She had even rung her parents, praying as she dialled the number that her mother would answer, but it was the Colonel himself who had picked up the phone. He listened to her story with incredulity, evidently taking it as some sort of personal affront, as if in a better-ordered society there would be some agency to prevent Things Like That from happening to People Like Us. He rang off in a marked manner, leaving Penny feeling as usual guilty and inadequate and regretting her impulse.

She had not turned on the portable television in the corner. Watching a comedy show would be crass, she had had her fill of violence, and there didn't seem to be much else. She certainly did not want to risk catching the News, to hear the rumours of the hunt, to see some picture of Anna blown up across the screen, or even – as musical director of Ramillies – of Adam.

Penny shied away from the thought. She mustn't think of Adam in that context, not if she wanted to sleep tonight.

He had been so kind to her in her distress, so warm, so comforting, and she had leaned on him gratefully. It was enormously reassuring to see Adam back to his old self. It was – wasn't it?

All in all she was grateful to be called downstairs to join them, even if the atmosphere seemed almost shocking compared to the bleakness of her own mood. Anna had ruthlessly threatened their livelihood, she told herself, and it was only natural that they should feel relief.

'Darling, Penny!' Ben exclaimed, jumping up to make room for her on the miniature sofa. 'You haven't been moping away by yourself all this time?'

'We can't have that,' Adam said gently, taking her hand and kissing it, as he looked anxiously at her troubled face.

'Just think what you're going to be doing in Vienna while we're stuck in some grubby practice hall, scraping out notes for your totally unreasonable husband, who won't believe he's got perfection till there's blood on every string.'

Jancis's tone was jaunty. Thin and elegant in black, she drained her glass and rose.

'You won't take it personally, Penny, will you, if I go for an early night? I'm not usually a party-pooper, but after today I feel completely drained.'

Chris followed her. 'I'm bushed as well. I really ought to get a good night's sleep before the police start the third degree to make me confess. Don't move – we'll shoe-horn ourselves out.'

Apart from Penny, they all laughed. When the door had closed behind the departing pair, Ben said, 'They go through this routine all the time. For some reason, Chris thinks his wife is less likely to find out about Jancis if they perform this charade for people who know perfectly well what's going on.

'But if you want to get rid of me too, I'll disappear in five minutes once the coast is clear.'

'Of course not.' Adam got up to pour more wine into Ben's glass, and his own. Penny, nursing her drink, said nothing.

'Well,' said Adam.

'Well,' said Ben. The light from the lamp at his shoulder turned his coffee skin to gold, and his deep brown eyes sparkled with – what, Penny wondered? Excitement? Anxiety?

'Have you heard yet what they think? The police, I mean?'

Adam shook his head. 'Not a word. Maurice is completely in the dark as well. It's all terribly organised and professional, with all the different sections doing their own thing, and not one of them seems to have a pipe or a magnifying glass.'

Ben grinned. 'Are they baffled yet, do you suppose?'

'Oh, come on, Ben. Modern policemen are never baffled. "Pursuing several active lines of enquiry", they call it nowadays.'

They both laughed again, and Penny could bear it no longer.

'How can you laugh?' she cried fiercely. 'It isn't funny, any of it. Someone's killed Anna. Someone's shot her, and she's dead.

'And there are forensic scientists out there, and fingerprint specialists, and ballistic experts, and clever, experienced policemen who are going to devote the next bit of their lives to finding out who pulled the trigger.

'Nothing's been stolen from the house. They won't believe that someone wandered in off the street and did it for fun, and neither do I. The person who killed poor Anna is someone she knew, and someone we know too, probably. So making jokes about it really isn't appropriate.'

'Oh, come on, Penny,' Ben said impatiently. 'There's no need for the conventional crap. You didn't like Anna any more than the rest of us.'

Penny stood her ground. 'No, I didn't. But she's been murdered, Ben. You don't seem to realise it, but nobody's going to say, "Oh good. Everyone will be much happier without her," and leave it at that.'

The men said nothing, exchanging embarrassed glances. Penny set down her untouched glass. 'I'm sorry if I've put a damper on things,' she said stiffly, and walked out.

9

Dragging herself out of bed, Judy opened the curtains on a milk-opal morning, the early haze fretted with streaks of fiery gold. She looked dully at this empty beauty, the gauzy mist which was from her bleak perspective no more than a foul and pestilent congregation of vapours. Heavily she turned away to get herself ready for the difficult day ahead.

There was no point in going back over last night. She had analysed every nuance of Maurice's behaviour a hundred times yet she kept returning to it, picking at the scab of rejection while knowing that it would only make her feel worse.

She could not bear to believe what she had sensed in Maurice's tone last night. He had persuaded her to embrace Life, though childhood pain had instilled in her the wisdom of keeping it at arm's length. She had opened herself to its pleasures, and now found herself defenceless against its pain.

Even if her interpretation was blessedly wrong, even if he was exhausted and shocked and anxious to talk business with Jonah and possessed by the need for delicacy and discretion (she had told herself all these things), the fact remained that she must not look to him for any close contact or support. Amid all the dangers she must stand alone, like someone on a tiny mountain plateau with an icy, vertiginous drop on every side. And the wind was rising.

She went down to start the chores of the day, almost welcoming them as a relief. Someone must have gone in early for the papers, because they were in a jumbled pile in the hall. She hadn't time to read them, but gave them a swift glance as she neatened and laid them out on the table in the Green Salon – *The Times*, the *Telegraph*, the *Daily Mail*: nothing, so far, on the front page of any of these.

It was the headline in the *South East Express* ('Double Death Mystery – Exclusive') which stopped her in her tracks. She picked it up, sank on to a chair and read through the front page and the two feature pages inside. It talked about inside knowledge, and further revelations. At last she closed it and set it back on top of the others.

It was only then she noticed the by-line – Liza Moxon. With the name, a foxy face with an uneven, ugly smile sprang vividly to mind, along with a shrill, rancorous voice. 'For that you pay,' it was saying, 'in blood.' Inside knowledge?

A smile which was not itself particularly pleasant crossed Judy's face; she thought for a moment, then went to the telephone.

'How many of you have seen this?'

The CID room, where Will Canning had called his 8 a.m. briefing session, was crowded with men and women, police officers who were either based in the Fotheringham headquarters itself or had been drafted in from the outlying districts.

Canning, habitually well-groomed, was looking even sharper than usual this morning in a lightweight suit and dark silk tie. His bearing always suggested a controlled, purposeful energy, but today he seemed the centre of an electrical field of exhilaration.

The newspaper he was holding up was the *South East Express*. It was required reading for the local force, especially the small ads section in which a surprising number of the criminal fraternity on their patch were naïve enough to advertise their possession of stolen goods.

Diane Braithwaite had glanced at the front page as she gulped a cup of tea on her way out this morning and was glad she could join in the ragged show of hands. It was the first time she had worked directly with Canning, and she was anxious to impress.

Nothing, of course, could be further from her thoughts than his status as a thirty-five-year-old bachelor, personable and allegedly straight. It went without saying that her interest was purely professional: with the reputation he was building, he would be a useful man to have in your corner. That was all.

She wasn't quite sure what to make of Moxon's scoop. The girl was clearly flying a kite, but she couldn't be certain whether Canning was about to rubbish her theory or endorse it.

'For the benefit of those of you who haven't got to it yet, it's suggesting a close link between this killing and the murder of Dominic Leigh four years ago. He was shot in the course of a robbery in a rented cottage five miles from Ramillies.

'DS Simcox was on the case at the time, so I'll hand you over to him for the background. Kennie – '

'Well, we – er – we had the theory that probably he'd, well, come back and disturbed somebody. There'd been another break-in,

93

around the same time – nearby, I mean – and we never nailed anyone for that. It wasn't an MO we recognised.

'Nothing much was nicked, either time. Leigh's TV was found by the door, so I suppose that sort of suggested he'd disturbed them, probably.

'We knew he was into drugs, so we sort of put out feelers, but the Drug Squad snitches couldn't come up with anything. And after that,' he shrugged, 'the trail sort of went cold. Just another robbery with violence, nothing like it since.'

He finished with obvious relief, and Canning stepped in smoothly. 'Thanks, Kennie. Now, the thing about this article – ' he tapped it – 'is that the connection the woman's made is legit. I'd like to know where she got her info, I'm looking into it, and if I find someone had the cute idea of leaking to the press I'll have their guts for garters. Perhaps it was a case of careless talk but if you don't keep your lip buttoned the life it costs may well be yours.

'However, the point is, she's right. Ballistics have been working half the night and the report says that the gun that killed Hartington is the gun that killed Leigh.

'It's an old gun – war souvenir, probably. It must have been well maintained, or the thing apparently wouldn't have fired at all. But it's old ammunition, which deteriorates like anything else, so we're not looking for a pro. The guy with the gun could have found that shouting *Bang!* was the worst he could do.'

The concentration in the crowded room was such that when he raised his voice on *Bang!* several people jumped. He grinned.

'Right, now to practical matters.' He detailed the three teams, directed to taking fingerprints for elimination, questioning and searching. Hands and knees stuff, he warned them, for this last detail, 'but find the gun and the beer's on me. You're looking for a key too – front door's locked and it isn't inside.'

Then he sent them on their way, holding back his sergeants, Simcox, Braithwaite and Emery.

Canning perched on the edge of the table as they gathered round and the other officers shuffled off to get their details. Close to, his bubbling confidence was even more apparent.

When he spoke, it was in a lowered voice. 'I didn't want to make a public announcement about this, in case we have a mole. The last thing I want is Moxon's sticky little paws on this one before we've got it sewn up.

'A pen was dropped by the body – you saw it, Diane. Now, it's got as nice a set of prints on it as the most optimistic prosecutor could wish, and they don't belong to the victim. But we have to take this methodically.

'Hicks and Atkinson, who found the body, were asked yesterday without undue emphasis if they'd dropped anything inside. They both said no, but obviously we've got to check.

'Kennie, I want you i/c fingerprints. Clear those first for elimination, and then, if the gods are smiling, move on to the rest. With luck, someone doesn't know it's been dropped.

'We've got a lot to play for. It's just possible that by this time tomorrow we might have cleaned up not one but two murders.'

He could not quite control the flicker of satisfaction about his mouth, and it crossed Diane's mind that he had a lot riding on this one. Could she, she wondered with the faintest qualm of unease, be certain that he would be as open-minded as he was efficient? Perhaps he wasn't quite so attractive after all – if she'd been thinking about that, which of course she wasn't.

'All that is on a need-to-know basis, OK?' he was going on. 'Tony, I want you to get the incident room opened up. We'll work from here, and you'll need to liaise with the technical side about communications and so on. Jim's deploying the scavengers – we'll swap over sections tomorrow if need be.'

The two men went off, and Canning turned to Diane. 'I've saved you to go over to the *Express* to lean on our Ms Moxon. I think it'll take the rottweiler touch, and I daresay you're in a mood to do it.'

'Er – yes, of course sir.' Diane's agreement was politely puzzled. 'I did have a bit of a run-in with her yesterday – '

His smile held something she did not understand. 'I thought you might have. You obviously haven't seen the inside page? No? Oh well, take five minutes to read it before you go across there.

'We'd like her source for the story, clearly, but given modern squeamishness about using prolonged physical torture I don't suppose you'll get it. And we want to know all about her interview with Anna Hartington – she hints at undisclosed information, though that's probably the usual bullshit. You can twist her arm with the fact that Judy Freeman heard her making threats about Anna paying in blood as she left. She phoned this morning, keen as the school sneak to curry favour by fingering somebody else. I don't suppose Moxon carried it through, but it's good enough

95

reason to pull her in if she doesn't co-operate. I'll leave it in your hands.'

'Yes sir.' She took the paper and retreated. What had the little cow said about her? Come to think of it, Jenks, who had been one of those claiming to have read the rag, had given her a sneering grin.

The room was empty now as Diane opened the paper at the inside spread and settled to read systematically through it. Page two was the interview with Anna Hartington. It was cleverly done; what, you were meant to wonder avidly, were the 'secret fears' the doomed woman had confided exclusively to the *South East Express*? Allegedly. Diane *might* have believed it if a tone of vitriolic hostility hadn't kept showing through the hasty 'tragic victim' workover.

Page three was devoted to her visit to Ramillies after the crime. This page was dominated by a shaven-head-and-shoulders picture of Gary Stone, son of one of the Ramillies domestic staff, and his description of Anna as rotten to the core, stuck-up, mean, and given to throwing people out on the streets without a home to go to. He had, apparently, a record for drugs and he certainly wasn't very bright, having also declared that he would have been happy to kill the woman himself for what she was going to do to his mum.

Well, no doubt that would have put him somewhere on someone's list for a chat. Perhaps it would teach him the folly of chatting to the press.

It was only then she noticed a short article at the bottom of the second page headed 'Desperate Diane'.

Bullying the crowd at the murder scene was DS Diane Braithwaite, butch heavyweight of the Fotheringham force, with a tongue that could burn the warts off a toad at a hundred paces.

Desperate Diane – who looks as if a cow-pie, horns and all, would be a dainty snack – could give lessons in how not to deal with the public.

Let's be charitable. Perhaps she was having a bad hair day. Perhaps she's a lovely person who normally heads up the police charm offensive.

Perhaps the pigs might fly.

Diane's face and her temper flared simultaneously. Everyone must be creasing themselves behind her back, and the tag was one that she might never live down. Compared to her at this moment, a rottweiler with toothache would be just a big girl's blouse.

She found the newspaper's number and grabbed the phone.

It was certainly one of the busiest mornings the Cranbourne General Store and sub-post office had ever known, at least since Jackie and Ron Vine had bought it three years ago.

The shop was a model of its kind and the Vines were cheerful, warm-hearted people who spent their days providing social work, stress counselling, consumer guidance and fiscal advice for the cost of a few extra pence on the price of a can of baked beans.

Jackie was genuinely upset about the situation at Ramillies. 'I've never had such a shock in my life,' she was saying for the umpteenth time. 'I was sitting right here at the checkout when Ron came through from the back and said, "You'll never guess what just came on the radio – "'

Maggie Jones, who had already succumbed to the curious human need to describe in detail one's own position in relation to any very dramatic event by telling Jackie how *she* had been in her garden when the police car went by, suddenly held up a warning hand.

'Sssh!' she said, jerking her head towards the rack of newspapers at the entrance to the shop.

Penny Beaumont had come in, looking tired and pale but managing a smile for an acquaintance she passed in the doorway. Then she had paused to glance at the local newspaper with its sensational headline.

She stopped, as if she had been turned to stone. Her face, still with the lingering half-smile in place, froze in shock. As the two women watched her, she held that position, motionless, for much longer than anyone could possibly take to read the brief report.

The women exchanged glances, then Jackie eased herself from behind the checkout and went across.

'Are you – are you all right, Penny, love?'

After a second Penny's head turned; she looked at Jackie out of wide, haunted eyes as if she had never seen her before.

'All right?' she repeated slowly, her speech thickened, almost slurred. 'Oh – oh yes, all right.'

She swung away and walked back out of the shop, making no response to Jackie's awkward, 'We were ever so sorry, Penny – '

'Oh dear,' Maggie said sympathetically. 'Might as well be sleep-walking, way she went off just now.'

'Poor duck.' Jackie sighed and shook her head as she eased her comfortable frame back into the seat of custom. 'And she went away clutching her shopping list too. Maybe I'll get Ron to run up with a few things they might be needing.'

Liza Moxon was enjoying herself. She hadn't expected warm, heartfelt congratulations from her colleagues: none of them liked her, but then she had made little secret of her contempt for them, small-time no-hopers who would spend their working lives here in the boondocks. What had come as a pleasurable surprise was the nakedness of the envy in their faces as they said, 'What did they pay you for that, then?' or 'Next stop Wapping, I suppose.' She *loved* that.

She was at her desk making plans for the day when her extension buzzed. When she heard who it was, her little narrow smile appeared.

'Yes, Sergeant Braithwaite? Coming on your knees for the stuff you've all been too dumb to work out for yourselves?'

She listened to the terse reply, then said with saccharine sweetness, 'Oh, I'm so sorry, I'm afraid you're out of luck. On my must-do list you come in at about nine hundred and ninety-three, so I reckon that should come about the middle of next week. Unless you're really *desperate*, of course . . .'

She lingered provocatively on the word, but the response wiped the smile from her face. She licked her lips nervously. 'I never! If she said I did, she's lying, that's all.'

But her confidence was shaken. She blustered on, though it was clear that DS Braithwaite had won her point, and despite the treatment she'd given to her wasn't as much in awe of the power of the press as she should be.

'Just stick around, pig!' she finished shrilly. 'I may be just a hack on a local rag today, but not for much longer. By the time I've finished with you, you'll be a national celebrity.'

She slammed down the phone and sat chewing at her ragged thumbnail which was bleeding already round the nail-edge. She would have liked to ignore the injunction not to leave the building, but there wasn't a doubt it would give that bitch a real kick to arrange a warrant to have her lifted. And it was Saturday; she could be cooling her heels in the local nick until Monday morning court time, while every other hack got ahead of her and the big fish she knew were just about to nibble would forget who she was.

Her face was black with temper as she turned back to her desk. There wasn't much point in making up a schedule now; instead, she took the gum she was chewing out of her mouth and fashioned it into the rough semblance of a female form before finding a pin and sticking it not very hopefully through it.

Gary Stone was still asleep when his mother, like a small but deadly tornado, whirled into his bedroom with a copy of the *South East Express* in her hand.

'Gary! Gary! Wake up, you stupid little git! What the hell did you think you were doing, running off at the mouth like that to the newspapers, telling them all that rubbish?'

She was shaking him. Gary, fuddled from sleep, sat up and raised his arms over his head to protect himself as she started raining blows on his head with the rolled-up paper.

'Ow! Ow! Stop it, Mum, that's not funny! That hurt! What'ya doing? You gone mad or something?'

'Not me gone mad.' Doreen desisted, to sink down breathlessly on to the end of the bed, her eyes still shooting sparks of fury. 'It's you gone mad, Gary Stone, getting your photo in the paper and all, saying those things.'

His peaky face showed a nascent grin of satisfaction as he took the mutilated paper from her and smoothed it out.

'Got my best side, have they?' he said jauntily.

Grimly, his mother pointed to the text and as he read it the smile faded and a look of almost comical dismay took its place.

'The sodding bitch has stitched me up! But we were . . .' he paused, conscious of his company, and went on, 'mates, real muckers. She asks me for the lowdown on Miss Hartington, just between friends, like. Then she does this to me – "criminal record", she says, when she knew it was only a slap on the wrist for possession.'

'That's just what it is, though.' With apprehension overcoming her anger, Doreen groaned. 'How d'you get to be so dumb, Gary? Even if your dad did have 'bastard' stamped all the way through like Blackpool rock, he was nobody's fool. But you – well, sometimes I think you must be a ha'penny short.'

It was a measure of his distraction that he didn't even think of making a quick comeback about her own lack of the smarts. He was reading through the article again with mounting panic.

'But – but she's as good as said it was me that done it! She can't do that, can she, Mum? I'll have the Law on her – '

Doreen met his beseeching gaze with exasperation. 'Well, did you say it or not?'

His eyes fell. 'S'pose I might of. I was ticked off, see – But it's just her word against mine.'

'And how many more times did you say it down the pub last night?' she asked shrewdly, and he said nothing, biting his lip.

'Oh, Gary,' she sighed. 'Weren't born to learn, were you?' Then, as she had done so many times before, she squared her shoulders and accepted the burden of the follies of her boy.

'Right. What's done's done,' she said briskly. 'Just have to do the best we can, won't we, when the police come knocking. You didn't do anything wrong, I know that, and they won't be paying too much mind to a little toe-rag like her. Just tomorrow's chip-wrapping, that's all this is.

'Get yourself out of bed anyway, and dress up smart in case they come round. Don't suppose you can grow your hair before they get here, but lose the rings and the stud. Put on your good chinos and that nice shirt your Nan gave you for Christmas.'

Too dispirited to argue, he got up obediently as his mother said, 'I got to go, Gary. Promised Judy I'd help up at the house with them all in this state. You stay here now, be polite if the officers come – '

She half expected a sarcastic reply, but he disappeared meekly into the bathroom. She looked after him, then with a shrug of resignation went off to her work.

Showered, shaved and dressed as he had been directed, Gary came downstairs and went to the phone.

'Kev? This is Gary. Listen – OK, so I woke you. Sorry. But I need a favour, mate, right?'

He outlined his predicament, obscenely and succinctly. 'So get over on the bike, will you, soon as you can? I gotta get to Fotheringham and back before my mum finds I've gone. Cheers, mate – I owe you.'

10

Diane had time to formulate her plan of attack on the way to the newspaper offices. She had a tight rein on her temper now, and the adrenalin surge had been a useful aid to clear thinking.

There was a tiny yard at the back of the building which served as a car-park. As she got out and locked her car she noticed a motor bike at the far side, a big black Suzuki. A youth in leathers was straddling it, with his huge black helmet perched in front of him and a smaller blue one on the seat behind. He was looking bored, as if he had been waiting some little time, and he watched Diane idly as she went to the door marked *South East Express*.

She was directed up a concrete staircase at the back of the dingy entrance hall. On the first landing, a glass partition gave on to the big main newspaper office. There were two rooms, little more than cubicles, at the back; the rest of the area was taken up by about a dozen desks with computers, telephones and unstable-looking piles of paper.

There seemed to be some sort of altercation going on at the farther side, and as Diane opened the door she could hear a male voice raised in anger.

Liza Moxon was seated, shrinking as far as she could go into the angle formed by her desk and the wall, looking more childlike than ever with her narrow face pinched with fear. A young man, neatly dressed but with a shaven head, whom she recognised from the newspaper photograph as Gary Stone, was standing menacingly over her.

He was scarlet with rage, and working himself up to greater heights of fury.

'You lying little bitch! Don't give me that! "No harm in it" – except it's going to bring the filth down on me again, i'n't it? You can't weasel your way out of this one, scumbag – '

'Gary, Gary!' She clutched at him, trying desperately to stem the flow of abuse. 'You've read it all wrong. It wasn't like that – you got to give me a minute to explain – '

The boy shook off the little pawing hands, raising his own as if about to clamp them round her skinny neck. 'Had enough of the fancy talk, I have – '

There were four other men in the office, standing in a bunch with hands in pockets or arms folded, like spectators enjoying the finer points of some arcane sport and gravely pondering marks for technical merit and artistic impression. None of them moved in response to Liza's anguished shriek; indeed, Diane was obliged to push her way past to go to the girl's assistance.

'Police,' she said briefly and grabbing Gary by one thin arm yanked him away with practised skill. 'Cool it, OK?'

He made no attempt to resist. 'I never laid a finger on her, honest. Ask anyone.'

'That's right, not a finger,' a voice said from behind Diane, but she did not turn.

'He was ready to strangle me, if you hadn't stopped him,' Liza claimed shrilly.

Diane surveyed her sardonically. 'Oh, we have our uses, Ms Moxon. Now perhaps I can hear what all this is about.'

'Put me in the paper, she did,' Gary said sulkily. 'Made out I'd killed Miss Hartington – '

'I think you'll find I said no such thing.' Under police protection, Liza's cockiness was visibly returning. 'There are libel laws, you know, and all I did was quote what you said to me.'

'Yes, but I didn't say it that way! You wrote it down so I sounded – sounded – '

'What?' Liza sneered. 'Violent? Stupid? How extraordinary!'

'I'll have you for that – '

He started forward and she shrank back in alarm. 'Don't let him touch me!' she squealed as Diane put herself sturdily between them.

'That's enough, from both of you. Now, you're Gary Stone, right?'

He nodded, sullen in frustration. Made kind by fellow-feeling, she felt a pang of sympathy.

'Gary, I said cool it and I meant it. All you're doing is letting her get you in more trouble. I can promise you the police take very little notice of this kind of malevolent trash.' She enjoyed saying that, and seeing Liza's furious glare. 'We carry out our own investigations, and if you haven't done anything you've no need to worry.'

'What about the assault on me?' Liza demanded. 'I want to prefer charges – '

'I'm afraid it's not really your decision, Ms Moxon.' Diane turned

102

to the men behind her, who seemed to be enjoying Liza's predicament. 'I didn't see any assault, did you, gentlemen?'

There was a general shaking of heads, a chorus of 'Ooooh, no,' and a grey-haired veteran said, 'Being very reasonable, he was, after such a nasty personal attack,' with the air of one who has waited a long time for such a happy opportunity.

'Fine. Then off you go, Gary, and forget it. She's not worth getting into trouble for.'

The boy held his ground for a second longer, then slouched to the door. But on the threshold he turned menacingly. 'Just don't you think you've heard the last of it, Liza,' he said, then went out and slammed the door.

'Letty Wells,' Canning repeated when Diane reported this nugget of information. He looked at her with some respect. Desperate Diane – the name would stick – was quite an operator. Attractive too, though he liked them five years younger and willowy, with ankles like racehorses.

'Has Moxon still got the standard number of teeth and fingernails? I thought revealing your sources was the ultimate taboo?'

Diane smiled demurely. 'Shooting fish in a barrel, really. Her threat to Anna Hartington was a gift, of course, and then I suggested I might personally contact the Press Complaints Commission. She's expecting offers from the national press and doesn't want anyone rocking the boat. And she'd been a bit shaken by another of her victims who had made a slightly more – er – direct complaint – Gary Stone, you know? He left breathing fire and swearing vengeance, so I caught her off balance and kicked while she was down.'

'All in the finest traditions of police-work.' He jotted down a note. 'Letty Wells. That might be useful. If we don't crack it today, I'll see that someone talks to her. And what about Hartington's "secret fears"?'

Diane shook her head. 'Bluff,' she said briefly. 'Moxon's hawking her wares, and that was her attempt at talking up the price.'

Canning raised his brows. 'Likes playing with matches too, does she?'

'I warned her, sir, but you can't make someone hear when they don't want to listen.'

He smiled. 'A philosopher too! Thanks, Diane. That was a useful morning's work.'

There was, of course, a multiplicity of reasons why those attending the last concert of the last Ramillies Festival would never forget it.

Somehow it seemed the evening was pervaded by the strange sharp scent of finality. Somehow the gardens seemed more richly luxuriant, the fountains more ethereal in their ballet on the velvet of the lake, the peacocks more majestic in their regal progress than ever before.

The air was heavy with humidity and cloying with the perfume of the philadelphus below the terrace. The heatwave was set to break, and there was a quality to the light which gave the petals of the pink geraniums an almost fluorescent glow.

Inside the ballroom, the atmosphere was charged. The silence for Anna, when the close-packed audience rose, seemed to stretch on and on; somewhere a woman gave a hysterical sob, then smothered it. There was a sense of heightened reality about the whole occasion.

Principally, though, it was the music that would live in legend, after sensation had gathered the dust of history.

It was, as Anna herself had demanded, a traditional programme: Schubert, Chopin, Mozart, with Beethoven in the second half. Jonah, pale and sombre, contrived without distortion to temper the gaiety of an impromptu, the brilliance of a waltz, with a poignant shading of sweet gravity. Altering the programme from Mozart's good-humoured Sonata in D, he played instead the Fantasia and Sonata in C Minor, a work which had inspired Beethoven himself by its force and complexity. The applause after the first half was fervent, but almost reverential in character.

The interval was short; few people left their seats, and when the orchestra filed in, players were fretting nervously with instruments reacting badly to the temperature and the humidity.

But from the opening bars of Beethoven's sublime Piano Concerto in E♭ major – the enigmatically named *Emperor* – they, and the audience with them, were lifted on the music, soaring into the empyrean where they were together immortal, all air and fire, right up to the moment when the resonance of the final dramatic chord faded, and music at Ramillies was dead.

There was a long, emotional silence. On the platform Jonah sat,

Adam stood motionless, both with their heads bent. On the upturned faces of the orchestra could be seen here and there the glitter of tears.

When the applause came, it was explosive, and the audience rose as one, as if they had rehearsed the movement. There were no cries, no shouts of 'bravo' or 'encore', but a swell of sound so intense and so powerful that no one noticed that, overhead, the storm had broken. It drowned the diapason of thunder, the harsh drumming of the rain.

The two men came up to bow again and again. After such expense of emotional energy, they looked alike drained and exhausted. But alike, too, was the radiance which touched them both, as if tonight they had stood together on holy ground.

Tonight, Penny couldn't smile. It just didn't work; she had practised before the concert in the mirror above her dressing-table, but somehow the corners of her mouth quivered and shook and the muscles jumped in an ugly, scary way. Solemnity was her best offer.

And now she had run back through the rain to the house alone. She had left Adam with Jonah and the other musicians, Adam higher than she had ever known him before on the strange cocktail of emotions tonight had produced. She was sitting again in her bedroom, lit only by the lamp beside her bed, towelling her damp hair and staring again into the mirror's shadows.

A grave, pale face stared back at her, like the face of a stranger. It was alien in its impassivity, as if panic and pain were not prowling there, savage as beasts of prey, only just outside the thorn-fence of her self-control. It was alien, too, because it was an older face, a calmer face, the face of good dutiful Penny Beaumont, not –

She jumped to her feet. She mustn't go down that road, she mustn't!

She made herself a hot drink, had a hot bath, went to bed resigned to wakefulness. But unexpectedly sleep came upon her, and when Adam at last returned she did not even stir, lying with her cheek cupped in her hand like a tired child. He watched her for a long moment, then switched off the light and quietly slipped into bed himself.

*

'No, no!' Adam cried in the thickened voice of nightmare. He was pushing away the sheet which was his only covering, as if trying to throw off something or somebody which had a hold at his neck.

Penny woke, opened heavy eyes. In the muted light coming through the chinks in the curtain she could see Adam's face, contorted in some distress. Drowsily, she reached out to soothe him; he jumped at her touch, then mumbled something and turned over. His breathing quietened.

But she was awake now, and black recollection swept in like an oil slick. It was almost six o'clock; she had slept for nearly seven hours, though she still felt unrefreshed. Goodness only knew what time Adam had got to bed. He could sleep for hours yet, now the strain of the concert was over.

She managed to collect up underwear, jeans and a shirt and slip from the room without waking him, and after dressing in the bathroom went downstairs.

There had been so much to think about with the concert yesterday that she had reacted to the newspaper headline with the numbness of shock. Now, as she sat with a mug of tea listening to the rain dripping monotonously from the eaves, she was hurting, with the gut-wrenching agony of raw grief she had fondly believed would never afflict her again. The unexpected, unreasonable pain racked her, as if a knife were being slowly turned in her stomach.

It had always been a passion beyond reason. She had cherished no happy illusion that Dominic saw her differently from the other women who had burned up in his passing; there was never going to be a happy ending. Their love – if love it had been – had no tomorrow nor yesterday, and what had seemed everlasting day was swallowed now in death and eternal night.

Yet even death, even long mourning had not broken his spell. Black magic, she had said to him once, and he had laughed at her.

'Then make me immortal with a kiss, sweet Penny,' he had said, and she had complied but with a shiver, as if she could see Mephistopheles patient at his shoulder.

There had never been anyone like Dom. The Golden Boy, the others like Jonah and Adam had called him mockingly; so beautiful, so clever, so divinely gifted. He looked like some pre-Raphaelite seraph, with hair like a blond curly fleece, soft as a lamb's, and his golden hawk's eyes. Israfel, he liked to call himself, because that was the archangel destined to sound the Last Trump. She had imagined him sometimes, poised on a cloud of flame, his trumpet to his lips, pouring out scalding notes while below the world spun down to fiery destruction.

When she was with Dom, the air seemed thinner and colder and so exhilarating that you barely needed food or sleep. The drugs were a part of it, of course. You could tell when he was on speed, when he moved so frenetically that his dancing seemed to create a firestorm which sucked in all the oxygen, so that you were almost fighting for breath. And then he would take the moggies that calmed him down and made him langorous and sexy, and his irises would glow amber like the eyes of a grey Persian in the dark.

He'd offered them to her, naturally, and she'd tried it once but had hated the loss of control and personality. She didn't need them; being with Dom was ecstasy enough and she preferred champagne.

He didn't press her. Some people could take it, some couldn't, he said, and though they never mentioned her name, she knew they were both thinking of poor Jizzy.

Jizzy had been Dom's woman when first Penny met him, living inside the circle of light that surrounded him wherever he went. But it hadn't lasted once Jizzy started main-lining. When she died of an overdose, Dom had remained detached. You couldn't live someone else's life, he had said, and everybody's karma was different. That was shocking, but it was more shocking to find that it heightened rather than diminished her desire for him.

Well, she had paid for it, but not enough, apparently, never enough. Would any amount of suffering buy her freedom from his restless ghost, or was Dom with his beautiful decadent face haunting her to cry 'Revenge!'? All that was certain was that for her there could be no painless resolution.

Because now she knew that the person who had killed Dominic, who had returned her to a life that was respectable and pleasant and secure and unsatisfying, was here in Ramillies. It was someone she knew, someone she had talked with, laughed with, and no deep instinct this time had warned her of blood on the hands she might have touched or shaken.

Or held, caressed . . . She had seen the torn photograph, the baton snapped in rage. She knew that music, to someone like Adam, had imperatives beyond reason. She knew, too, for he had told her, that he had loved her when she was still Dom's girl, sparing him a smile or a laughing comment at a party.

Could Adam, kind, loving, gentle Adam – She must not even frame that thought, or she would never be able to pull herself together again, whatever the Colonel might say.

Perhaps it was all much simpler than that. Perhaps after all someone would find that Anna, too, had interrupted a burglary and they would wake from this nightmare with the shadows gone. But as she stared at the rain streaking the little window, her face was as bleak as the weather outside.

Since the days – before she ran away – when her foster-parents used to drag her to their house-church meetings and pray over her so unctuously that she had shaved her head for ease of washing, Sunday mornings had not been a significant feature in Liza Moxon's life.

They were the blank space that came after Saturday night and before Sunday lunch time when – normally under sheets she had meant to take to the laundromat the day before but somehow hadn't – she would struggle out of bed and stagger round to the Newt and Aardvark where she and her friends had a regular date with a vodka and lime to zap the morning-after feeling.

But this weekend, the night before had been a quiet evening in front of the box and early bed to escape shattering boredom. Which was how she came to be conscious at this uncivilised hour – seven o'clock, for chrissake – and wandering aimlessly round her seedy two-roomed ground-floor flat in bare feet and the outsize black T-shirt which served as nightwear.

She flicked on the radio and with the phony matiness of a radio jock providing familiar protection against the horrors of silence, eyed the dirty dishes and pans piled around the kitchen area with unease. But strong-mindedly overcoming it, she went to the cupboard to get a mug. They had all been used.

Liza swore, then went to fetch one of the three she had abandoned at various intervals on top of the piles of newspaper on the coffee table. The first she picked up had a scary colony of vaguely green organisms thriving on the bottom which would need to be scoured away; rejecting it in favour of one supporting less intimidating fauna, she swilled it out in the cluttered sink and made some strong instant coffee.

She pushed some clothes along the sofa to make space then sat down, her thin shoulders hunched forward and her small mouth drooping. She hated, more than anything else, having nothing she must do. There was too much in her short life that she would, from choice, never have time to think about again; she crammed her days and nights with activity so that she was seldom alone in this miserable place unless she was asleep, and not always even then. Its disorder depressed her; she didn't want to live like a pig, it was just that the way she had structured her life she didn't have time for regular cleaning and tidying and when it got to this state you needed to be feeling upbeat and full of energy to tackle it. Then of course when you were feeling like that the last thing that crossed your mind was to stay in and do housework. It would be different, of course, when she got her smart flat in London. If. She tried to blot out the negative thought.

She had been on a roll yesterday morning, sure that her luck had turned, that she was on course for the golden future she always fantasised about as she was dropping off to sleep: Cinderella, rescued at last by an editor substituting half his publishing kingdom and an open cheque-book for the princely hand in marriage. Now it looked as if she was back with the pumpkin and the eight white mice and the ashes of a dead fire.

After her scoop, she had seen herself fielding offers from all the famous newspapers, playing off one against the other, auctioning her talents, even ... But all they had done was send down their own big-name journalists, and now it wasn't her story any more, it was public property. There had been one tentative approach, from Personnel at one of the lesser-known tabloids: hoping for better things she had let herself sound underwhelmed, he was offended, and now she wasn't sure whether, even if she grovelled, the offer was still there.

A scowl drew her dark brows together. How could she go back, to the covert – and not-so-covert – sneers of the sad people at the *Express*? She knew they hated her, and she knew why, too. She wasn't a nice person. She had learned her life-skills in a school where if you let your guard down, there were teeth in your jugular next time you checked. She had to be tougher and meaner and brighter than anyone, because quick wits and a sharp tongue were all she had.

She didn't have anyone in her corner, didn't want anyone. She could be very entertaining when she chose, and there were acquaintances who might describe themselves as friends, but the last thing she needed was emotional baggage to slow her down when she was running for the train out. And if she missed it, if she wasn't going to be the princess after all but just Cinders sweeping up the crumbs of local news, she might just as well run a hot bath (if the geyser was working) and retire to it with a razor blade.

There was one chance, one last card that might turn up trumps. That was what had kept her playing hermit in this dismal cell. She had given her address and telephone number to anyone who would take it, including some who were reluctant, at the murder scene on Friday. She had talked about money and fame, offering public interest as a user-friendly fig-leaf to cover the nakedness of greed and vanity. Surely there must be someone with a story to tell?

And once she had it, she was back in the game. The big mistake had been handing her story to Emrys just because the *Express* was paying her wages, and she wouldn't make that blunder again. Next time, if they wanted the story they would have to take her too.

If there was a next time. The trouble was that the grubby white telephone had remained relentlessly silent and she could feel the chill breath of the black dog of depression, which lurked always at her shoulder, ready to snap, then gnaw, and ultimately devour . . .

The rat-tat-tat at the door was so unexpected that she leapt to her feet and looked around her in dismay. She hadn't thought of a prospect arriving unannounced at her chipped green front door in Albert Lane, the little alleyway which ran up the side of a Chinese takeaway, but it certainly wasn't a mate popping in just to be neighbourly. No one in this locality so much as opened their curtains on a Sunday before midday.

You would only come at this hour if you didn't want to be seen. And if you didn't want anyone to know you were talking to press, the story you had to tell had to be good.

Calling, 'Just a minute – don't go away,' she grabbed armfuls of clothes, clearing the sofa and a battered armchair, and thrust them into a cupboard from which she snatched a fringed black Indian skirt which she pulled on.

She even glanced in the mirror which hung on the wall near the door, ran her hand over the soft stubble on her head and licked her finger so that she could smooth her heavy brows into shape, then crossed her fingers at her reflection for luck. This could be where that golden future began.

Or not. With pathetic optimism, she opened the door to her killer.

11

It was at ten o'clock that the police came to arrest Adam.

Penny, her eyes huge in a face grey with shock, was sitting at the breakfast table which was still littered with used dishes and the Sunday papers she had gone to Cranbourne to fetch before Adam came down as a defence against the awkwardness of conversation.

The police had taken him away, politely enough but without explanation. She had tried to talk to them, ask them questions, but it was as if there were armoured glass between them which prevented her engaging them as fellow human beings. She felt like hurling the middle-class adage she had been taught in childhood, 'The police are our friends,' but suddenly and chillingly she found herself outside that cosy circle.

They had shown her what they said was a search warrant and she had looked at it obediently because that was what they seemed to want her to do, though she had not the faintest idea what she was meant to be looking for. She could hear them upstairs now, three big men moving heavily about, opening and shutting doors and moving furniture.

Opposite her, strategically angled like cats watching a mousehole, were two police officers, a man and a woman. She was Sergeant Braithwaite, she said; a stocky woman with bright blue, wary eyes. The coarse-looking man beside her, whose salient features were a notebook, a pen, an untidy ginger moustache and a faint self-satisfied smile, was Constable – Jenkins, was it? Something like that. She had listened passively to their introductions, which were cool, impersonal. They used forms of words designed for their protection while laying her, stiffened by fear, open to dissection like the worm stiffened with formaldehyde and pinned to a cork board in her school biology class. It was that hostility which quashed any half-formed, disloyal doubts.

'Perhaps you can give me some idea of what happened on Friday morning, Mrs Beaumont?' The words were polite, the tone an assault.

'Friday morning.' Panic clouded her mind. What was there to differentiate Friday morning from Thursday, or even yesterday morning? Yet hesitation would sound at best feeble-minded, at worst suspicious.

Playing for time, she said, 'Usually we get up together, though this morning I woke early, about six, and Adam was still asleep. But Friday – let me think. It was – oh, it was the morning after the concert, that's right, and Ben came in – Ben Lousada.' She was gaining confidence, elaborating. 'We talked for a bit, then Adam went out – '

'Went where?'

'Well, over to the practice rooms, probably, or to the hall – '

'But in fact you don't know?' The man made an obvious note of that; the woman glanced at papers she had in front of her. 'So what was your husband's programme that morning?'

'He had an orchestra rehearsal later.' Penny hesitated, but, something warning her that this was a question to which they already knew the answer, added, 'And before that he should have had a meeting with Anna – '

'Ah yes. A meeting that was, perhaps, unlikely to be very amicable?'

'It didn't happen. He didn't go.'

'Why not, Mrs Beaumont?' The question was aggressive and the manner of its asking overbearing.

Penny straightened in her chair, as if a genetic memory of fighting men who had suffered interrogation and revealed no more than name, rank and serial number were bracing her spine, and responded with a certain hauteur, 'I'm not in the habit of cross-questioning my husband, sergeant. Perhaps he was too busy, or he knew that Anna was busy somewhere else – '

'Or dead, perhaps?' The detective did not wait for her indignant rebuttal, but said with shrewdly calculated abruptness, 'Do you know what kind of pens your husband uses?'

With the wind taken out of her sails by this change of tack, Penny stammered, '*Pens*? Well, he has a Waterman's fountain pen, black enamel – '

'Does he ever use pens like this?' Braithwaite held up a yellow plastic pen with a black top: commonplace, totally innocuous. It could, in this context, only spell deadly danger.

Penny said coldly, 'No. And I can assure you, I would know. I buy all that sort of thing for him, and he's never had one of those.'

'I see.' She paused artistically for a moment, as if weighing her words. 'The thing is, Mrs Beaumont, that a yellow pen with your husband's fingerprints on it was found lying beside Anna Harting-ton's body.'

The shock was like a punch to the solar plexus. Penny had to stop herself from doubling up, as if she had indeed been winded, but it produced a visceral response.

'Then it must have been planted there,' she said fiercely. 'Pre-cisely how desperate are you to make a quick arrest?'

It would have helped if there had been outrage at the suggestion, but the constable did not even raise his eyes and the sergeant did not lower hers. Penny went on, more shakily, 'I would advise you to be very careful before you make accusations like that. He wouldn't have been down at the cottage anyway.'

'No? Yet you said, didn't you,' the woman leaned over ostenta-tiously to check her colleague's notes, 'that you didn't know where he went after breakfast on Friday?'

Biting her lip, Penny could think of nothing to say.

'But you do know, you claim, what pens he had. You would know, for instance, what pens he would have in the pocket of the jacket he put on when he left here this morning.'

Drowning in a sea of confusion, she clutched a passing straw of certainty. 'If he had put his pens in there, he would have his fountain pen, of course. And he would probably have his silver propelling pencil. The other pens he has are fine point fibre-tips; he likes those.'

'But he wouldn't have had one of these yellow ones? Or, say, a clear plastic ballpoint with a blue cap?'

Penny shook her head. 'Definitely not.'

The man, whose head had been bent as he scribbled indus-triously, looked up and the faint smile was quite marked now.

Braithwaite did not smile. She said, with what seemed almost like personal rather than professional triumph, 'Strange that you should be so definite. You see, we checked just before he got in the car, and one of his pens was a clear ballpoint with a blue top.'

'But he could have picked that up anywhere!' Penny cried hotly. 'You know how it is with pens – '

Then she broke off, and what she had said hung on the air between them.

'Yes. Of course. Well, Mrs Beaumont, perhaps we could turn now to the question of relations between Anna Hartington and your husband – '

As she spoke, there were footsteps on the stairs; the door from the hall opened and one of the searchers came in carrying a plastic bag holding a white handkerchief and a key. He looked at the sergeant, who nodded permission, then said to Penny, 'We found this key wrapped in the handkerchief in the pocket of a grey linen jacket. Do you recognise it?'

Penny looked at it dully. It was an ordinary-looking key with a clip attached, as if it had come from some sort of key-ring. She shook her head.

'If it was in that pocket it could be from a practice room or cupboard up at the house. He hasn't worn that jacket since Friday so he probably forget to put it back, with all that – happened.'

The constable took down what she had said as the man thanked her courteously and went out to the car.

'Now, Mrs Beaumont.' Like a bulldog which has been interrupted but not diverted from its attack, Sergeant Braithwaite was returning to her questioning when there were more footsteps on the stairs, hurrying this time, and another of the detectives burst into the room. He was young, with a bright enthusiastic face, and if he wasn't actually smiling, there was no mistaking his satisfaction.

'Look what we found at the back of one of the desk drawers!' he crowed.

He held up another of the ubiquitous plastic bags. Inside was a torn-up photograph, on which the savage red pen-marks were plainly visible, together with the snapped halves of a pretty Victorian conductor's baton.

Suddenly Penny's head felt very cold, very cold and very light, as if at any moment it might float away off her shoulders. She got to her feet unsteadily and heard a high voice say, as if from a great distance, 'I think I'm going to faint,' then recognised it as her own.

When she came to, her head was between her knees and she was being supported on one of the kitchen chairs by the policewoman. Her head hurt; as she straightened up cautiously she put her hand to it and found a rising lump under her hair.

'You hit your head on the table as you fell,' Braithwaite said. Her voice had softened markedly. 'Are you all right?'

'Yes – yes, I'm fine.' Penny sat back and closed her eyes. 'I'm sorry. That was stupid.'

The young detective said urgently, 'I think we should take her into hospital.'

Hearing his defensive tone, Penny opened her eyes and caught the look they were exchanging. She smiled bitterly.

'How touching, that you're all so kind and concerned! You think I'm going to claim you beat me up, don't you?'

Braithwaite tensed, and Penny had the curious feeling that there was antagonism there which did not simply relate to the current situation. 'Our reason for suggesting that we should take you to be checked over is your own welfare – '

'Oh, don't bother,' Penny said wearily. 'The bump on the head is nothing, but you're fussing about that yet perfectly happy about the mental beating-up you've been giving me, though I haven't done anything wrong. It's quite funny, really.'

She began to laugh, and once she had started the sergeant's protests about her expressed willingness to co-operate made it seem funnier still and she found it hard to stop. When she did, she found that tears were rolling down her cheeks and smudged them away with her fingers.

'Brian,' snapped Braithwaite, 'Mrs Beaumont's in shock. Make a cup of tea, will you?'

Shocked himself by this demeaning demand from a female who should understand her place in a kitchen, Jenks opened his mouth to protest. Encountering a glare of unambiguous savagery from his superior officer he thought the better of it, rose and picked up the kettle with an artistic, if unappreciated, mime of someone working out what to do with a mystery object.

The younger officer went out to the car and the last of the team, satisfied with the results of the search, followed him out into the drizzling rain. Diane Braithwaite came to sit down again at the table, and the car swished away on the damp stones. A silence fell.

After her outburst, Penny felt a strange calm descend, as if they had found themselves sitting together for some purely social reason. 'Braithwaite,' she said inconsequentially. 'That's your name, isn't it? I knew a Braithwaite once. He was Sarn't Major in my father's regiment.'

She did not remark the hostile bristling of the other woman, as if her hackles were rising preparatory to launching an attack on condescension, perhaps, or snobbery.

'I thought he was wonderful,' Penny went on dreamily, as if the distraction of an old memory were somehow therapeutic. 'He was a darling man, the nicest man I ever knew. He sounded terrifying on the parade ground, but he was really gentle and funny. I always wished he was my father, because he wouldn't be angry when I got things wrong, or cried when I'd fallen off my horrible pony. He used to keep chocolate biscuits in his office in an old tin – '

'An old tin with the Queen's Coronation on it,' the other said gruffly.

'That's right! But how on earth – oh, of course, Braithwaite! Are you his daughter? Oh, lucky you! I remember you a little, I think. Diana – no, Diane.'

A dark flush settled on Diane's cheeks. 'I think I – er – remember you too.'

Lost in her own thoughts, Penny hardly heard her. 'You always won prizes at the regiment's children's sports, didn't you, and I was never very athletic. That was something else I couldn't get right, as far as my father was concerned.'

Her voice wobbled, but she controlled it, saying in a high, hard voice, 'You see, I've always been a complete failure in his eyes, starting with being a girl instead of another boy. Perhaps if I'd married a soldier he'd have forgiven me, but musicians as far as he's concerned are bohemians, probably communists and certainly incomprehensible wimps. And how, how on earth I'm going to tell him about this – this – '

Tears were starting to well up again in her eyes. Diane jumped to her feet. 'Jenks, whatever do you think you're doing with that tea?'

Jenks, with the air of a dog which knows it has been kicked as a displacement activity, brought over the mugs with tea-bags still floating on the top and dumped them down on the cluttered table so that they slopped. He sat down himself, and looked from one to the other with a smirk.

'Well, well, fancy you two being old chums! Daughters of the regiment, don't they call it? Shame, isn't it, that you're not meeting under happier circumstances when you could have had a good old chin-wag about the good old days, couldn't you?'

Satisfied with the pall of embarrassment he had cast, he blew delicately on his tea and slurped it. Neither of the women touched theirs; after a few more awkward minutes, Diane got to her feet.

Penny found it hard to convince them that she would prefer that they did not fetch someone to stay with her, but at last they went. On the table before her, the sordid mugs of tea stood with a cooling, oily film gathering round the slimy dark brown tea-bags.

It seemed strange to be alone. Her ears were almost ringing with

116

the silence, which was only broken by the steady drip-dripping of the rain.

Her eye fell on the paper in front of her, dominated by two pictures, both publicity shots, one of Anna and one of Dominic. Dom's was the familiar one which had been used, she remembered with pain, at the time of his murder. It was his own favourite and hers; he had been photographed in profile, in the act of raising his trumpet to his lips, and the background was very dark, showing in strongly lit contrast the bright hair and the glittering instrument.

The trumpet shall sound; the quotation came unbidden, and completed itself in her head without conscious thought, *and the dead shall be raised*.

She shuddered uncontrollably. Unimaginable evils were even now writhing up from this newly reopened grave.

Doreen Stone was whizzing round the warren of little rooms on the top floor at Ramillies, christened by Eden Hartington the Players' Ghetto. Despite the weather, it was still warm and her face shone with heat and exertion as she stripped sheets from beds with practised skill and wielded hoover, duster and damp cloth with goodwill if not precision.

She was just closing the door thankfully on the last of the vacated rooms (was it a hobby, she wondered, to assemble small piles of nail-clippings in unexpected crevices, or some sort of heathen superstition?) when she heard someone coming up the wooden stairs and Ben Lousada appeared.

He had obviously been out running. He was wearing shorts and a singlet, his legs were splashed and his dark hair was plastered to his head with rain and sweat. He had climbed the stairs quite slowly; even from a distance she could hear his laboured breathing.

He did not see her in the dark of the long corridor and turned the other way towards his room. But he was a great favourite with Doreen and she hailed him.

'Do yourself a mischief, you will, out running like that till you're exhausted!'

He started at her voice and was frowning as he turned, but when he saw her his usual cheerful grin appeared and he came towards her with one hand clasped melodramatically to his bosom.

117

'Oooh, what a turn you gave me!' he cried. 'Me nerves is in a shocking state.'

She eyed him indulgently. 'What you doing, still here then, Ben? Thought you'd have been off like a shot, back to the bright lights and all the girls who've been sitting in every night waiting for you to get back.'

Well, I would,' he said confidentially, taking the duster out of her hand and clasping it in his own, 'but it's you, Doreen. It's the thought of leaving you – I just couldn't hack it. Give me another couple of days, I said to myself, and she'll stop fighting it.'

She giggled comfortably. 'Oh, that'll be right.'

He looked disappointed. 'Aren't you going to say, "Oooh, you are a one"? I've always wanted someone to say that to me – that or "You're a proper caution" but nobody ever has. And it's not for want of trying, trust me.'

'Get you done for sexual harassment, more like.' She retrieved her hand and her duster and flicked his nose with it so that he sneezed. 'How long're you staying, then?'

He winked conspiratorially. 'Basically, as long as I can get away with it. I'm skint as usual, and while it may not be the Hilton the price is right. But Judy's beginning to tap her foot – I doubt if I can swing it much longer.'

Doreen sniffed; she wasn't Judy's biggest fan. Tough-minded herself, she thought her a feeble creature, and never felt quite comfortable with her either. For instance, she'd told her long ago to call her Doreen, but she just went on calling her Mrs Stone in that rather frosty posh voice, and even though Doreen always pointedly called her Judy, she never seemed to take the hint.

'Just wants everybody out of the way so she can have a clear field with poor Mr Hicks, that's what she's after if you ask me.'

Ben's dark eyes danced. 'Doreen, you're a wicked gossip and I love you. How many people haven't gone?'

'Only about three – they're packing. But there were enough people down the hall when I came up here, all with their luggage and falling over those big music cases they have and swearing. Shocking, some of the language was, and from people you would think ought to know better.'

'There's not a sound or a sign of anyone downstairs now. It's like a morgue – oops, sorry.'

Doreen sighed. 'Poor soul,' she said. 'Awful, innit?'

But it had reminded her once more of her own concern, and she gathered together her black plastic bags and cleaning implements. 'Got to get going. See you later, Ben.'

She struggled awkwardly with her burdens down the narrow stairs. She ought to be getting back in case the police turned up – though her spirits had risen when they hadn't come round hot-foot yesterday – but she was so hot and sticky that she really fancied a cuppa and a sit-down first, and a bit of a chat with Judy if she was there. Maybe she would know what was going on.

Judy was there, just back from a Sunday expedition to the supermarket at Fotheringham and obviously in a sour mood. She barely thanked Doreen for helping her unpack and put away the contents of a depressingly large number of carrier bags, even though Doreen had done her hours and by rights should have been sitting down with a mug of Nes.

'It seems ever so quiet now, Judy,' Doreen said, finding a space in the freezer for a stack of ready meals. 'You'll soon have the place to yourselves again, won't you?'

'I wish!' Judy's tone was bitter. 'Oh, I understood everyone was to be away by lunch time, but Jonah hasn't said a word about leaving and Ben Lousada still seems to be hanging around for some reason. Maurice obviously doesn't like to ask them, but he just hasn't thought that it's a lot more work for me. Chris and Jancis were still around too, though perhaps they've gone at last. But certainly when I went out this morning the only house-car they'd left me was that awful old Land-Rover, and it's ripped my skirt – look!'

She showed the triangular tear in her flowery print skirt, and Doreen tutted sympathetically, then added with apparent casualness, 'Do you think the police have anyone in particular in mind, Judy?'

But it was still too direct an approach.

'I really wouldn't have the least idea, I'm afraid, Mrs Stone.'

There it was again, that funny emphasis on her name, as if Doreen might not know what it was. Well, if she wasn't going to learn anything useful she might as well go home and be safely out of the way of any more demands on her time. It was just on one o'clock anyway – Gary would be wanting some lunch.

Just as she was formulating the thought, a door somewhere in the house opened and someone shouted urgently, 'Judy! Maurice! Is anybody there?'

'That's Jonah,' Judy said. 'Whatever – '

119

Followed by Doreen, she hurried out into the hall where Jonah, standing at the open door of Anna's sitting-room, greeted her with agitation.

'There you are! I couldn't think where everyone was. It's awful – they've arrested Adam!'

He dived back into the room again, and through the open door could be heard the newscaster's voice – '. . . a report from James Weatherby in Fotheringham.'

In front of a backdrop of the Fotheringham police headquarters, an earnest young man was talking to camera.

'In a dramatic move this morning, police investigating the murder of Anna Hartington during the Hartington Music Festival near Fotheringham, Sussex, arrested Adam Beaumont, conductor of the world-famous Hartington Philharmonic Orchestra. Speaking a short time ago, Detective Inspector Will Canning announced Beaumont had been charged not only with the recent killing, but also with that of musician Dominic Leigh, whose murder four years ago in the same area had remained unsolved.'

A clip of DI Canning exuding satisfaction at a press conference appeared, just as Maurice came in with Ben, whom he had met in the hall, and joined the others in stupefied silence as Canning repeated the information they had heard already, refused to answer further questions and retired into the building behind. The reporter wrapped up the item and handed back to the studio.

'The Football Association has announced today – '

Jonah snapped off the set, but it was Ben who found his voice first, gesturing towards the Sunday newspapers which were spread out on the coffee table.

'Was there any hint they were fingering Adam?'

Jonah shook his head. 'I've got all the main papers there, and I haven't seen a thing. Playing it close to their chest, no doubt.'

Judy exclaimed, 'But *Adam*, for heaven's sake! That's – that's ridiculous!'

Maurice, today looking tired and pale and suddenly much older, echoed weakly, 'Ridiculous!'

An awkward silence fell. It was Ben who said, 'Penny! What about Penny? She must know all about it. Why hasn't she phoned us?'

'Oh dear, I put the answerphone on,' Judy said. 'It was just going all the time. She wouldn't have been able to get through.'

'Perhaps she's at the police station with him,' Maurice suggested.

120

'I suggest we check,' Jonah said grimly. 'That went out some time ago, and once the press got it her phone would be jammed. And they'll be on her like a pack of hunting-dogs.'

Ben spun round. 'I'll get over there,' he said.

'Take a car, Ben, in case she's trapped already. We'll all come – the men at least, in case we're needed.'

The men hurried out, Maurice uncertainly bringing up the rear.

Doreen said awkwardly, 'Well, I'd best be getting back. Give me a call when you need me again, Judy.'

Judy didn't seem to have heard her. She was gazing longingly after Maurice's departing back, and giving her an old-fashioned look Doreen went home.

Penny knew she ought to be doing something – phoning people, marshalling the defences she and more importantly Adam needed. But somehow, here she was still sitting at the table.

It was like having a wound which has been pumping out blood; if the bleeding stopped, you weren't going to move in case it started again. But the catch was that the remission was temporary and you couldn't sit here for ever.

Adam had a right to her loyalty. Loyalty went deep with Penny; it echoed through nature, nurture and philosophy. He had loved her, cherished her, done nothing to forfeit that right. Surely Penny Beaumont knew where her duty lay.

Unless, unless . . . What if she had married her lover's killer – slept with him, tended his needs, loved him in her fashion – when she herself was the reward for his crime? When she had inspired the bullet that killed Dominic – and Anna too, for they said that once the taboo was broken it was easy to breach again?

Penny Drayton-Smith, with Dominic's cynical whispers in her ear, had almost – almost – come to despise honesty as naïvety and truth as folly. Almost, but not quite. Adam had restored a gentler faith but was his in fact a greater, almost unimaginable betrayal?

The Adam she knew could not do it. Yes, she still believed that. But then there was another Adam whom she knew not at all, an Adam who resided in a mind-world where sounds and their strange, pure mathematical relations and combinations had a significance and power which outweighed all the normal human emotions. Did it also supersede the moral law?

There was a pain around her heart, as if the bleeding she had imagined had started up again. As she groaned, burying her face in her hands, she heard the sound of an engine and looking up saw a car drawing up in the middle of the stable yard. Was it the police – or even, please God, Adam come back, released and cleared?

Galvanized into action, she went over to the little window and peering out saw a man festooned with cameras climbing out. Catching the movement at the window he spun round, camera at the ready.

Protective instinct prompted her recoil, but she wasn't sure whether that was before or after the flash and the clicking whirr of the automatic shutter. Snatching at the jaunty blue gingham curtains she drew them together so violently that the rings clattered on their pine pole. Almost in the same movement, she reached across to the door to drop the catch on the lock, one moment before the assault began.

First there was the doorbell, then someone began hammering on the door and shouting, 'Come on, love, we know you're in there! Let's have a look at you.' Then another voice: 'Just come out and talk to us, dear, for a moment, that's all, and then we'll leave you alone.'

She heard more cars arriving, and then the phone began to ring. She did not answer it, but it did not stop, ringing on and interminably on. Mesmerised, she stood watching someone trying the door handle and breathed a prayer of thankfulness that she had reached it first.

Then the doorbell rang, and kept on ringing, on and on until it seemed to be playing a sort of crazy duet with the telephone providing syncopation. It was five minutes (she timed it on the cheerful sunflower clock on the kitchen wall) before the torture of noise and fear drove her sobbing to her knees. And still it continued.

Penny didn't raise her head after that, even when a car pulled up just outside, and the bell stopped pealing and she could hear shouting and angry exchanges above the noise of the still-ringing phone.

'Penny, Penny, are you there?' The voice was close, on the other side of the door, and familiar – Ben Lousada's voice, she remembered, like someone recalling a friend from another world, another time.

Creeping closer, she pressed herself against the door and whimpered, 'Oh, Ben!' Though she knew it was inaudible, she could not find strength to make herself heard.

'I'm sure she's moving just behind the door,' she heard him say, then there was another voice.

'Penny, it's Jonah Dancey. Tap on the door if you're there.'

She looked doubtfully at her shaking hand, but at last raised it to knock feebly.

'Well done. Now listen.' The voice was strong and reassuring. 'It's going to be all right. I want you to stand behind the door – behind it as it opens – and let me in. Maurice and Ben are keeping them back and we'll have you safe in a moment.'

She responded instinctively to the authoritative tone. She managed to stand and even, at last, to find the strength to release the catch and turn the heavy metal handle.

As soon as it opened a chink, Jonah was inside, slamming the door to behind him

He looked stricken at her appearance. 'Good God,' he said, as he looked at her, ash-pale, swollen-eyed and trembling. 'This is outrageous.'

There were coats hanging on pegs beside the door; he grabbed one of them, and handed it to her.

'Over your head,' he said briefly. 'The car's right outside the door and Ben's fighting mad already. God help the reporter who lays a finger on you.'

She couldn't speak. Clinging to him, she plunged into the rattling, flashing maelstrom of cameras and shouting voices. She could hear Ben's threatening yells above them all, then she was inside the car with the door shut. The others jumped in and Maurice, at the wheel, drove off with scant regard for the safety of photographers who thrust themselves and their cameras into his path.

The rain had stopped now. In Albert Lane, a girl in distressed black jeans and a black laced bodice was knocking on a chipped green door next to a Chinese takeaway.

'Funny, innit?' she said to the youth behind her whose single lock of bright scarlet hair curled down on to his shoulders from a naked scalp. 'She said her tongue would be hanging out this morning. Stayed in last night, didn't she – you'd think she'd be stir-crazy by now.'

'Maybe she stayed in and got guttered on her own.' He wasn't interested. 'Come on, Nicky, there's a bottle with my name on it down the pub.'

'Liza!' Nicky rattled the letter-box. 'Liza, are you in there? Wake up! We're going round the Newt – you coming?'

The boy had turned away. 'Suit yourself. I'm off, anyhow.'

'Hang on a minute,' she said, and dropping to her knees pushed open the letter-box and peered in.

12

God, he was smug!

Diane Braithwaite, watching Canning's virtuoso performance on the News, peered more closely at the set. Was it possible that his tie (heavy silk with a fat, confident knot) was smirking too, or was that just a mark on the screen?

No, she definitely didn't like him, after all. He was far too sure of himself, and if there was one thing you should have picked up on the way to your flashy cap-badge, it was that in police-work you could never be sure of anything.

Diane had a couple of hours off, so she had come back to her flat in Fotheringham to grab some lunch. She liked her flat. It was undemanding, neat and functional; she had furnished it with neat, functional pieces of furniture and had the walls emulsioned white throughout. But one wall in the sitting-room was taken up by a startling abstract in black, white and orange which had set her back most of a month's wages and was, she considered, worth every penny.

She left the News on as she went to and fro to the galley kitchen, making a sandwich, opening a beer, and glanced at it from time to time.

Somehow it was hard to keep her mind on the problems of the world when so many of them seemed both monotonous and hopelessly intractable. It was the problem of Penny Drayton-Smith which kept pushing its way into her consciousness, like some unwelcome caller getting a foot in the door. She had tried her best to exclude it, but now it was well and truly in – lounging on the sofa, so to speak – and she wasn't happy.

When she had heard that the husband of her childhood bugbear was being arrested, Diane was less than devastated. She hadn't paused at the time to analyse her feelings but, 'You may be prettier than me and more charming than me and do the right thing more often than I do but at least I'm not married to a murderer,' would pass for a reasonably accurate summary.

When you put it like that, it wasn't exactly heart-warming, was it? Not for a grown woman and a police officer at that. In fact, even if you allowed for arrested development on this one, it would be sort of a nasty attitude for a ten-year-old.

She wouldn't even be considering it now, if Penny hadn't talked about her father. Dad was a star as fathers go, of course, no doubt about it, and Diane had never known what it was not to feel loved and treasured. But the lay figure she had constructed to represent Penny Drayton-Smith would have despised him; secure within the Teflon shield of social status, she wouldn't have remembered or even noticed someone as lowly as the RSM. It would have been all right to hate someone like that.

But it wasn't all right to hate a vulnerable kid who had grown up with the agony of a coldly critical father, who felt she had been nothing but a failure all her life. She wasn't the spoiled Princess for whom everything had always been perfect – indeed, she must have been a lot tougher than she looked not to have gone completely off the rails. You had to feel sympathy for someone like that.

Of course, it was Diane's job to question Adam Beaumont's wife as thoroughly as possible. Thoroughly – but that wasn't the same as mercilessly. She knew there had been a strain in her questioning which, while being perfectly within the rules, she might not have inflicted on another innocent woman in an obvious state of shock. She'd certainly had a bad fright when Penny fainted.

Damn, damn, damn. Desperate Di screws up again. She scowled absently at the television, now showing a pressure group explaining why the grant of £1.5 million was too little, too late. She really wasn't doing very well, and she didn't like herself much, just at the moment.

She was turning to pick up the beer bottle when she heard, 'News is just coming in of another killing in the Fotheringham area where conductor Adam Beaumont was arrested earlier today,' and spun round.

'The body of a young woman was discovered at her home in the town this morning. Her identity has not been disclosed, but the police made this brief statement a few minutes ago.'

Canning wasn't looking smug now. He was standing in a seedy street somewhere, his hair ruffled and his tie slightly squint. He

125

gave nothing beyond the bald facts already stated and in answer to a question about links between the killings, said only that the police were keeping an open mind.

Diane, already shoving the last of her sandwich ungracefully into her mouth and grabbing her handbag, paused only to hear the newsreader add, 'We shall of course bring you an update on this story on the next news programme – '

She zapped it with the remote control and was scurrying down the stairs when she heard her phone ringing. She didn't need to go back to find out what that was about.

The situation at Albert Lane was chaotic, the atmosphere sour. Police cars were blocking off the end of the cul-de-sac and a couple of uniformed constables were struggling to control the gathering crowd, since the thin blue line just at the moment was seriously stretched.

A television van was parked on the far side of the street and there were men with cameras draped like bunting about their persons pushing in front of resentful rubber-neckers who had believed themselves assured of a ring-side seat for their Sunday afternoon's entertainment.

Canning, shirt collar unbuttoned and tie nowhere to be seen, was pacing about the lane, snarling at anyone unlucky enough to cross his path.

'Yes of course, move the blasted car aside for the SOCOs,' he snapped as one of the harassed young men approached to announce that the scene of crime van was waiting to get in. 'Good God, is there no one with any initiative?'

The constable, who had been bawled out ten minutes earlier for letting the Chinese restaurant owner have access to his premises without checking first, raised martyred eyes to his fellow sufferer as he went off to obey instructions.

It was all the fault of the low-life scum who had found the body, Canning mused savagely as he stood aside at the door of the squalid little property to let the men in white overalls take over. He stopped just short of blaming the wretched Liza Moxon for allowing herself to be so inconveniently murdered, but there was no doubt he would have strung the other pair up by their thumbs, given half a chance, with a whoop and a holler.

Instead of telephoning the police, as it was every citizen's duty to do, they had been inspired instead to phone three of the grubbiest tabloids to auction their exclusive story. Now they were in a car with a reporter from the *Daily Filth* or whatever the rag called itself, who was having a wonderful time protecting his investment while making life as difficult as he dared for the investigating officer. The next time Canning had half an hour to spare he was going to go through the statute book with a fine-tooth comb to find something to pin on them. Pity they had phased out boiling oil.

Because they had phoned the police eventually, of course. Only, egged on by their mentor, the policeman they had selected to receive their confidence was the Chief Constable, interrupted at a lunch party he was giving for the Lord Lieutenant and several other local worthies.

Jack Peckham was in orbit by the time Canning reached him, and he had been forced to endure the most uncomfortable interview of his gilded career. Seething at the injustice of it all, he had been unwise enough to ask what he could possibly have been expected to do about it.

Peckham, smarting himself, had countered unfairly, 'Never mind the stable door, Canning. Get after the bloody horse, and see if you can wipe some of the egg off our faces.'

Despite priding himself on his sense of humour, Canning failed to appreciate this unconsidered gem. There was nothing remotely amusing in arriving at the crime scene to an ironic cheer from the waiting press, or in conducting the enquiry under a merciless media spotlight. And having put himself forward to claim the glory for clearing up two murders, he now found himself trapped in the humiliating position of trying to explain away a third.

He wasn't a fool either. Of course this prompted nasty niggling doubts where there had been happy certainty. Beaumont had rehearsed the orchestra all day and conducted a concert at night, then stayed drinking with the musicians till after two. Perhaps he'd done it then, and popped back to be, as he claimed and she had confirmed coincidentally in her statement, innocently asleep when his wife woke up early this morning. Yes, a time of death of three in the morning would be handy. Otherwise –

He spotted someone who must be the pathologist coming in with his bag of instruments. He was a burly fellow with a healthy complexion, more like a farmer than a medical man, and as he passed Canning caught his arm.

'Dr Pardoe? Have you spoken to the police surgeon?' he

demanded peremptorily, without introduction. 'We need the time of death as a matter of urgency.'

The other man eyed him with sardonic amusement. 'Ah, Canning, I presume. You were described to me as a young man in a hurry. Yes, I'm Donald Pardoe. How do you do?'

Canning reluctantly performed the ritual courtesy. 'Time of death?' he prompted.

'Right. When was she last seen?'

'Around six yesterday evening, I understand.'

'And they found her about twelve this morning. Well, since you're in such a hurry I can confidently state that death took place between the hours of six last night and twelve today.'

He chuckled happily at this hoary pathologist's joke, but Canning's sense of humour still seemed to be in acute failure.

'Perhaps we could trouble you for something just a touch more precise?' he forced out.

'Patience, man, patience! Just let me get in there and see the poor lass, then I'll fit it together with what Dr Patel has given me already. We'll have something for you before too long. Keep smiling!'

With maddening serenity Pardoe strolled unhurriedly inside.

Judy was fed up to the back teeth with Jonah Dancey. He had simply taken over as if he, not Maurice, were the new master of Ramillies.

He'd ordered her – that was the only way to describe it – to go and make strong sweet tea for Penny. Not that she wouldn't have offered – poor Penny looked a complete wreck and naturally she was happy to do anything she could – but it was the principle of the thing, that was all.

She'd pointedly asked Penny how she took her tea. 'Weak and naked,' Penny said with a shaky smile but before Judy could even nod her satisfaction, Jonah had steam-rollered her as well.

Then of course when she'd made it according to instructions, and offered it to Penny with a disparaging, one-woman-to-another smile, he'd poured in a great slug of Maurice's best brandy, Penny had drunk it like a lamb and begun to perk up.

'Do people know about this stuff?' she said, sipping a second cup. 'Is it legal?'

Which presumably was a joke, since all the men laughed, though it seemed silly rather than funny to Judy.

Then Jonah had made all sorts of phone calls: to a friend of his who was a top solicitor, to a friend of his who did public relations, to that ghastly Larry to say he'd be staying for a bit to help out.

Well, thank you *very* much.

So Ben had jumped on the band-wagon too, and said, 'Would you like me to hang about as well, Maurice? Be a gofer – it's one of the things I do best.'

She'd tried to catch Maurice's eye but he wasn't looking at her and agreed with what looked almost like enthusiasm, though surely it should have been obvious that Ben was taking advantage of the situation to do a bit of sponging.

So Ben in his self-appointed role had taken himself off to see what was happening over at the stables and now he was back reporting that the press infestation had gone – folded their tents, he had said oddly, then something about Arabs silently stealing away, though what they could have been doing there she was at a loss to understand.

Penny, who had stopped shaking but was still pale and quiet, looked up eagerly.

'Oh, thank God for that! I'll get back home then. Thank you so much, you've all been wonderful – '

'I'll take you across, shall I, and see you in,' Judy offered eagerly, but Ben and Jonah both spoke at once.

'Forget it!'

'No, I don't think that's a good idea.'

Then Maurice, to Judy's surprise and chagrin, got up and came to sit beside Penny on the sofa, putting his arm round her shoulders.

'Stay here, my dear. We'll be more than glad to have you, and – well, you never know what may happen. If you're here, we'll be on hand to deal with anything that crops up.'

Jonah nodded. 'Why don't you go across with Ben now and get whatever you're going to need? Judy will find somewhere for you to sleep, won't you, Judy?'

He smiled at her winningly and Judy achieved a weak grimace in reply.

'Well of course, if that's what *Penny* wants to do.' She risked the tiny emphasis, but no one seemed to notice it. 'I'm afraid it will have to be in the Players' Ghetto – none of the other rooms here have been cleaned . . .'

So there it was. Judy, who since the news of Adam's arrest had been finding it difficult to seem suitably distressed, was further now than ever from blissful togetherness with Maurice. Now they were no longer under the shadow of suspicion, her spirits had lifted to the point where she could almost convince herself that his present remoteness was dictated purely by discretion. Eventually all these people would leave and surely they would have their happy ending, just like in *Lovers Meeting*.

She would re-read it tonight for consolation when at last she got to bed, if she wasn't too exhausted with all the cooking and cleaning up.

Diane Braithwaite arrived not long after the pathologist. She had been considerably shaken by the news of Liza Moxon's death.

Prickly as a thorn-bush, streetwise as an alley-cat and with an instinct for savagery that would put a pole-cat to shame, the girl had seemed the ultimate survivor. How had anyone ever got close enough to slip something around her neck and pull it tight?

And yet... She had been young and pathetically naïve; Diane had seen how readily the brittle shell could be punctured. Liza had been afraid of physical violence, afraid of the power of the law, but most afraid of failure. A damaged person, Diane had concluded at the time, but had reckoned only that the shell would grow tougher and in the course of her career the world would have to pay ruinous compensation for what had happened to make Liza Moxon what she was.

But what she was now, was dead.

Canning advanced on Diane just as one of the constables came up with the reluctance of the messenger expecting to fall in the cross-fire to tell him he was wanted on the car phone to report progress to his agitated superior officer.

He swore. 'I'll have to go, I suppose. Peckham seems to have nothing better to do with his time than hinder the investigation, but he's the boss so we'd better humour him.

'Diane, you get over there and lean on Dr Death. He's one of these jokey beggars, and I want him kept up to the mark. I need a preliminary report on time of death a.s.a.p.'

'Sir,' Diane said, carefully non-committal. There were no prizes for guessing why Sir was acting twitchy about timing. She walked on up the alleyway to the open door.

The flat was so tiny that the forensic team was having problems about space to work in. Three of the men in the white paper overalls were standing outside, one dusting the door for prints, the other two watching over the shoulders of the pathologist and his assistant as they crouched over something a couple of feet inside the doorway which looked as if it might be a tangle of black rags.

Diane knew a couple of them as Mike and Dixie; they greeted her advent with cautious optimism.

'Have you taken out Wonderboy's batteries and put him back in his box?' one asked hopefully. 'He's getting up everyone's nose, even Pardoe, and he's so laid back he's almost horizontal.'

'He's just been called to the phone. He'll be back in a minute.'

Diane glanced towards the kneeling men, caught a glimpse of bulging eyes, a protruding tongue, a face purple, contused and mercifully unrecognisable. For them, it was all in a day's work, but she swallowed hard and looked away.

'How do you reckon it happened?' She wanted something to think about, quickly.

Dixie shrugged. 'Answered the door, turned round to lead the way in and wham! That's my guess. Couple of quick twists on something round her throat – a rope, maybe – and that would be it. Tiny frame, not much bigger than a child – she'd be taken by surprise and chummy could be away again in a couple of minutes, door shut and no one any the wiser.'

She nodded, then looked at the man who was busy on the door with a big fluffy brush.

'Getting anything off that, Mike?'

'Far too much. Dozens of prints, all over. Door hasn't been washed since it was painted, I'd say, and that wasn't yesterday. There's one quite nice set, though, which could be recent, just where you might hold the door on the way out. Probably innocent enough, but we'll get a shot of them, and have a good hunt around inside as well when we can get access.'

Canning was returning, two spots of temper showing vivid in his cheeks.

'Anything, Diane?'

She grimaced. 'Not really. Some prints on the door, but that's not much good unless we have something to link them with.'

Mike said, 'Dr Pardoe's coming now, sir,' as stripping off his latex gloves, Pardoe straightened up and stepped outside.

'You can contact the wagon now, lads,' he said. 'We've done all we can at the moment,' then in answer to Canning's eloquently

131

raised eyebrows, added, 'You can meet me later at the mortuary, inspector, but I'm not expecting any surprises. It seems straight-forward enough.'

'Was she assaulted?'

He shook his head. 'No visible signs, though that's something we'll check more thoroughly later, of course. No bruises, no sign of a struggle. Nothing under her nails. Taken completely by surprise, I would say – perhaps by someone who just came to the door? But that's your end of the business.'

'She was giving out cards with her address on to everyone at Ramillies on Friday,' Diane recalled suddenly.

Canning ignored her contribution. 'Time?' he said with the air of one who, having exercised superhuman forbearance, deserves good news.

'Well.' Pardoe flipped back through his notes. 'When Patel saw her, rigor had only just progressed beyond the face and jaw. It's still not complete, so given that the ambient temperature is broadly speaking normal, I would estimate death took place about five, maximum six hours ago. We'll do the measurements and calcula-tions, of course, but I don't think we'll be able to fix it closer than seven to nine a.m.'

Canning's face fell. 'Not earlier?' he said, and there was a pleading note in his voice. 'Not, say, around three in the morning?'

Pardoe shook his head. 'Unless some extraordinary factor shows up, no. I'm sorry – is that what you were hoping for?'

Canning laughed hollowly. 'Yes. Yes it was, rather. Still, we just have to take whatever you boffins give us and do the best we can with it.

'Diane, Peckham's called us for a conference. He's talking about "loose ends" he thinks need tying up.'

He was making no effort to disguise his annoyance, and his tone was sharp as he spoke to the men at the door. 'And don't hang about on those fingerprints. The quicker you get us the information the happier we'll all be.'

'Yes, sir,' Dixie said woodenly and they watched in silence as Diane followed Canning out to the cars. He ignored the shouted questions and the clicking cameras, not even, Diane noticed, paus-ing to make sure they got his better profile.

132

13

You could have cut the atmosphere in the room into slabs, like cold porridge.

Canning sat immediately on Peckham's right, his mouth set in a straight, hostile line, his face pale with fury as he surveyed the dozen officers whom Peckham had called in to this foetid little conference room in the bowels of the police building. The random composition of the group made the cosmetic nature of the exercise embarrassingly apparent.

Diane was the only woman. She knew a few of the men; Jenks was there, and Kennie Simcox, and she surmised shrewdly that Peckham had simply hauled in everyone who was off duty, so that he wouldn't have to take anyone off the Hartington enquiry. A provincial force like this wasn't really equipped to deal with two murders – or, in fact, three, since they would have to disinter the Dominic Leigh case as well.

Peckham was looking greyer, wearier and more strained than ever. Had he once, Diane wondered, been sharp and clever and good at thinking on his feet? If he had, he was surely past it now and his tactic of relying totally on Will Canning wasn't going to work this time. If you could get a print-out of Canning's body-language, it would read in screaming capitals, YOU'RE OUT ON YOUR OWN THIS TIME, SUNSHINE.

The superintendent's hands were actually shaking as he asked his inspector to brief them on the current situation.

Canning provided the details briefly and unhelpfully. The girl was strangled with a ligature of some sort, subsequently removed. No evidence of a break-in or struggle; no eyewitnesses so far. Seven to nine a.m. for time of death; a guesstimate, he stressed. Even so, it was evident that the implications had not escaped his listeners.

'The problem is,' Peckham said gloomily, 'that it's just possible, isn't it, that we may have jumped the gun in charging Beaumont?'

Diane had never heard the word 'we' sound so like 'you' and the look Canning directed at his superior officer would not have been out of place in a knife-throwing act.

Jenks declared boldly for the side in whose hands, in his

reckoning, power most significantly lay. 'But, sir, I thought we had found a pen with his prints at the scene of the crime? And the key in his pocket?'

'We did,' Canning snapped, and Peckham sighed.

'We did, of course. But Beaumont's managed to get himself fixed up with this smart London lawyer, and he's giving us a lot of grief. He suspects already that Beaumont may well have an alibi for this latest killing, and that's obviously not the only trick he has up his sleeve.

'And I have to say I'm concerned myself about the evidence with the key. Odd to have taken such trouble not to get your prints on it, then leave it lying around in your pocket for us to find.'

'So he made a mistake,' Canning said tartly. 'Just as well they do, sometimes, or our clean-up rate would be even more embarrassing than it is at the moment.'

'But they've warned us he's going to be demanding that Beaumont is released on bail when the case calls in court tomorrow. And apparently it's Mrs Hardy-Hume who's chairing the bench.'

At the mention of her name the temperature in the room seemed to drop several degrees. Canning's lips tightened further and a muted groan came from a couple of others who bore the scars from previous encounters with that redoubtable lady. She was Master of the local hunt, with a tongue as stinging as a whipper-in's lash, but despite being a caricature of the old-fashioned magistrate, she was no fool, and the expression 'zero tolerance' had probably been invented to describe her attitude to iffy police evidence. Both the police force and the criminal fraternity were unshakeably convinced she was biased in favour of the other side.

'We may have managed to tie him in to Moxon's murder by then, whatever the time of death.' Canning was sounding bullish. 'They've got prints they're checking for me now as a top priority, and if they place him at the locus we're home and dry.'

Peckham, wittering now, was clearly unconvinced. It was also becoming clear to everyone in the room that this so-called 'case conference' had no purpose beyond that of assuring the Chief Constable it had taken place. His audience, seeing their precious off-duty time trickling away, was becoming noticeably restive, so the sudden ringing of the telephone at his side came with the impeccable timing of the bugle-call of the US cavalry towards the end of the last reel.

He held it out to Canning. 'Forensic, for you.'

134

Diane was watching the inspector's expression as he listened. It was guarded at first, then more relaxed, and finally as he finished the brief conversation, he allowed himself a thin smile which might almost indicate satisfaction.

'Beaumont's prints?' Peckham, who had also been watching him narrowly, dared to hope.

'Not Beaumont's, no. Gary Stone's.'

The name meant nothing to Peckham, and Canning briefly explained who he was, and added. 'They ran the prints from Moxon's flat through against the prints they collected at Ramillies, and there it was – as neat a tie-up as anyone could wish for.

'So I think we've just been barking up the wrong tree in linking this murder to the other two. Stone's prints are all over the place, and Sergeant Braithwaite here actually heard him threaten reprisals at the newspaper office.'

'But surely . . .' Peckham paused, reluctant to hole the lifeboat, but there was an obvious point which really couldn't be ignored, however little Canning might like it.

'It's a bit unlikely, wouldn't you say, that suddenly we have two separate killers operating on this same patch?'

Canning's expression was mulish. 'I can't see why. Different MO, different social stratum. He's got a criminal record, you know – young thugs like that rub out their totties every day of the week.'

Diane glanced round the table. No one spoke; no one was going to speak, though she knew as if she could read their minds that they didn't believe a word he was saying. Yet every head was doggedly lowered; it was never a smart political move to tangle with the bosses, and Canning wasn't the type to forgive and forget.

Damn! Tell the truth and shame the devil, her old dad had always said, and most of the time it was lousy advice. She groaned inwardly and cleared her throat.

'Er – isn't it just possible there might be some third party involved? There's such a strong connection, with Moxon claiming – falsely, as it happens – to have inside information from Anna Hartington. And most of the evidence we have against Beaumont is circumstantial – '

'There's nothing wrong with circumstantial evidence,' Canning snarled. 'If all the strands weave together it's a rope strong enough for hanging. You should know that, sergeant. Ignorant remarks really aren't helpful.'

Jenks, with a sidelong glance at her, smirked. 'Well of course,' he said venomously, 'it's naturally very hard for DS Braithwaite, being a chum of Mrs Beaumont's.'

Both senior officers turned to stare at her, and both spoke at once.

'How come I haven't heard about this?'

'You never mentioned that to me, sergeant.' Peckham's reproach was pained.

Diane could feel colour infuriatingly flooding her face. 'But I'm not,' she protested, knowing that she sounded unconvincing. 'I hardly know the woman – that is, we knew each other when we were kids – '

'Daughters of the regiment, they call it,' Jenks said with relish. 'It was quite touching, really, the way they sat round swapping stories about biscuit tins once the interview was over . . .'

Canning rose decisively. 'Thank you for your contribution, sergeant. I quite understand your dilemma, but a police officer with your years of service should know that personal feelings can have no place in a police enquiry. We'll see to it that you aren't placed in such an invidious position in future.'

Ignoring her indignant 'But – ' he said to Peckham, 'I take it, sir, that you will have no objection if I charge Gary Stone?'

Still Peckham hesitated. He had once been a good policeman, and the instinct which had made him one was still there. But ground between the upper and the nether millstone of an impatient Chief Constable and an implacable inspector, he crumbled into submission.

'Do what you think is best,' he said hollowly, and Canning, with the spring restored to his step, left the room.

Looking even more outré than usual, Letty Wells made her way to her accustomed place, a bar-stool in the regulars' corner of the Tart and Strumpet.

She had draped several of her flimsy scarves, regardless of pattern or colour, round the décolletage of a salmon-pink lace cocktail dress. It was topped by a ruffled garment in blue chiffon which, in an earlier and happier incarnation, might have been a négligée. Her lips were painted askew and the diamanté clasp holding back the thin, dishevelled white hair at one temple was unfastened.

Annie, the cheerful barmaid, greeted her with affectionate concern. 'You all right then tonight, my love? Watch now, you're losing your slide.' She leaned across the bar to fix it securely.

Letty's smile was a little wan. 'Thank you, my darling. All I need is kindness and my hair putting up in curl-papers, like the White Queen.'

Accustomed to ignoring Letty's gnomic utterances, Annie said, 'Your usual? Maybe that'll cheer you up a bit.'

Letty sighed, delving into the silver-mesh purse hung over her bony wrist to count out the cost of a double gin and Dubonnet. 'I've a lot on my mind, Annie. I've got a decision I have to make and I'm too old for making decisions.'

Summoned by another customer, Annie made a sympathetic face and said, 'Talk to you later, then, Letty. Yes sir, what can I do you for?' and moved down the bar. It was still early, but already it was much busier than the usual Sunday night, with everyone out trawling for the latest on the astonishing events which had rocked Cambourne's accustomed rural tranquillity.

It was almost an hour later that Doreen Stone made her entrance, with Kevin Pulley her gentleman friend protectively at her shoulder. Though it was her usual night, no one had expected that she would put in an appearance. Gary Stone's arrest was the hot topic of conversation, and as she made her way across to the regulars' corner a silence fell which positively vibrated with the frantic efforts of people searching for something innocuous to say.

Doreen had gone to town on her appearance this evening. She was wearing a silky tunic in a vivid pink print over black velvet ski-pants, and under the flame-coloured candy-floss of her back-combed hair huge silver pendant ear-rings dangled. If her eyes were red, the kohl pencil outlining them disguised it, and the musk-laden waft of her perfume preceded her by several yards.

With Kevin hovering supportively, she walked sturdily up to the bar, a confident smile nailed firmly into place.

'Make mine a treble, Annie love,' she said in the husky voice that spoke of fags and gin and good times. 'I'm drinking to forget how pig-stupid your average British copper can be – and he's paying.'

She jerked her thumb over her shoulder at Kevin then turned into the ripple of amusement she had engineered.

'Just been working out what we'll do on the money my Gary'll get for wrongful arrest. Might sue them myself for stress – and Kevin can try for expenses for the size of the drinks bill.'

'Don't worry, Kev, the next one's on me.' Bill Morland, another of the regulars, put his arm round her shoulders and gave her a squeeze. 'You lay it on them, Doreen, that's right. You're a great girl.'

The awkward moment passed, and after that she could almost forget her worries amid the jovial backchat; if recollection jolted her stomach from time to time, she gave no sign of it.

It was some time before she became aware that Letty, usually the life and soul of every party going, was sitting silent in her corner, her faded blue eyes as distant as if her gaze were fixed on something beyond normal sight.

Doreen was fond of Letty. She was such a sparky old girl; it would be nice to think you might face old age with that same defiant spirit, in the unlikely event that the fags and the booze didn't carry you off before you ever got to that stage.

Letty was looking really down tonight, though, no doubt about it. She came up behind her and put an affectionate hand on her shoulder. 'Cheer up, dear, it may never happen! You're very quiet tonight, Letty – that's not like you!'

Letty's eyes seemed to take a moment to focus and Doreen noticed that where the red lipstick had not covered them, her lips were pale and the skin around her mouth which had escaped the dusting of tan powder had a bluish tinge.

'Here – you feeling all right, love?'

Letty's responding smile wasn't very convincing, but her tone was jaunty. 'Course I am! This is my second double and things are looking better all the time.'

Doreen was still anxiously scanning her face. 'Something's bothering you, isn't it? Come on, tell Doreen. Might stop me thinking about my troubles.'

Letty squeezed her hand in quick sympathy, but her mind was still on her own problem, whatever that was.

'If you knew something,' she said slowly, 'something you'd promised someone faithfully not to tell what would you do if you thought that maybe you should?'

Around them there was talk, laughter and the clink of glasses, but Doreen was giving what Letty had said her undivided attention. It might be nothing more than an old lady's ramblings, but she paid her the compliment of taking it seriously.

'I think I'd ask whoever it was to let me break my promise,' she said.

Letty's lips twisted as if in pain. 'He's dead and gone, my darling, dead and long gone.'

Doreen frowned thoughtfully. 'When someone's dead,' she said at last, 'the way I see it is, all bets are off, aren't they?'

Someone tapped her on the shoulder, offering her another drink. 'Ta, Lennie,' she said, then half turned back. 'Want to tell me about it?'

Letty shook her head. 'You've said what I needed to hear, my darling. There's somebody wanted me tell them everything before, but I didn't. I'll tell that lovely girl – young Adam's wife. What did she say her name was?'

'Penny,' Doreen said, turning to take her drink. 'That's right, love. You go and talk to Penny. She's just the one who can tell you what you ought to do.'

Letty nodded. 'Penny,' she repeated. 'She knew my wicked, lovely Dom, and it's her I owe it to, really. I'll tell lovely Penny, that's what I'll do.'

She took another sip of her drink, then pressed her hand to her lace-covered bosom. Perhaps it was time she laid off the sauce for a bit. She couldn't seem to get rid of this funny indigestion.

Perhaps it was the moonlight, streaming in through the light curtains to flood the room with its milky radiance. Perhaps it was the airlessness of the humid summer night. Perhaps it was neither of those things.

Whatever it was, Jonah Dancey could not sleep. Insomnia was a familiar foe; at the best of times he was a light sleeper, easily disturbed, and once he was even half-awake he found his mind springing to action, like a greyhound which had been crouched quivering in expectation of the opening trap. Worries, problems, snatches of music with their awkward sections and difficult phrases would repeat themselves relentlessly and fruitlessly, faster and faster, until he was goaded to read, to get up, to pace the floor or to play his piano until the merciless whirligig slowed down.

He had pills he could take when sleep was of physical or professional importance, and they were good, sand-bagging him effectively at night without sabotaging his clarity of mind or dexterity next day. But he was afraid of them, afraid logically that frequent use might dull their potency and more afraid, illogically, that the nightly battle was part of the magic.

Like many great performers he was superstitious. What the gods had given, the gods could take away, and no sacrifice was too great to be laid on these particular altars. If what they demanded was the ordeal of the night watches, then Jonah would not risk all that he had sacrificed already for the fulfilment of his dreams by defying them.

His hunger for oblivion was almost painful. He had tried to read; he was so tired that his eyes would close and the book fall from his grasp, but whenever he lay down thankfully he was wretchedly wide awake once more.

Music was always the answer, as it was to most of the questions he asked himself, and this was when he usually went to his piano, and exercised his mind into submission. There was the piano in the Green Salon, but would playing it waken the entire household? He would play softly, of course, and the walls were thick.

It was like suggesting to an alcoholic that there was a bottle of whisky in a cupboard downstairs. He went out into the warm silence of the house.

The Players' Ghetto was in the attic, so should be safe from disturbance. From Maurice's room there came no sound, though he paused at the door as he passed. You wouldn't expect Maurice to snore, somehow, but he did hope that the man had sufficient instinct for self-preservation not to be down with Judy in her flat 'below stairs', as she had described it to him with that irritating, self-deprecating titter she had. She was a goose-grass female if ever he saw one, remorselessly clinging, and Maurice would need to be brutal to escape.

He could see his way downstairs without switching on any lights, and when he opened the door to the Green Salon the light was so intense that he was briefly dazzled. Bright and cold and pale, the full moon was shining straight in at one of the long windows.

It was an eerie, alien light. For all its beauty, Ramillies had never had a benign or welcoming atmosphere, and now it was as if the veneer of comfort and colour had been stripped off and only an impersonal hostility remained.

A fanciful night-thought. But he had said something about it once, long ago, to dotty old Letty Wells. 'An unloved house, my darling. Right from the start, unloved, because it was built as a dream and became a millstone.' When she said it, he had laughed, but then he hadn't been tired and tense and alone in the middle of the night.

It took an effort of will to walk across to the Steinway where it stood by one of the windows which looked out to the lawns and flowerbeds outside. He told himself that the perspiration on his forehead was a response only to the heat of the night, and unlatching the window bent to tug experimentally at the sash. It ran up smoothly and silently in well-crafted grooves.

The air outside was cooler, a little damp, and he gulped it gratefully, savouring its freshness and the heavy scent of the nicotiana in the border below.

When he saw the movement it was so unexpected, so ethereal, that he thought at first that his eyes were playing him tricks, then, crazily, that here was some ghostly projection of his fancies.

On the lawn beneath the arching trees a slight figure was dancing, gracefully, pliantly, as if to some unheard music, her face upturned to the moon as if in worship. Her pale hair was a cap, moon-silvered like the short shift she wore, and she swayed and drifted like a leaf blown on some spectral wind.

Confusion gave way to recognition and enchantment. Jonah sat down on the piano stool to watch her, then after a few minutes slid back the heavy cover on the piano, raised the lid and without taking his eyes off her began to play, very softly, Debussy's *Clair de Lune*.

He saw her start, freeze, then look towards the sound. He saw her see him watching her as he played and feared that she might flee like a nymph surprised. But he played on, and after a moment of hesitation the dance began again, now shaping itself as if music, player and dancer were one.

He played it twice through and she danced until he lifted his hands and the final chord faded on the air. Her head drooped on to the hands crossed over her breast.

'Penny!' he called softly.

She raised her head. She was looking in his direction, but her eyes were in shadow and it was impossible to make out her expression. At last she came towards him.

The moon's brilliance was beginning to fade. There was a cloud showing dark now against the still-bright sky, and the lightest of zephyrs sprang up, stirring the folds of the nightshirt she was wearing. Her bare feet were wet and covered with grass clippings, and she shivered.

'I've discovered your secret,' he said lightly. 'You're really a dryad, Penny Beaumont.'

Still he could not read her face, but she shook her head violently.

'Not Penny Beaumont.'

With sharpened attention he stared at her. 'Not Penny Beaumont? Back to being Penny Drayton-Smith?'

The shaken head was even more emphatic this time.

'Not Penny anyone. Neither of them is *my* name. One's my father's name and one's my husband's and tonight I'm not my father's daughter or my husband's wife. Tonight I don't belong to anyone. Tonight I can dance in the moonlight and be nobody's.'

Did she know how seductive she was? He was used to having women attempt to charm him, many of them both rich and beautiful, but most frequently the emotion they aroused in him was contempt. This was different.

'I'm glad you can escape, and that you let me help you.'

She turned her head away impatiently. 'Oh, I can't escape. I'm tethered with a million tiny strings. Tomorrow I'll be good again and do what everyone expects of me. It's only tonight, with the magic of the moon . . .'

'What will you do if they find Adam guilty?'

Her head tipped up to him again and this time he caught the glint of her eyes. 'It depends if I believe them, doesn't it, when I hear the evidence at the trial? But if he killed Dominic, and I was in some sense the reward for his crime – '

Penny's voice faltered and her hands flew up to cover her face.

'Ah, Dominic,' he said heavily.

She dropped her hands. 'Yes, Dominic!' Her voice was fierce. 'I know what you think. I know what you all thought.

'But none of you understood. None of you saw that I needed him to set me free, free to be myself, not somebody else's creature. He didn't have an image of how he wanted me to be. He didn't ask me to be anything at all.

'And without him I'm not strong enough to resist being moulded to other people's expectations. Except tonight, when the moon is full, and I'm demented anyway with worry and misery and pain. I'm no carefree tree-nymph, Jonah. I'm a maenad, blotting everything out except sensation, indulging myself in moon-madness.

'But the moon's going and the spell's fading and tomorrow there is brutal daylight and bloody reality.'

Somewhere in the trees a peacock stirred and called mournfully.

A cloud hid the moon and when it was light enough to see again, she was gone.

It was about half an hour after that when Letty Wells began to stir uncomfortably in her bed in the tiny cottage at the end of the lane which she had moved into after Bert died. She had slept only fitfully; the indigestion remedy she had taken hadn't shifted the odd, niggling discomfort which had made proper sleep impossible.

She sat up at last and switched on the light, and it was at that moment that the pain seized her. She had never imagined pain like it, a great, searing, engulfing flame which seemed at the same time to be crushing the walls of her fragile chest, forcing the air out of her lungs. She cried out, reached for the telephone beside her bed.

She began dialling, but before any friendly voice could answer a merciful blackness descended. The receiver slipped from her hand and swung to and fro, to and fro, like a pendulum marking the passing of time.

14

Mrs Hardy-Hume's teeth were large and slightly yellow and arranged in a manner which suggested that a whinny was the most probable vocal outcome of any attempt at speech; her smile was an alarming spectacle.

At the moment she was bestowng it upon the tall, slim and confident man in the Savile Row suit who stood below her in the well of the court. Her gaze lingered fondly on the massy gold links which could be glimpsed fastening the cuffs of his Thomas Pink shirt. Even his battered legal briefcase seemed to have an air about it which the much more respectable one favoured by the representative of the Crown Prosecution Service most definitely lacked.

'A well-urged argument, Mr Dunstable,' she said in the tones which could carry not only to the back of any court but also across three meadows, when necessary, in the hunting field. As he inclined his head and sat down with a murmured, 'I am obliged to your Honour,' she turned to her supporters on the bench.

'I think that for our deliberations in this case we should With-

143

draw,' she intoned majestically, and swept out as the small court-room, packed with journalists, struggled awkwardly to its collective feet and minions of various descriptions sprang to open the doors which would have impeded her unhesitating progress. Her companions on the bench, an earnest, tentative-looking young woman and an elderly gentleman who had spent most of what had been ironically called the hearing wrestling with his deafness-aid, followed meekly in her wake.

As Adam Beaumont was also escorted out, by a different door, the subdued atmosphere gave way to a swell of sound. A bold journalist elbowed his way forward to speak to Will Canning who with Brian Jenks at his side had been sitting in the front row, but with a snarled, 'No comment,' they both rose and went forward to join the lawyers at the table below the bench. A 'make-my-day' glare from the duty sergeant discouraged him from attempting to follow.

Will Canning was looking black. He had been forced to sit silent and listen while, as he saw it, a murderer's lawyer had danced intellectual circles round the decent, plodding efforts of the CPS. The only contribution he had been permitted to make was an unhappy shake of the head when asked if any evidence had been found – or even looked for – to suggest whether or not the pen might have been shut under the lid of the piano keyboard when it was taken across to the cottage. The young fellow who had his way to make in the CPS had looked at him with sad spaniel's eyes and tried, ineptly, to make the best of it.

Jenks had at least been a soothing companion. His muttered, 'Bloody snob,' as her Honour left might have been contempt of court but demonstrated solidarity, and when Canning asked Spaniel Eyes how he rated their chances, Jenks expressed the face-saving opinion that it wouldn't matter how watertight the case might be, you'd have to put a plum in your mouth if you wanted Madam to listen to a word you said.

Oliver Dunstable, who had lounged across, hands in pockets, in time to hear this, grinned broadly and addressed himself to his learned friend.

'Well done, laddie,' he said. 'You put up a good show, considering what they landed you in.'

Spaniel Eyes looked pathetically grateful, but Jenks, his hackles rising almost visibly, snatched at the bait.

'And what, precisely, are you inferring by that? Sir.'

Canning winced, but before he could speak the other man drawled, 'I can, of course, sympathise with your need to go round with a hand-gun dog, inspector, but I should have thought it was in your interests as well as everyone else's to keep it muzzled in public places. Particularly if it is incapable of mastering the simple distinction in meaning between the verb "to infer" and the verb "to imply". I implied that the evidence you offered was seriously flawed. I infer that this was the result of careless investigation.'

He turned his back and sauntered off, leaving Jenks opening and shutting his mouth like a codfish and Canning crimson with embarrassment and rage.

'Speak when you're spoken to, constable,' he said in a savage undertone, and turned back to the prosecutor.

But as the young man pointed out – and Canning himself knew perfectly well – the case for opposing bail had fallen flat. The pen had been rendered doubtful evidence and as for the key, the sworn statements Dunstable had produced proved that Beaumont's jacket had been accessibly draped over the back of a chair in the orchestra's rehearsal room for most of the morning. The outcome was virtually inevitable; a mutilated photograph and a snapped conductor's baton were not of themselves convincing proof of murder, and as far as the second charge of murdering Dominic Leigh was concerned, the linking ballistic evidence was all they had to offer.

By ten o'clock Adam Beaumont had benefited from the statutory presumption in favour of bail, and had been released. Canning could only hope that when it came to Gary Stone's turn Mrs Hardly-Human would not hold their previous failures against them.

She didn't. The duty solicitor representing Gary Stone made the best case he could, but the evidence of fingerprints and threats were enough to meet even Mrs Hardy-Hume's exacting standards.

'Should have said he was a drop-out from Eton, they should. He and Beaumont would be buying each other drinks in the Tart and Strumpet by now if they had,' Jenks, unrepentant, opined on the way back to headquarters.

Canning grunted. Whatever you said about the woman – and who didn't – she was both experienced and astute.

'They're letting him out on bail!'

It was Jonah who had taken the call from Oliver Dunstable on

145

the phone in the kitchen, where they were all awkwardly nursing cups of coffee amid the remains of a late breakfast. There had been no indication as to what time the case would call, and Adam had decreed that none of them should be in court, but still it would have seemed callous to find other occupation.

The news fell, thought Penny, like a pebble into a deep, still pool. Little effect at first, then the spreading ripples.

Light-headed from lack of sleep, she had herself found it difficult to take in what Jonah had said. She had not for a second expected this outcome and nor, from the looks on their faces, had the others. Did her own face, she wondered inconsequentially, look similarly foolish in shock?

Jonah concluded his conversation and turned. 'Well, it's – it's wonderful news, isn't it? I'm stunned. Dunstable's a good man and he did say yesterday that they had a strong case but I must admit I put that down to professional optimism.'

'But – but what does it *mean*?' Judy demanded querulously. She had been looking sullen; Penny had noticed that even though she had taken a seat next to Maurice, he had not once spoken to her directly.

Ben, who had been for his usual run before breakfast and looked as if he were the only person to have enjoyed a good night's sleep, had been almost offensively bright at breakfast. Now he shaped his lips into a silent whistle.

'Well, well, well.' There was something in his voice that Penny could not quite define. 'Presumably that means they don't have any very solid evidence against him. The usual cock-up by the fuzz, do you suppose?'

The silence that fell was pregnant with unease, as if they were all thinking in unison the same uncomfortable thought.

It was Judy who articulated it. 'I can't bear it!' she cried hysterically. 'Does this mean we all go back to being under suspicion again? It's just too much!' Tears welled up in her eyes.

Jonah was leaning against the wall at the far end of the kitchen, as if by calculation distancing himself from the common reaction. He said coldly, 'You mean, you would prefer it was Adam because that would be so much more convenient for the rest of you?'

'Oh, it's all right for you, Jonah! You simply don't know how hard it is when you're terrified of – '

Maurice intervened swiftly. 'Oh, I'm sure Judy didn't mean it

146

like that, did you, Judy?' and earned a tear-washed gaze of melting gratitude. 'It's just the shock – I feel quite taken aback myself.'

'Of course,' Ben went on, as if thinking aloud, 'maybe it doesn't mean as much as you might think. They've fingered Doreen's son for the girl's murder, after all, and Adam's lawyer guy would only have to convince the magistrates that Adam wasn't about to make a habit of it and they'd have to give him the benefit of any doubt, wouldn't they?'

'If so, I should have thought that two murders was quite enough to count as a habit, if they were remotely convinced by the evidence against him,' Penny said sharply. She was far from certain what she herself thought about it all, but she was loyally angry as well as disappointed by Ben's attitude.

Ben's voice changed completely. 'Darling Pen, I didn't mean it the way it sounded. Sorry, sorry, sorry! Me and my giant-sized mouth – it's only that size so I can get my foot in it. It's brilliant that they haven't thrown away the key and I'm going straight down the bookie's to bet my next unemployment giro that it never even gets to court. Shall I come with you to get him back?'

'Dunstable said he'd bring him. He's not sure how long the formalities will take, and he's going to tell the press Adam's off to a secret destination in London so that we won't have the feeding frenzy down here all over again.'

Penny cast a grateful glance at Jonah, though of course it was really Dunstable she had to thank for sparing her a trip that would be difficult for a whole variety of reasons. But she was grateful to Jonah anyway; she had greeted him this morning feeling shy and somewhat foolish, but he had behaved as if their curious encounter had never taken place.

Judy had begun to clear things from the table and Penny got up to help her.

'Will you go home to your family, then, Penny? I'm sure you'll want to get away at the first possible opportunity. I know I would.'

Judy's hint was distinctly unsubtle, and Maurice looked up, shifting uncomfortably.

'No, actually.' Penny tipped her chin. 'My brother's in America, and when I phoned my parents last night they said they were going to the house in Spain until things settle down a bit. I don't know what the conditions of Adam's bail will be but I'd be surprised if anyone liked the idea of him leaving the country.'

'Well, cheers!' Ben said ironically. 'Supportive or what?'

'Naturally, we'll go back to the cottage – '

Maurice intervened with almost embarrassing haste. 'I won't hear of it, Penny. Good gracious, if you were vulnerable to the press before, think what it could be like now! And the last thing I want is to be rattling round in this huge, ridiculous house. I've never liked the atmosphere anyway; it's nothing but a great, demanding white elephant.

'In fact, Jonah, I was going to ask you. How soon do you think I could call a meeting of the Trustees about winding the whole thing up? There's Aubade – my publishing imprint, you know. Of course, Anna was perfectly entitled to ask me to close it down as a loss-making operation, but if it's not necessary . . . In any case, I haven't the least intention of staying here a day longer than I have to.'

His audience was clearly astonished at the vehemence of his tone, and Judy, who had looked a little more cheerful after his earlier intervention on her behalf, sagged into all too obvious misery again.

Ben cleared his throat. 'Er – call me hypersensitive, but wouldn't it be a cool idea to wait until after the funeral? Hey, you knew Anna – she'd have wanted a send-off from here with all the razzamatazz.'

Behind his glasses, Maurice's expression was hard to read. 'That would really be for the Trustees to decide, wouldn't it?'

Jonah said soothingly, 'Let's talk about it later, Maurice. I'm quite sure the Trustees will be anxious to do what's best for everybody, but obviously they won't be in a position to make decisions about the orchestra until – '

He stopped, and Penny said crisply, 'Quite.' Suddenly, she had had enough. 'If you're sure that's all right, Maurice, I'll just go across to the cottage and pack some things for Adam.'

She fetched her keys and went from the kitchen down the passage to the back door which gave on to the courtyard. She glanced across at Doreen's quarters, wondering about Gary's fate, but they looked deserted. She must be at the court.

The cottage seemed already to have a sad, neglected look about it. She didn't want to come back here, to be alone with Adam, and even if it was obvious to everyone – except, apparently, the predatory Judy – that Maurice was terrified of being left alone with her, she was grateful to him. It would be much easier to be over at the house among strangers.

Strangers! The word took her by surprise, an odd word when applied to people she had known for so long and lived with so closely. Yet since Anna's murder, she had been thinking of them in that way. How much did she know about Maurice, Judy, Ben or even Jonah?

Or Adam. How well could she really claim to know the man she was married to, if she couldn't even feel absolutely certain –

But this would never do. Whatever would the Colonel say? She hurried up to the little bedroom and hastily packed a small suitcase. She had no temptation to linger.

When Penny came in again at the back door she could hear voices in the kitchen, but it was only as she reached it that she realised Maurice and Judy were alone.

'But Maurice, you are my whole life, my very soul,' Judy was saying dramatically. 'Without you, I am nothing, and your coldness is breaking my heart. I have wept until sometimes I think there can be no more tears left to cry.'

Penny stopped dead, reluctant to eavesdrop further on the purple prose of Judy's reproaches but aware that revealing herself would plunge all three of them into hideous embarrassment. Everyone had known, even before Anna's death, that they had a thing going, but she was pretty sure they cherished the belief that it was their secret.

'Judy, you know we have to be particularly careful, especially now if they're having second thoughts about Adam. We've gone over all this before.'

His tone sounded to Penny more exasperated than lover-like; if she were Judy she wouldn't be convinced.

She wasn't. Her tone had sharpened, ever so slightly. 'But Maurice, you still love me, don't you? We still have our beautiful plans? Because if not – '

Maurice said heartily, 'Well, of course we do, darling, but – '

This was awful; she mustn't listen any longer. With extravagant care Penny, holding her breath, tiptoed back along the passage and edged open the back door. Then she slammed it hard before marching noisily back again, contriving to swing the suitcase against the wall with a thump and a loud 'Oops!'

When she reached the kitchen there was no sign of Maurice. Judy, with her back turned, was busy at the sink.

'I'll – I'll just take this upstairs,' Penny said, hurrying out of the kitchen.

Diane Braithwaite was by herself in the office with a pile of files stacked high in her in-tray trying not to feel paranoid even if Brian Jenks had been invited to accompany Canning to court and the other sergeants were out doing field-work while she had been bluntly instructed to read up on the background of the Moxon case (and the Moxon case only) and prepare a report.

Not that it wasn't interesting reading. Once it had been established that Liza had been in care as a child, the social work department had produced any amount of documentation to fill in the details of her short life.

She had been, most evidently, a clever, difficult child with a perfect genius for putting people's backs up; a theme of ill-suppressed irritation ran through all the reports written by anyone who had ever been forced to deal with her.

Diane could understand – only too well – that exasperation, but as she read these stark, impersonal accounts of an unloved and unwanted child, she felt her eyes stinging and wanted to protest, like a passionate child herself, 'But it's *not fair!*' Liza Moxon had been given so little, yet with positively scriptural ruthlessness even that which she had was taken away by the bastard who had deprived her of the very air she breathed.

The congested face, the bulging eyes swam up before her again and shuddering she turned to attack the pile in front of her with renewed determination. Ignoring the witness's statements, she flipped through till she came to the one labelled 'Gary Stone'.

It wasn't a very thick file. There was his 'record' – one conviction for the possession of heroin – and the papers relating to that, then a transcript of the statement he had made in custody.

He had declared that this statement had been made of his own free will. This was presumably said as the result of prompting, but unlike other statements she had read, this breathed an almost frantic desire to co-operate.

He had admitted, readily, that he had been to Moxon's flat (well he would, wouldn't he, with his prints all over everything) but claimed that this was a one-night stand after she had picked him up in the Newt and Aardvark (where did they get these names?) and took him back, as he elegantly phrased it, 'to have it off'.

Then she'd dumped him in it in the paper next day, and after that he'd never been back. In the tones of a wronged Village Maiden, he claimed (probably with justification) that he had been Used; in modern terms that meant the immorality of wanting him not for his body alone but for what he could tell her about the set-up at Ramillies. And if he had known then what she was like, he'd have kept his mouth shut.

Yes, he had threatened her, but no, he had never gone to her flat again. And no, no, no – several emphatic denials – he hadn't killed her. Hadn't, indeed, wanted ever to see her again. He *hadn't killed her*, right?

Well, again, he would say that, wouldn't he? Diane closed the file and sat with her chin propped on her hand, deep in thought.

She was more convinced than ever, after reading that statement, that Gary was innocent. She thought he *was* a bit of an innocent, actually, and when it came right down to it she just didn't believe he was the type. She had seen him make as if to strangle Liza Moxon in front of a room full of witnesses (which wouldn't help when it came to court) and he had reminded her of the sort of dog which growls and snarls on the end of a lead while its owner tries to drag it away, but wouldn't know what to do if the lead snapped. And yes, of course that was a bloody stupid, unscientific way to reach the conclusion that he wasn't guilty.

But he just wasn't. She knew it in her bones.

She went back to the statement, read again the part where he talked about being quizzed over the people at Ramillies. The girl had clearly been digging into a past which someone hadn't wanted revealed, a past that might be considered to be safely buried.

But, the thought suddenly struck her, if you wanted the past to remain buried, why on earth would you use again the gun that had killed Dominic Leigh? Everyone nowadays knew enough about ballistics to know that a bullet could be matched to another bullet, and the gun that fired them identified.

So where did that get her? She began to make connections, tentative, of course, but they hung together. She needed to check the file on Adam Beaumont, but she had been emphatically warned off. Both Peckham and Canning were convinced that, whatever she said, she had an agenda which was part of the Old Pals Act. Funny that, really.

Diane was still frowning over logistics when the door burst open and Jenks stormed in, his face dark with temper.

'Bring on the Revolution!' he said savagely. 'I'd bring the guillo-
tine down on that sodding bitch's neck and whistle the "Red Flag"
as I did it.'

'Er – Mrs Hardy-Hume?'

'Hardly-Human is nearer it. Patted the toffee-nosed reptile they
brought down from London on the head and let the murdering
bastard go.'

'They didn't refuse bail?'

'Oh, well done. How you come up with these things, I'll never
know.'

She brushed aside the sarcasm. 'Peckham warned Canning yesterday we were on shaky ground. What did Beaumont's lawyer
say?'

'Oh, spouted some rubbish about the pen being inside the piano
when it was taken across. In a pig's ear! And then wheeled out the
old chestnut about the key being planted to frame him when he
wasn't wearing his jacket, or slipped into his pocket without him
noticing. All stuff with whiskers on, but of course when you're up
against class prejudice you might as well say "Goodbye Charlie"
and forget it.'

'Tough,' she agreed absently. 'Brian, do you know if there were
any other prints on the pen?'

'Clean as a whistle,' he said triumphantly. 'Just Beaumont's, in a
couple of different places.'

'I see. Right.' They were clearly not thinking along the same lines.
No one, she suspected, was putting two and two together and
coming up with five the way she was, and what he had told her
just now had strengthened her conviction that she just might be
right.

'What's Peckham saying about all this?' She tried to make it
sound a casual enquiry.

Jenks was scornful. 'You don't need to ask. Came out to ambush
us whenever we got back and went doo-lally – all white and
trembling, stupid old git – then called Canning into his office and
blew his socks off. Canning stormed out and drove off in his car
without a word to anyone, and can you blame him, with a geriatric
rabbit nominally in charge? It's time Peckham was painlessly put
down – and I wouldn't worry too much, personally, about the
painless bit.'

'It must have been a real blow for him.' Diane, purposely not specifying where her sympathy lay, stood up. 'I'm – er – just going to get a cup of coffee from the machine. Want one?'

Brian snorted. 'Coffee! It's not coffee I need, I'll tell you that. In any case, I have to report up to the incident room for my next detail. Some of us have more important things to do than sit at a desk all day pushing paper and swigging coffee.'

Ignoring the gibe she went out, but she did not turn in the direction of the coffee-machine. She made her way to the door marked 'Detective Superintendent Peckham', knocked and went in.

Peckham was looking worse than she had ever seen him, his face ashen and crumpled, scored by lines of pain and anxiety. Despite the fact that he had brought it all on himself by giving a subordinate too much power in the hope of an easy life, she could not help feeling sorry for the man.

'Yes, Diane?' he greeted her warily. 'Is it something important? I'm under a lot of pressure at the moment.'

And it shows. She didn't say that, of course, but asked delicately whether it would be possible to speak to him freely and in confidence.

It was almost comical how easy it was to read the emotions which flickered across his face as he struggled between dismay at the prospect of being drawn into some new crisis and the hope that she just might, by some miracle, have a solution to offer.

'Is this going to be helpful, sergeant?' he said at last, sternly. 'Because I really do not have time or energy to waste on anything that is not strictly relevant to the problems in hand.'

'I hope it may be helpful, sir.'

So he let her explain, his shadowed eyes fixed on her face as she outlined her thinking, and at the end of it looked more torn than ever.

'You do realise, don't you, that this would put you directly on a collision course with Inspector Canning?'

'Need we tell him?' she suggested demurely.

'It would be most improper, of course,' he said, though his weary face had brightened perceptibly at the thought that High Noon could be delayed if not postponed indefinitely. 'And I'm not quite sure that I see how it could be managed. We agreed – and Canning circulated everybody – that you shouldn't be any further involved in Beaumont's case. No, I don't want to discuss it.' She had opened her mouth to speak. 'Still, desperate diseases demand desperate remedies, and I have to say, strictly between these four walls, that I fully share your doubts about the quality of the evidence.'

'Perhaps you could ask for the papers I want and then pass them on to me,' she suggested. 'And the other thing I felt needed to be done was to interview Letty Wells. She was Moxon's source for the newspaper story and I'd like to talk to her. Unless it's been done already?'

'I'll check.' Picking up his phone he pressed an extension button and held a brief conversation.

'Nothing's been done about that. Sergeant, you're looking tired. And hungry. I think you ought to take an early lunch hour, and don't hurry back.'

'Sir,' she said, grinning in response to what was almost a smile.

It took barely twenty minutes to reach Letty's cottage at Cranbourne. It was a pretty little house, but showed the signs of an elderly occupant with a garden where bright cottage flowers fought bravely against the encroaching weeds.

Diane opened the gate and went up the short crazy-paved path to the front door. It was a cheerful red, but the paint was chipped and blistered in places and the brass knocker had not been polished for a long time.

No one answered when she knocked, and looking more closely at the deep-set windows on either side of the front door she realised that beyond the wide window-sills the curtains were drawn across.

Damn. She must be away from home. There was a house next door; Diane rang the bell, but was no luckier there. She'd have to come back later, and hope that the woman hadn't decided on a summer fortnight at Brighton.

15

When the telephone rang, Penny was in the Green Salon, dozing on one of the brocade-covered sofas while Jonah at the piano played something exquisitely quiet and intricate – Bach, perhaps? She had come in, a little tentatively, when he was practising scales; she didn't like to disturb him at what was, after all, his work, but Judy was in no mood to welcome company, Ben and Maurice had disappeared and the alternative of sitting alone in her monastic cell in the Players' Ghetto was not appealing.

She was grateful that he nodded at her but did not speak or break off, though once she had sat down he switched from practising to playing. For her benefit? It wasn't everyone who could boast of having had a personal recital from Jonah Dancey.

She smiled at the indulgence and leaning back on the silky cushions shut her eyes and allowed his music to fill and quieten her troubled mind. She only realised she was asleep when the telephone startled her awake.

They heard Judy answer it in the hall and a moment later she put her head round the door. 'Is Penny here – oh, Penny, they've been trying to track you down. It's someone from the hospital at Fotheringham. They wouldn't say what it was about.'

'Hospital?' The sick tide of panic swept away all trace of healing tranquillity. Her mind flew to Adam – not suicide, surely? Oh please, let him not have tried to kill himself!

Her hands were shaking so much that she could barely lift the receiver, and at first what the woman at the other end said made no sense at all, except that – thank God, thank God – she obviously wasn't talking about Adam.

With Judy and Jonah watching anxiously from the doorway she took a deep, calming breath. 'I'm sorry, I'm a little confused. Could you repeat that for me, please?'

As the woman patiently complied, Penny frowned in puzzlement, just on the point of interrupting to say there must be some mistake, when she remembered. Of course! Letty Wells was the splendidly raffish old lady who had sat beside her at Simon Byrd's ill-fated concert, and they had talked about Adam – and Dominic, afterwards. So she listened, made the appropriate noises, promised she would do what she could then hung up.

She hadn't quite stopped shaking. 'Oh dear!' she said ruefully. 'I must have sounded incredibly stupid, but it gave me such a fright! I was sure something awful must have happened to Adam.'

'What was it all about?' Judy's nose was almost quivering with curiosity.

'It's Letty Wells. Do you know her? She has a wild attitude to clothes and bags of charm.'

Judy laughed shortly. 'Oh, we all know Letty. She's one of Ramillies' most long-standing hangers-on.'

Jonah had gone quiet and Penny shot her a look of pure dislike. She really was a poisonous woman when you got to know her.

'I thought she was wonderful, as a matter of fact. Anyway, apparently she's had a heart attack and isn't at all well, poor old duck. For some reason she seems to have something she's anxious to talk to me about.'

'That's the car!' called Ben, appearing above them, hurrying down the staircase. 'I saw it from my window. Let's all go out front and give Adam a hero's welcome.'

There wasn't time to feel awkward, but even so Penny was glad the others were there. She hugged her husband, kissed him, shook hands with his solicitor and thanked him effusively while Dunstable gave a wholly unconvincing performance of becoming modesty. He refused all offers of refreshment and got back into his Jaguar. They waved him off, then walked back up the steps into the house.

Ben said, 'Now I'm going to root Maurice out of his office and twist his arm to find some champagne to celebrate. Jonah, come with me just in case he needs persuading. Judy, do you think you could go and find some glasses?'

Judy gave him a look that should have dropped him where he stood but they both obeyed orders and Penny and Adam found themselves alone in the hall.

He laughed mirthlessly. 'I think that was Ben's notion of a tactful way to leave us alone together.'

Penny managed to laugh too. 'Well, let's go and sit down and wait for them. Let's hope that Maurice is feeling in a generous mood, and that we didn't clean the cellars out completely with the last party.'

Oh no, what a stupid, banal thing to say! Despising her own inadequacy, she led the way across to the Green Salon.

He was looking very pale. You couldn't have a prison pallor, could you, she found herself thinking wildly, not after two days? And anyway, that was out of date. That was 'that little tent of blue which prisoners call the sky' stuff, and now they had to have fresh air and exercise and facilities and things or someone called in a commission. Didn't they?

She didn't know the first thing about it. He had undergone an experience she couldn't even imagine and she didn't know what to say. It seemed crass, even impertinent, to ask, 'What was it like?'

Penny took her seat on the sofa once more. 'Dunstable's very impressive, isn't he,' she said brightly. It was the first thing that came into her head.

Adam did not join her. He stood looking down at her, his face still and set. 'Penny, don't prattle.'

Silenced, she bit her lip.

'I'm sorry. It's just that I didn't have time to speak to you before they took me away on Saturday, and I want to say this now in case something else happens and I don't get another chance.

'I've landed you in a sordid mess, and the best I can manage now is damage limitation. Go away, Penny – go to your parents, or something.'

'But what are you going to do? It could be months before the trial.'

He shrugged. 'Stay here for a bit, if Maurice will have me. Look for a flat in London.'

'Don't you want me?'

An emotion she could not read passed across his face. 'Not if it means watching you suffer on my account.'

'Whereas, of course, if I wasn't with you I'd be having a good time, whooping it up – parties, night-clubs – '

He ignored her sarcasm. 'If they convict me, Penny, I want you to get a divorce.'

There was a huge hard lump in her throat. 'I promised for better, for worse, remember?'

'This is something else. "Above and beyond the call of duty", I think the Colonel would call it.'

'It's not something to joke about, Adam,' she flung at him bitterly, determined that she would not cry. 'Anyway, why should they convict you? Obviously the evidence against you is so shaky they couldn't even convince the court to let them keep you in. Dunstable said just now that the next step was to make them drop charges.'

Looking infinitely weary, Adam sank into one of the deep wing chairs opposite. 'I can't afford to think that, Penny. Can you understand? I've forced myself to face the worst, but I can't deal with hope. "Be absolute for death" – do you remember, darling, that *Measure for Measure* at Stratford?'

'Either death or life
Shall thereby be the sweeter.'

157

Her voice broke as she completed the quotation, because of the unguarded endearment, and because he had brought so vividly into her mind that carefree day from another life: the picnic on an idyllic spring evening with the swans on the river and the daffodils and the pussy-willows; the black, bitter brilliance of the play which made her grip his hand in the darkened theatre, moved to luxurious tears by make-believe emotion.

It was no make-believe now, and the tears would be tears of agony.

At this singularly inopportune moment the champagne procession arrived, Maurice at the front with his arms wide in greeting to the man who still stood charged with his wife's murder.

'Good to have you back, Adam. Let's hope that Dunstable manages to make the police admit they've made a mistake forthwith.'

Ben was clowning around with the champagne, as if charges had been dropped already. Judy was managing to smile as she handed round glasses, but still wore the hang-dog expression which must surely, Penny reflected, make Maurice want to kick her. Jonah, as if uncomfortable with the situation, had gone to the window and was staring out.

The atmosphere was charged with tension, despite the flurry of laughter as they all gathered round to drink a toast to Adam's freedom now and acquittal in the future.

But, Penny thought, was there anyone who didn't think, as they raised their glasses, that if it wasn't Adam it had to be someone else? Anna was still dead, and Dominic, and the little journalist. She had a sudden, hysterical impulse to suggest as the next toast 'Absent friends'.

Frustrated in her attempt to talk to Letty Wells, Diane Braithwaite got back into her car to contemplate her next move. She had a report to write for Canning on the Moxon files, but that could wait. He wasn't going to like what she had to say in any case, and Peckham had officially given her a long lunch hour. She'd better make the most of her chances.

Dominic Leigh's murder. That had to be the starting point. Whatever Canning believed about poor, inadequate Gary Stone, she found it totally implausible that Moxon's death was unrelated.

She hadn't worked out the why, still less the who, but she was convinced that until they understood the motive for killing Leigh they would be groping in the dark.

There would be reports, of course, but it wouldn't be easy for her to get hold of them. Someone else was no doubt combing through them already and it was common knowledge that Desperate Di (oh yes, that had stuck all right) had got her knuckles rapped and been taken off that case.

Kennie Simcox! That was who she needed. They weren't exactly chums, but they'd been in the same section for some time now and had a good working relationship. And he'd been at Peckham's 'case conference' yesterday; he must have his doubts too. He'd been doing fingerprints at Ramillies, but he must have wrapped that up by now.

She looked at her watch. Quarter to one; she knew the pub Kennie favoured at lunch time, and she just might strike it lucky if he was working from headquarters today.

The pub was fairly quiet when she went in and there was no sign of him. She ordered a sandwich and a slimline tonic, but before she could collect it a group of four detectives came in, including her quarry.

They joined her and, mindful of the landlord who recognised them and whose ears were almost visibly flapping, talked generally while he served them.

Diane drew Simcox aside. 'Favour to ask you, Kennie. Can we have a private word?'

The response from the others was raucous.

'Whey-hey!'

'Remember you're a married man, Kennie!'

'No need to be spiteful, lads, just because you haven't got his irresistible sex appeal,' she countered, while Kennie turned pink but meekly followed her across to an isolated table in the corner.

'I want you to tell me all about Dominic Leigh's killing.'

He gave her an old-fashioned look. 'Thought you'd been warned off.'

She snorted. 'This has nothing to do with whether or not Penny Beaumont and I knew each other a hundred years ago. That was only a nasty little trick of Jenks's. I'm just not happy with the case against Adam Beaumont.'

Simcox grunted non-commitally.

159

Irritated, she pressed him. 'Well, you were there yesterday and no doubt you heard that they released him on bail today. What do you think?'

'Think?' He took a sip of his half-pint of lager. 'If they want me to go round thinking about a case Canning's in charge of, they're going to have to pay me danger money.'

'OK, so you thought it was garbage, the same as everyone else did. I'm the only one prepared to stick my neck out. That means you owe me.'

He groaned. 'Oh, all right then. What do you want to know?'

There had been, indeed, as he had said at the original briefing, very little to tell. The glass-panelled front door had been found standing open with one panel smashed from the outside to reach the Yale. A TV set stood abandoned just outside on the path. The video was unplugged and Leigh had been shot in the sitting-room. The sick joke had been, Kennie said, that for a musician he had a rotten sense of timing.

'Shot in the back or from the front?'

Kennie considered. 'Back, I think.' Then, with a sudden grimace, 'Oh yes, I can see him now. Back, definitely.'

'Nobody thought that was funny? Turning his back on someone who was burgling his house?'

Kennie looked harassed. 'You know as well as I do that when things turn violent anything can happen. And there had been that other break-in just days before, not much taken, similar thing, except of course it didn't end in murder.'

'Where was that?'

'Some old lady's house in Cranbourne. I was looking at the report the other day, but I forget the name now. Hetty something, was it?'

Diane suddenly sat up straight. 'Not Letty Wells?'

'That's it! Letty Wells. Why, do you know her?'

'Not yet, but I want to talk to her. Particularly after what you just said. Anyone whose name crops up by chance twice in the course of a murder investigation needs to be grilled over a slow flame. She seems to be away from home, but perhaps I can manage to convince Peckham it would be worth my while to track her down. He's not very happy either.'

'I wouldn't mind being not very happy on his salary,' Kennie said darkly, and sighed. His wife had her heart set on Florida for their autumn week, and what Gemma wanted, Gemma usually got.

'Now how are we going to occupy ourselves this afternoon? Satan finds mischief for idle hands to do, as my old gran always used to say.'

Ben seemed determined to keep the party going. He was performing a useful function by filling in the awkward silences and Penny, though she had not forgiven him for his attitude this morning, found him hard to resist when he was exerting himself to be charming, and she was grateful to him. Sort of.

Judy wasn't. Judy was going round with a face that would curdle custard.

'I've got plenty to do, anyway. If you need keeping out of mischief you can help me put sheets on Adam's bed.'

She had offered not very enthusiastically, to sort out one of the double rooms on the first floor, but Adam had said hastily that a cell in the Players' Ghetto would be fine.

'Luxury, after the last two nights,' he had said with a twisted smile and everybody looked away as if he had made a remark in bad taste.

Penny, who had not argued at the time, said now, 'Oh, don't be silly, Judy. Tell me where the sheets are and of course we'll do it ourselves.'

Judy pursed her lips with a sideways glance at Maurice. 'Well, I am the *housekeeper*, of course, so it's my job to look after guests, but with Doreen Stone not turning up . . .' She sighed a martyr's sigh.

Changing the subject hurriedly, Penny asked if she could use the machine to do some washing this afternoon and Ben said eagerly that if she absolutely insisted he would let her do a few things for him too.

Adam took no part in this discussion, had indeed been quiet all through the snack lunch Judy had provided for them.

Jonah glanced at him then said, 'Why don't we all get out of here for the afternoon? We could take the station wagon and drive to the Downs and have a proper walk with lots of fresh air. Would you like that, Penny?'

Why should she feel her cheeks getting hot? Before she could speak, Ben demanded dramatically, 'Now why didn't I think of

161

that? Just what we need, and I won't hear a word against it. Say yes, Penny, go on. We haven't seen the fuzz since yesterday morning and they can't possibly expect us to stick around just in case they have a rush of blood to the head and want to ask us more stupid questions. If we stay here any longer we'll all go stir-crazy – oops, sorry, Adam.'

Jonah said smoothly, 'Afterwards we could have tea at that little place at Wellbrook, if it's still going. Remember, Adam, we went there one day from here.'

'Yes, I remember.' Adam met his eyes and said steadily, 'With Dominic.'

'Right,' said Ben. 'Who's on for an excursion? Charabanc provided.'

'Give me five minutes to start the wash.' Penny had got suddenly to her feet and went out now, hotly pursued by Ben with extravagant blandishments.

'I'll have to stay,' Judy said aggressively. 'I've got far too much to do to take the afternoon off, with the supper and everything . . .'

She trailed into pointed silence and the look she gave Maurice was challenging. He glanced in her direction but did not quite meet her eyes.

'Surely we can all help you with it when we get back,' he said in placatory tones, but this was plainly not the answer she hoped to hear, and she refused curtly.

Maurice looked agitated at her tone, but when Jonah said, 'Right then, everyone, ready in five minutes. I'll fetch the keys,' he did not linger to coax her to come. With the reluctant air of a man forced to call 'Tails' at the toss of a double-headed coin, he went out on Jonah's heels and Adam more slowly followed them.

The house seemed very, very quiet after they had gone. Mechanically Judy cleared the table, stacked the dishwasher, wiped down the Formica surfaces then draped the dishcloth neatly over the edge of the chipped enamel sink to dry. She glanced round the room, tidy now.

It was a horrible kitchen, old-fashioned, inconvenient and ugly. Though money had been lavished on the rest of the house, none of it had been spent in here because it was 'Only Judy' who worked here. They'd spent the minimum on 'Only Judy's' tiny flat too, where all the fittings were cheap and nasty and if it was cosy and pretty now it was thanks to Judy herself.

Her job, which had defined her adult life, had been tolerable because she had been foolish enough to believe she was sharing in the glamour surrounding the Hartingtons when she was in reality nothing more than a servant without a life of her own.

Oh, she'd known for a long time what Anna meant when she said 'friend'. Anna meant someone with no power to complain, who could be exploited and mistreated and underpaid. Armoured with this cynicism, she should have realised that where Maurice was concerned, although her duties might be very different her position was the same.

The romances which were her favourite reading were her education about the workings of the human heart. And they had been right, quite right, about the glory of the passion she had known. The memory of that passion now prompted a shaft of agony; they had been no less accurate about the pain and humiliation of rejection. She could write a book about that herself.

Now with the heat of her anger refining her perception, she had seen Maurice as he really was. He hadn't been in love with her, he had used her and now was trying ineptly to keep her sweet because he was terrified of what she might do. She had thought that, like Carla and Alex in *Lovers Meeting*, they were being kept apart by fate until the inevitable happy ending.

But here again she had been deceived, she saw that now. Now she was as furious and strong and vengeful as Sacha in *A Woman Scorned*.

It was a perfect day for a walk, sunny but not as hot as it had been, with a cooling breeze. The physical exercise was refreshing and they chatted pleasantly as they talked about uncontentious subjects, like the view and the people they passed and other walks and other views.

Adam was subdued but not silent. The fresh air had put some colour in his cheeks, and if he had feared what ghosts they might encounter by returning to the tea-shop, these fears were ill-founded. It was busy and cheerful and served irresistible cream teas, and despite Penny's sudden anxiety, no one recognised them.

It was getting dark by the time Jonah drove them back to

Ramillies. As they approached, Maurice said uneasily, 'I do hope Judy hasn't gone to too much trouble over supper. I'm not sure I can eat a thing.'

There was general agreement. Penny said firmly, 'If she has, we all just have to eat it, even if we burst. We should have made her come, you know. It would have done her good.'

Gloomily Maurice agreed.

Dusk was gathering when they got out of the car in the courtyard at the back, but there were no lights in the kitchen.

'That's the phone!' said Penny suddenly, trying to open the back door. But it was locked, and by the time Maurice found his key to let them in it had stopped ringing.

Jonah hung up the car-key on its board and went on down the passage to the kitchen.

'I wonder where Judy is,' he said. There were no signs of preparation for a meal.

Sulking, was Penny's guess, and Maurice said,'She's probably in her flat. We didn't give her any idea when to expect us back.'

He went through to the hall, switching on lights as he went. The rest of them straggled behind him.

There was a letter on the hall table, addressed to Maurice in Judy's handwriting, and as he snatched it up an awkward silence fell.

He read it, then looked up, his face blank. 'She's walked out,' he said, and held the letter out to Jonah. 'You might as well read it aloud. It's not personal.'

'"Dear Maurice,"' Jonah read, '"As you know, I have been feeling very upset since Anna's death, and do not feel able to continue in my duties. Perhaps in the circumstances you would be prepared to recommend to the Trustees that they waive the formal period of notice. Once I have found somewhere to stay they might be kind enough to send on the wages I am due.

'"I shall also, of course, contact the police to tell them where they can find me and assure them of my fullest co-operation. Yours, Judy."'

Jonah did not comment, only folding up the letter and handing it back.

Ben gave his customary whistle of surprise. 'Well, well, well! Who'd have thought the worm would turn?' Then seeing Maurice's stricken face, he said humorously, 'Hey, my man, hang loose! You can always get another housekeeper.'

From the look on Maurice's face, however, it did not seem as if that concern were uppermost in his mind.

Penny, worn out when she went to bed, fell asleep almost immediately. She tumbled into vivid, almost lurid dreams, confused and disturbing; she tossed restlessly, drifting to the surface then plunging back into troubled sleep once more.

The screaming of the peacocks in the garden would not normally have roused her. It was a common occurrence; a cat or a passing fox was enough to cause agitation in their roosts among the lower branches of the trees.

But tonight it disturbed her and then she was, tiresomely, awake. She could hear them all fuss about in the garden below and then after a little while settle down again.

Was Adam, in the room next door, also lying awake?

Apart from their brief, initial conversation they had not spoken alone together. He had not sought her out; perhaps he was as uncertain as she was, and he had been quick to reject the idea of a shared bedroom.

After all, he had offered her a divorce.

Her freedom. That was what he was offering, and that was what she had talked about last night in that strange moonlit encounter with Jonah which neither of them had referred to today by so much as a glance.

She couldn't be sure that Adam was incapable of killing when it came to his music. He simply wasn't normal where that was concerned. If she asked him, face to face, and he looked her straight in the eye and denied it, perhaps she might be convinced. But how could she ask that question, without making her distrust of him plain?

Dancing last night, she had felt briefly relieved of all the corrosive cares and responsibilities which shaped her life. Just for those moments out of time, it was the way she had felt with Dominic: detached from reality, a free spirit.

Yet even with Dom, even if he had not been doomed, it couldn't have lasted for ever. He would have tired of her, she would have tired of him, or someone would have wanted some kind of commitment to some kind of future. Their affair had been like an exquisite, fragile soap-bubble, its evanescence its charm.

If Adam didn't want her she could have an untrammelled,

irresponsible life once more. Self-pityingly, she had said last night that it was what she wanted.

So why wasn't she feeling a huge sense of relief? Why, all day, had she felt so bleak and despairing, struggling as she laughed and chatted not to give way to the tears which were gathering now?

Penny had got up to fetch a handkerchief when she heard once again a peacock's weird, chilling cry. But it sounded oddly muted, and as she paused to listen it came again.

It sounded almost as if it were inside the house. Had a peacock, fluttering around in one of their nocturnal panics, found a door somewhere left open and wandered in?

She opened her door quietly and padded out on to the landing in her bare feet. She hadn't looked at her watch, but the window at the end of the corridor was pale with the first streaks of dawn, letting her see her way to the wooden back staircase which led down two floors to the kitchen below. She listened; there was no noise, but was that a draught of fresher air coming up?

She had no idea where the light switches were, and it was darker here. The shadows in the corners were thick and she found herself looking round nervously as if someone might be hiding there, or coming down stealthily behind her. Perhaps this wasn't the cleverest thing she had ever done –

Then she heard the dry, rattling scratch of claws on a hard floor, the rustle of, as it might be, sweeping feathers, and then as she neared the bottom, an enquiring 'Sqrrk?'

The back door had been pushed open, and in the darkened passage the peacock gleamed, white and unearthly, with one clawed foot raised uncertainly and its serpentine head cocked to one side. It was very elegant, very beautiful.

Very stupid. As Penny moved gently with her arms spread wide to shepherd it out of the door, it took fright. Giving a squawk of outrage and alarm, it began a tottering, panicky run down the passage, for all the world like a dowager in uncomfortably high heels, a train and a tiara, for some unaccountable reason taking to headlong flight.

Smiling to herself, Penny managed to head off the idiotic creature and shooing it out got the door shut behind it. The catch was a little tricky, and Maurice, with all he had on his mind, had probably forgotten to lock it.

But when she bent to lock it herself, the key was gone. Frowning, she straightened up and her eyes went to the board where the keys of the three house cars were kept. One of them was missing.

She felt unease prickle her scalp. It was strange that someone should have gone out in the middle of the night, and strange things, just at this moment, were inclined to make you feel vulnerable and afraid.

Oh, probably it was Maurice. He might well know where Judy would be, and have gone to try to persuade her to come back.

Her brow clearing, she went back to bed. It wasn't any of her business if he couldn't recognise a lucky escape when he saw one.

16

The infuriating thing was, Penny simply couldn't get back to sleep. Eventually she bowed to the inevitable, stopped trying and picked up the book at her bedside, an escapist page-turner which gripped her attention sufficiently to blot out the tormenting and futile thoughts.

By eight o'clock she was up and dressed and going down to the kitchen on tiptoe, since everybody else seemed to be asleep. She switched on the kettle and while she was waiting for it to boil went curiously through to check the back door.

It was locked now, and the car-key was back in its place on the board. She shrugged and returned to make her mug of tea, but she had barely taken the first sip when the phone rang and mindful of the somnolent household she grabbed it up.

A woman's voice asked for Mrs Penny Beaumont, and when she identified herself, said that this was Sister Mayhew from Fotheringham Hospital.

Conscience-stricken, Penny exclaimed, 'Oh dear! Is it about Letty Wells? I'm so sorry, I did mean to come in to see her yesterday, but – well, a lot of other things happened and I'm afraid it went right out of my head.'

Sister Mayhew carefully didn't sound judgemental. 'I'm ever so sorry to call you so early, Mrs Beaumont, but we did try yesterday evening and couldn't get you.

'I'm afraid Mrs Wells is very frail and she's fretting to talk to you. To be honest, we're getting just a bit worried about her – '

Penny felt worse than ever. 'Sister, I'm on my way. I shan't even stop to finish my tea.'

As she snatched one of the car-keys from the board and hurried out, Penny thought she heard footsteps coming downstairs. Seized with a sense of urgency, however, she didn't stop to see who it was. She would only get involved in a conversation and she just had the awful feeling that every minute counted. She mustn't keep poor Letty waiting any longer.

She didn't hear the voice calling sharply, 'Penny! Penny, wait!' or swearing savagely at the sound of her starting up the car.

It was so seductive, that was the problem. She was in pain and she was tired. Oh, she was so tired. Oblivion, the velvety darkness round the edge of her consciousness, was the enemy but it had disguised itself as a compassionate friend. Let me take away the pain, Letty, it was saying inside her head. Let me cradle you, soothe you.

Letty jerked open her heavy eyes. Dotty old bat, she scolded herself. Just like going to sleep in a snowdrift, that would be – you'd never wake up. And don't you forget what you still have to do, Letty Wells. Nice time you'd have explaining to St Peter that you quit on the job before you'd sorted out the mess you and Bert had made between you.

She hadn't told the girl with the ferrety face anything when she came sniffing round, or at least not anything she hadn't pretty much worked out herself. And that was a mercy, because the poor little muck-raker was dead now, and feeling responsible for her would be another thorn in her dying pillow, as her terrifying Scottish granny had been inclined to say when she was a naughty child. But at least St Peter couldn't set that down to her account.

Then she drifted into thinking about golden keys and angels and trumpets and somehow bad, beautiful Dominic with his golden eyes and his trumpet were in it too.

When the door of the single side-ward opened she woke with a start, hopeful for a moment, but it was only Sister Mayhew again. Her face fell.

But Sister was smiling. 'We've got to get you ready for a visitor, Letty. I've just spoken to Mrs Beaumont and she's on her way now.'

Then, as Letty looked alarmingly about to sit up, despite the wires attaching her to a monitor which was pulsing silently, she

168

said, 'No, no, dear, you just lie there like a lady and save your strength for talking to your friend, while I smarten you up. But not a word out of you, mind. Give me a chance for a change.'

She moved quietly about, tenderly wiping the old woman's face with a damp flannel, straightening the sheets and chatting with cheerful inconsequence as she did so.

'We've got ever such a nice young policeman here this morning. There was a bit of a to-do last night by all accounts, with someone trying to break in at one of the doors down on 'A' corridor. Of course the alarm went, and by the time the night sister got there there was no sign of anyone, only a broken pane. One of those druggies, no doubt, the same as it always is, but now this lad is here doing all sorts of measurements and asking questions no one has any answers for. Doesn't look old enough to be out on his own, he doesn't.'

Letty half listened as her pillows were deftly smoothed. Sister Mayhew usually left that sort of thing to the junior nurses, but Letty had made herself a special favourite.

'There,' she said as she finished combing the front of her patient's straggling hair. 'That's better, dear.'

Letty's bluish lips curved in a smile of great sweetness, but she was not satisfied, reaching out one hand to the bedside table where there was one of her hair-slides with a jaunty red bow attached.

'Oh, of course!' Sister said, and she was just fixing it when Penny came in.

Just from the set of her shoulders Letty could tell she had been bracing herself, but even so shock at Letty's appearance was evident in the girl's face. Oh dear, enough to frighten the horses now, was she?

With barely a nod to the nurse Penny came to sit at the bedside and gripped Letty's thin hand.

'I'm sorry. I should have come yesterday, Letty, but they let Adam out on bail and that just put everything else out of my head.'

Sister Mayhew, on her way out, paused. 'Please try not to over-excite Letty, Mrs Beaumont – '

Letty's weak voice was derisive. 'Chance would be a fine thing! And what do you imagine I want to save myself for, anyway? Off you go, Sister, and let me do what I want. I'm a big girl now.'

After a glance at the monitor screen Sister Mayhew, shaking her head and smiling, left them alone together.

'Now, my darling, I've a long story to tell you. My silly old heart's

169

playing up, so don't go interrupting. I don't want to pop my clogs before I get this lot off my conscience.'

Penny squeezed her hand in wordless sympathy, and she began.

'It was my darling Bert, you see, wicked old thing. Not much to look at, but he was the love of my life, Bert was, and he made me promise – '

As she confided the secret she had kept uncomfortably for four years, she saw the look of sweet concern on the girl's pretty face change to a mask of consternation, and felt a brief guilt. But there was a hint of steel about that delicate chin which perhaps Penny herself hadn't recognised yet. She'd cope if she must, and dealing with this difficult legacy might be good for her, at that.

When she reached the end of her account, Letty was very very tired, and the exertion hadn't done anything for the pain in her chest. There was one other little thing she wanted to say to Penny, but she'd have to let that go for the moment. Her eyes were closing from weakness and she felt Penny's kiss on her forehead.

'Dearest Letty, I'll do what I can. Don't worry any more. Have a good sleep now.'

Letty heard the quiver in the girl's voice and wanted to reassure her, but she couldn't risk speaking just now, and she heard her go.

It was only five minutes later that the monitor started blaring its terrifying alarm.

When Diane got into work, there was an unwelcome message on her desk telling her to report to Canning first thing. She grimaced. Had Peckham or Simcox shopped her, and ought she to take time to slip into something bullet-proof before she went?

Will Canning certainly looked far from pleased when she appeared but, it transpired, she had wronged her colleagues. His scowl related to her report on the Moxon case.

'You're someone who just can't bear to be wrong, aren't you, sergeant?' was his greeting.

Takes one to know one. No, perhaps she wouldn't say that. 'Sir?'

'You don't want to accept the evidence we have and the line we're taking on this case, do you? I'm reluctant to believe you would write this report in a deliberate attempt to clear your friend's husband, but – '

'Sir, may I just explain? Penny Beaumont isn't a friend. I knew

170

her when we were children, and if you really want to know I couldn't stand her.'

'If you say so. Then how come the whole tenor of this is that Gary Stone didn't do it, someone else – unspecified, naturally – committed all three murders and by implication Adam Beaumont has to be innocent?'

It is hard to speak clearly through gritted teeth. 'Because that was what the facts suggested to me. The evidence against both Stone and Beaumont is weak – '

'Of course it's weak, sergeant, at the moment.' His voice rose. 'We are in the early stages of investigation and we haven't had either the time or the resources to consolidate it yet. But at least we know now where to look, and we'll find it, believe me.'

Should she just say,'Yes sir,' meekly? It would certainly be wiser, but – oh, to hell with politics!

'But *are* we looking in the right direction, sir? Doesn't it seem odd that the pen is apparently clean, apart from two sets of fingerprints? If it was a normal pen in use you'd expect lots of prints and lots of smudges, wouldn't you? But just for the sake of argument, suppose someone wanted to frame Beaumont – wiped the pen then got him somehow to pick it up – that's how it would look, isn't it? And the key being left casually in his pocket too . . .'

He hadn't thought of her point about the pen. His eyes flickered and she drew back instinctively. But after yesterday he was prepared to listen; humiliation is an effective, if pitiless, teacher.

'All right, Diane. What's all this about?'

She told him her theory: that X, whoever he or she might be, having literally got away with murder, was not about to resurrect the question of Dominic Leigh's death by using the same gun to kill Anna Hartington, unless someone else was lined up to take the rap.

'But why kill Liza Moxon?'

'She was dumb enough to pretend Anna Hartington had told her something, and she was digging as well. With Beaumont fingered, we weren't looking any more – but she was.'

Canning had done her the courtesy of listening intently, and now he paused, thinking over what she had said. Then he pounced.

'Ah, but there's a flaw. What you haven't begun to explain is why your friend X should kill Anna at all. OK, let's suppose for the sake of argument that Beaumont was framed – why do it, if you're afraid of having the Leigh case stirred up? What's your motive?'

171

He was, damn him, perfectly right. She hadn't thought of that angle, and she didn't have an answer for him.

Content to have outsmarted her, Canning's voice softened.

'Look, Diane, you know how seldom a conspiracy theory is the right one. But I'm impressed; that was a good bit of lateral thinking. We need people with ideas, and you've highlighted areas we need to cover before the defence homes in on them.

'Now, I want you to set up door-to-door enquiries in the area round Albert Lane. I can't spare you more than a couple of people, but I want them chatting to everyone they can find. See if we can pick up relevant sightings of Stone – he's a memorable lad, after all. See if anyone saw his bike parked outside – you know the sort of thing.'

'Right, sir.'

He gave her a smile which was meant to disarm all hostility. 'I know you're sceptical, but just consider how hard it is to frame anyone convincingly and I'm sure you'll see we're on the right track. Thanks, Diane.'

As she went up to the incident room to collect her team, she was still uncertain. Perhaps the man was right. After all, he was the one who had experience of murder enquiries. She didn't.

Then she stopped. It was, he had pointed out, extremely hard to frame someone convincingly. In this technological age it was probably, in fact, getting close to impossible.

And that was precisely the point. It hadn't proved convincing evidence, had it, or Adam Beaumont would even now be on remand awaiting trial.

She'd try to get the door-to-door stuff under way and then slip off to check up on Letty Wells as a matter of urgency.

Penny was almost too shocked to feel grief as she drove away from the hospital, though it was plain that the end of the road for Letty wasn't far ahead. But she had presented Penny, there for a compassionate sick visit, with a hand-grenade with the pin out.

She wasn't going back to Ramillies, not yet. Not until she had thought things through, gone to the police, perhaps. If she and the murderer were to be the only two people left who knew this, the sooner she shared her knowledge the better.

She swung the car into a quiet lane and parked in a field gateway. There was a low stone wall, crumbling a little, beside it; she perched herself on top, facing a pleasant prospect of trees and fields with the low, rolling Sussex hills beyond. There were butterflies dancing in the meadow below, flirting their wings in the sunshine; there was the low hum of wild bees, and somewhere a cricket was chirping. Deaf and blind to these idyllic tokens of summer she gazed out over the tranquil landscape.

Letty didn't actually *know* anything, of course. She had emphasised that; to ease her conscience, perhaps? But she had guessed shrewdly, Penny believed. That belief gave her no pleasure, but oh yes, knowing Dom, Letty's was a shrewd guess. Letty had forced her to see, with a sick sense of shame, what she had always refused to admit to herself.

She had allowed herself to be dazzled by Dominic, even – or did she mean especially? – once he was dead. He had been Israfel, the archangel, living on a different psychic plane, so golden and so divinely gifted that he could not be subject to the moral judgement of mere mortals.

Penny had grown up painfully in the last couple of hours. The man she had so naïvely romanticised had been a squalid petty thief who had not scrupled to steal from an old lady who believed him her friend. Viewed in that light, glamour vanished and she saw him at last as he was: amoral, drug-addicted and ugly of soul. How could she ever have loved a man like that?

It had, as Letty said, all started with her darling Bert, who had come back from the war in North Africa with the backpack he had 'liberated' from the dead Italian soldier who had tried to kill him and failed. 'Quicker on the draw, he said he was, thought he was John Wayne,' Letty's thready voice had said fondly.

He hadn't felt guilt about it – 'We didn't, my duck, not in those days. None of this stress stuff they go in for now' – and the Italian pistol had been his pride and joy, lovingly stripped down and cleaned regularly, kept swaddled in an oily rag. He'd only fired it a couple of times, up a mountain somewhere, just for the hell of it, but he kept the ammunition in a sealed container in the tin box along with the gun, just in case he fancied another go sometime.

There was something else in the tin box too. A picture, quite a little picture, but Letty could tell it was quality. They'd argued; it was loot, Letty said, stolen by the Eytie, and it should go back.

But Bert wouldn't hear of it. They'd only say he'd nicked it himself, and then where would he be, with all his service medals taken away, if they didn't court-martial him. Anyway, he liked it, and he was fond of saying, 'A thief who steals from a thief is pardoned for a thousand years,' which was a Spanish proverb he'd heard in one of his silly Westerns.

So she'd promised never to tell, because she loved him and anyway the rightful owners were dead more than likely. So there it stayed, in the tin box in her hall cupboard; she'd never breathed a word to a soul because they could take your medals away even after you were dead, and Bert would have hated that.

She kept those in the tin box as well, and she liked to take them out sometimes and have a little weep and give them a bit of a polish. She would clean the gun as well, just the way she had seen Bert do it, because that would have pleased him too.

And then one day Dominic had dropped in, unannounced, and seen what she was doing before she could hustle the box away. He hadn't been shocked; she'd had to tell him the story, of course, and he had laughed and joked about her being a dangerous woman, and treating her with more respect in future.

And then she'd shown him the picture. The great golden eyes had gone very wide, and he had said, 'That's a Poussin,' which, since she wasn't really into art, hadn't meant all that much to Letty. But she could recognise covetousness when she saw it, and she'd wrapped it up hastily and put everything away again.

It had been barely a week later that she came back home with a friend to find the house burgled. The friend had insisted on summoning the police who had, said Letty with the Londoner's scorn still in her weary voice, done just what the Old Bill always did, asked lots of questions and then did nothing.

The telly, the video and the box were all that was missing, and Letty hadn't mentioned the box. 'I knew it was Dominic, you see. He'd taken the telly and the video to make it look right, but it was the picture he was after. I just knew – he always needed money for those dreadful drugs, stupid boy – but I couldn't shop him. He was a lovely boy, really, and "a thief who steals from a thief . . ." I wish he hadn't taken my old Bert's medals, though. I really missed them.'

Her voice had trailed away, and Penny half rose, anxiously, but with an obvious effort Letty finished what she had to tell.

She had been very frightened when Dominic was shot. She didn't *know*, she said again feebly, could have been any gun, could have been just ordinary house-breakers and a bit of bad luck. She'd managed to put it out of her head, mostly.

Then there had been the ferrety girl asking questions. She hadn't told her anything much, but she began to worry again, and then Anna was killed, and the girl as well.

The old woman was looking alarmingly tired, but Penny had to ask. Her mouth dry, she said, 'Letty, who killed Dominic?'

But Letty didn't know. She hadn't wanted to know, hadn't tried to guess. She had shut her eyes with obvious thankfulness.

So there it was. As she sat on the wall in the growing heat of the morning sun, Penny felt icy cold.

Diane couldn't get away from Albert Lane as soon as she had hoped. Canning had been naïve in describing Stone as a memorable lad; youths with shaven heads were indeed memorable, but since to anyone over the age of twenty-five youths with shaven heads were as identical as hard-boiled eggs, getting a reliable and positive identification proved extremely difficult. There were three sightings of shaven heads on the intervening days between the murders, but nothing that even the most optimistic prosecutor could cite as proof that the shaven head in question had indeed been attached to their particular suspect. Nor could anyone remember seeing a bike, and as for Sunday morning, all they got was pitying looks when they asked if anyone had been around to see an early caller to Albert Lane.

Mr Chan, the owner of the Chinese takeaway, was the only person able to describe Gary's distinctive tattoo and pinpoint the day he had come in to buy two bags of chips. However, since this was the evening when Gary had freely admitted to visiting Moxon's flat, it didn't exactly move things on.

They couldn't even get anything on Liza Moxon to add to what had been gleaned already from the social work department and her colleagues at the newspaper. This was a neighbourhood where minding your own business was a prudent virtue; the only person who knew her at all was the public-spirited Mr Chan, who was happy to share with them that she preferred chips to Chinese, and vinegar to brown sauce.

By half-past twelve, however, they had done all they could and Diane went again to Letty's cottage.

It still looked the same, and though she tried several nearby houses this time she still couldn't raise anyone. All out at work no doubt. She'd have to come back this evening, wasting more time.

Or – of course, dumb-dumb! – she could go round to the pub. That was where Liza Moxon had met Letty in the first place; she was probably a regular, and at the Tart and Strumpet they might well know where she'd gone.

They did. Annie, behind the bar, was more than ready to share her unwelcome news. Her kind brown eyes brimrned with tears as she told Diane that Letty was in hospital, and by what one of the neighbours had said last night, not likely to come out again.

Diane did not swear until she was back in her car, but when she did her fluency would have elicited respect from even the most hard-boiled of her father's squaddies. She drove back to Fotheringham in a very bad temper.

17

Things were just refusing to come together. Will Canning, smarting from a press briefing where he had had nothing new to offer in answer to a statement from Dunstable proclaiming his client's innocence, flung himself into the swivel chair by his desk and spun it round savagely to face out from the sixth floor window of the police building over the roofs of the town below.

He'd had a couple of very edgy phonecalls from the CPS too. They were definitely getting their knickers in a twist over Beaumont, and unless he could come up with something soon the next thing would be the charges withdrawn.

But they just hadn't bloody found anything. Thousands of pounds of taxpayers' money that had been: dragging the lake, combing the area, talking, talking, talking, and all to generate a pile of paper telling him absolutely nothing he wanted to know.

They hadn't made progress with Stone either. They'd leaned on his dubious friends, but even highly unprofessional offers of sympathetic treatment in future encounters hadn't produced anything useful. They'd questioned him again, but he just repeated his story with increasing stubbornness, and now his lawyer blocked most pertinent questions anyway. And truth to tell, Canning himself was beginning to have a faint, uneasy feeling about that one.

He was sure about Beaumont, though. The mutilated photograph, the valuable baton broken; he had held them in his hands and they positively reeked of the sort of fury and hatred which was half-way to violence already. He knew that smell.

Not only that, but one after another the musicians in Beaumont's orchestra had proclaimed his guilt by their fervent, unconvincing denials that he could possibly do such a thing. There could be no doubt that in cutting off his career, Anna Hartington had struck at the very core of the conductor's being. Oh yes, he was sure about Beaumont.

As for Leigh's killing – well, other than the bullet, hard evidence would be tricky after all this time, but equally Beaumont would be pushed to prove he hadn't been in the right place at the right time. And then, of course, he'd married Leigh's girl. Juries loved that sort of motive.

He'd fancied him for Moxon's murder too, much more than that spavined specimen Stone. Whatever he might say to Peckham, the different MO was neither here nor there; in a densely populated area you'd have to be a fool to fire a gun. Just park your car in the quiet alley, knock on the door, follow her in, loop the rope round her neck and twist. Easy.

Not that they'd found the rope – stuffed in a dustbin somewhere by now, most like – or recovered the gun, either. From the marks on her neck forensic could identify the rope as a common type, bought in a DIY superstore perhaps or hacked off a clothes-line, and the pistol they were guessing was an elderly Beretta, Italian issue in the Second World War – was presumably some old soldier's souvenir, tucked untraceably away somewhere for fifty years.

They'd had no joy on that front in their searches of the Beaumonts' cottage, but then that proved nothing, either way. He'd really like to take the big house itself apart, but he didn't fancy his current chances of being granted a search warrant.

Anyway, there was that damned alibi. The wife could be lying, of course, but he'd seen what she looked like; put Goldilocks in the witness box and they'd believe her if she told them that the earth was flat and three little green men had given her a lift to court in their spaceship.

Will ran his hand down his face wearily. Unless they got a break soon he simply couldn't see a way ahead that didn't involve wiping the slate clean and starting again from scratch. And that went for his career prospects too.

He was interrupted in these depressing thoughts by a phone call from the sergeant at the front desk.

'I have Mrs Beaumont here, sir. She wanted to talk to DS Braithwaite, but I explained she's off the case. She seems a bit uncertain but I thought you'd want to see her.'

'Indeed I do. Excellent! Get her brought up here, sergeant, will you please?'

He set down the phone and jumped to his feet, straightening his tie and smoothing his hair automatically. What was that word? Synchronicity, that was it. Maybe his luck had turned.

Even with no make-up, even wearing old jeans and a chain-store T-shirt, Penny Beaumont was a remarkably attractive woman. With the shading of strain and tiredness under her eyes and that pale clear skin she looked delectably fragile. With appropriate gallantry he settled her in a chair, ordered coffee to be brought and resumed his seat opposite her.

She was clearly ill-at-ease, sitting on the edge of her seat and fiddling with her wedding-ring, drawing it up her finger and almost off at the tip. Significant, he wondered?

'You asked to see DS Braithwaite,' he prompted.

'Er, yes. Yes, I did.'

'I'm afraid she's working on another case now. I know you two girls are friends, but – '

The smooth brow furrowed. 'Friends? I wouldn't say that, no.'

'But she's the sort of person you feel you could talk to? Oh, thank you, Jane.'

He took the tray from the secretary, handed Penny one of the cups. She put it down untouched on the desk in front of her.

As he sat down again he looked her full in the eyes and smiled suddenly. It was a technique he had refined in his bathroom mirror and deployed usually to gratifying effect.

'Perhaps you could talk to me instead?'

She didn't simper. The look she gave him was wary, very cool.

Undeterred, he offered her a biscuit, which she refused, took one himself, leaned back casually and bit into it. Relax, woman, relax!

Even that didn't persuade her to start talking. He balanced the biscuit in his saucer and tried a fresh tack.

'Shall I guess what your problem is? Would it be easier that way round?'

She looked at him in some surprise, then said, 'Fine, why not?' Surely that couldn't be sarcasm in her voice?

'I must confess that while I was waiting for you, I was asking myself why you should be here. You haven't really been much involved in significant events, after all. Your information has been run-of-the-mill background stuff. With one important exception.'

She raised her arched brows.

'Before you knew when it had taken place, you alibied your husband for Liza Moxon's murder.'

'So I gather.'

He leaned forward across the desk, trying to foster the illusion of intimacy. 'So what I asked myself was, what might you want to say to Diane Braithwaite, your – acquaintance, if you like? Might I be right in guessing you thought she would be a sympathetic person to talk to about making perhaps an "adjustment", shall we call it, in your only significant statement?'

Penny was sitting bolt upright now, and her level blue gaze made him wonder uneasily if perhaps the air of fragility was misleading.

'Are you really being impertinent enough to suggest that I have been lying to the police, inspector?'

His silence answered her and she sprang to her feet, almost knocking over the coffee cup.

'I don't tell lies,' she said stonily. 'And even if I did, I find it insulting that you believe me moronic enough to lie to protect anyone who might be a triple murderer, whether or not I were married to him. I can assure you, my sense of self-preservation is much too strong.'

For some reason she hesitated as she said that, and unwisely he picked her up on it.

'Are you sure, Mrs Beaumont?'

Canning could not know it, of course, but the look she turned on him bore an uncanny similarity to the celebrated Drayton-Smith Dagger, a stare which had kept an entire regiment in permanent and terrified subjugation.

He found himself on his feet, stammering apologies. 'I'm sorry, I shouldn't have suggested – of course you wouldn't. Forget I ever said it, and let's start again.'

He gathered his wits sufficiently to offer a hopefully winsome smile. 'Please come and sit down. You had something you wanted to say to me.'

She surveyed him icily. 'No, inspector, I don't think I did. Forget I ever came here.'

179

Then he was looking at a door which showed all the signs of having been shut in a very marked manner indeed.

When it opened again five minutes later and Tony Emery came in, his superior's expression was black enough to give even that stolid young man pause.

'Sorry, sir – is this a bad moment?'

'Is there any other kind?' Canning's tone was bitter. 'If it's good news you can sit down.'

'To be honest, I don't know what it is,' Emery said, but he sat down anyway. 'Judy Freeman – the housekeeper-secretary woman, you know – '

'Yes, I remember her. Face like a tea-cake.'

'They put her through to me just now. She sounded a bit stressed; she's walked out of Ramillies, apparently, staying in some guest house in London.

'She claimed she felt obliged to phone us. Spouted all the usual guff about duty as a citizen, but the gist of it was that she and Maurice Hicks have been having an affair and now she's feeling guilty.'

'Is she, indeed! Now, Braithwaite said in her initial report that she wondered about that.' He glanced vaguely about the papers on his desk, shifted one or two hopefully, then abandoned the search. 'Anyway, she said she got the impression there was something going on, but of course it wasn't worth investigating once we'd got Beaumont.'

'Not really what we're looking for, right? That's why I didn't know if it was good news. Anyway, she claims he was mad about her, frantic to marry her.'

'He was? Well, takes all sorts.'

'What stood in the way, according to Freeman, was Anna having all the money, since neither of them had any of their own.'

Canning frowned. 'If Freeman's got such a delicate conscience, how come she didn't shop him before? Or alternatively, if they're madly in love why is she telling us now?'

'She *says* she's scared.'

'*Says*?' he queried the emphasis.

Emery hesitated. 'If I was a betting man,' he said at last, 'I'd lay a fiver that if one was crazy about the other, it wasn't that way round. There's a hysterical tone to the whole thing that suggests to me that he's backed off and she's out to make him pay.'

'Hell hath no fury?'

'Something like that. The catch is, it doesn't mean she isn't telling the truth as well. And it's a nice neat motive.'

Canning groaned. 'But look,' he said desperately, 'we've established that Beaumont has a perfect motive; he's unbalanced where music's concerned and Anna was a threat. And there's hard evidence with the pen and the key – '

The straws he was snatching at were looking soggier all the time as the waters threatened to close over his head.

Taking his courage in both hands Emery voiced the theory that was steadily gaining credence with the detectives on the case. 'Sir, I don't suppose it's remotely possible that those could have been planted, is it?'

For a wild second Emery thought he was going to admit to having doubts, allow them to open the case up again. Then Canning's eyes went cold and distant.

'No, I don't suppose it's remotely possible either, sergeant. But obviously we can't afford to ignore any information that comes our way. Get back to the Freeman woman and ask her for any details she can give us, then phone Hicks, politely of course, to see if he could drop in this afternoon sometime. Just for a pleasant chat.'

Jack Peckham replaced the telephone receiver with infinite care, as if his caller might be able to appreciate his delicacy.

The Chief Constable had been fretting before and with the news of Adam Beaumont's release was, not altogether unreasonably, pawing the ground. He had mentioned only in passing that his wife was a member of the Friends of Ramillies and that she was relentlessly bending his ear, but however professional you might try to be (and by and large, the man did try) that sort of thing didn't help.

And then Lord Carswell, the chairman of the Ramillies Trust, had been on to him, hinting that HRH, having been at the recent concert, was concerned about the situation too. The Chief Constable simply hated the idea of HRH being concerned, and he wasn't precisely relaxed about his domestic situation either. Right at this moment, Will Canning's name was mud.

Peckham's home life wasn't any bed of roses either. His wife, while always of course devoted and loyal – that went without saying – was apt to be, well, robust in her opinions and had sniffed in her own inimitable way, Well, 'I warned you about that young man, didn't I? *Much* too pleased with himself.'

And indeed she had warned him, several times. It just wasn't terribly helpful at the moment, that was all.

As always when he was under strain, his shoulder was aching even more than usual. He sighed heavily, shutting his eyes and permitting himself a fleeting vision of the boat he planned to acquire for his retirement – a tubby, solid, clinker-built day-boat, moored on the south coast – but much in the way a dusty traveller might contemplate a mirage, knowing it to be no more than that. Then he returned to wrestling with his problem.

Sooner or later he was going to have to take Canning head on – sooner, at this rate – but the trouble was that he had no clever suggestions to make about where they should go from here.

When Diane Braithwaite appeared, unannounced, his face brightened with sudden hope, but the words 'Got something for me?' died on his lips as he realised that hers was not the expression of one bringing home the bacon.

'Letty Wells,' she said without preamble. 'I should have moved faster. I thought she must be away on holiday, and only discovered today that she'd actually been taken into hospital with a heart attack. She had another one late this morning and according to the nurses it's probably curtains.'

'So whatever she told Liza Moxon goes to the grave with her?' With the way the luck was running at the moment, he wasn't even surprised.

'Well, perhaps not.'

'Not?' He looked alarmed. 'I'm not at all convinced about psychics, Diane, and the publicity it attracts is always – '

'*Psychics*?' Diane snorted. 'No sir, neither am I. The thing is, she spent some considerable time this morning talking to Penny Beaumont. We don't know what she may have said, of course, but the Sister said Mrs Wells was desperately anxious to tell her something.'

'Penny Beaumont!' This was even worse than psychics. He could feel his blood pressure rising right to the top of the mercury column and almost expected to hear it hit a bell at the top with an audible clang. 'You had a go at her once already.'

'I know that, sir. And before you remind me, yes, I know we had to put in a special report because she fainted. But – '

'Diane, are you mad? I've got the Chief Constable's wife going into orbit about the situation with Beaumont himself, and if Penny Beaumont starts screaming about police harassment – '

Diane stood her ground. 'There's something else, sir. You probably won't have seen the report – there's no reason why you should – but when I was at the hospital they happened to mention there had been an attempted break-in last night. Maybe it was just one of the usual suspects looking for drugs, but it was on the block which has the women's medical wards.

'Someone silenced Liza Moxon because they thought she knew something, and it's just possible that last night someone was trying to get to Letty before she could talk.'

'I think you're reaching, sergeant.' He used the distancing formality.

Diane gave him a straight look, and he could see both contempt and disappointment in her eyes.

'I've been accused of somehow doing favours for Penny Beaumont – that is, when I wasn't brutalising her. I didn't, but perhaps I can make use of the connection now. May I do it with your permission, sir, or am I on my own?'

It was tempting, very tempting, to refuse to endorse what she had clearly decided to do whatever he said. The outcome would be the same either way, but he would have covered his back.

But once upon a time, before he had been reduced to cowardice by fear and pain, he had been a decent man who believed in the job he was doing. Perhaps one day DS Braithwaite would find that she was old and tired and cynical too, but because he had once been fired by that kind of idealism, he could not altogether betray his younger self.

'OK, Diane, you have my blessing. But I'm the one who's going to have to take the rap if you get it wrong. Remember what happened last time, and leave the hobnailed boots on the doorstep.'

'Penny Beaumont was in shock the last time I spoke to her, and I should have realised that. But her father was one of the toughest colonels that regiment ever had, according to my dad, and I doubt if she's actually such a delicate flower as her looks might suggest. But don't worry – I'll play it gently.'

She swung round and marched sturdily out. Peckham could only hope she had a dictionary to look up the meaning of the word. It was unlikely she'd come across it before.

*

Penny did not often lose her temper but when she did the aftershocks could go on for days.

This time, however, as she headed back towards Ramillies, her anger was fading fast. Stalking out like that had been seriously stupid, since she was obviously going to have to give the information to the police. Soon.

Not just yet, though, she thought mutinously. That creep with his transparently synthetic charm and his ludicrous accusations! She wouldn't tell him what day it was if he came at her with a pair of red-hot pincers.

But for her own sake Penny shouldn't have let him get to her. Telling the police was to have been her safeguard, and thanks to Inspector Slimeball here she was on her own still, the vulnerable recipient of Letty's dangerous confidences, and haunted by the conviction that the killer was either someone she knew or someone she knew very well.

She didn't have to consider Ben or Jonah. Ben had no connection with Dominic and Jonah hadn't even arrived at Ramillies until Anna was already dead. That left Maurice and Judy and several members of this year's Festival orchestra – like Chris Medway – who had also been there four years ago. It left Adam too.

Of course, as she knew better than anyone, he had an alibi for Liza Moxon's murder, and if she had been the third victim of the same killer then Adam was blessedly innocent, however much Inspector Slimeball might prefer one tidy trial to two.

She wanted to believe it, but the black doubts persisted. Like Will Canning, she had seen in the photograph and the baton a frightening hatred; she knew, even better than he, that Adam's music was, quite simply, his life. If someone was trying to murder you, you were entitled to kill in self-defence.

Letty had been definite: she hadn't put Liza in possession of any dangerous secrets. And Gary Stone was still locked up so there must be solid evidence against him. More solid, in fact, than anything they had against Adam.

Or else Adam had a better solicitor and a different background –

Stop it! she told herself fiercely. You can't afford to go to pieces now when you've got a problem to solve. Whatever would the Colonel say?

Actually, she knew exactly what the Colonel would say: it was his invariable answer to any problem. Draw up a battle-plan. Define objective, strategy and tactics. She'd been inclined to confuse these, constantly provoking one of his 'and-you-a-soldier's-daughter' rants, but she had them straight now. Probably.

The objective could be simply stated. Staying alive just about covered it. Making sure she didn't become the next victim.

The strategy she had worked out already was still sound enough: to see to it that it wasn't worth killing her because others would know all that she knew.

So far, so good. It was only at the tactical level things had broken down, and there was no point in fussing over whose fault it was. Retreat in good order, regroup and advance.

Where her own safety was concerned, it wasn't vital that it was the police she talked to. What was essential was that she should tell other people, and for their safety the more she told the better.

So she could start by telling everyone at Ramillies when they were all together, and then not only would everyone know but everyone would know that everyone knew, which sounded complicated but made a lot of sense to her. She was still scared, but she was in control.

She had reached the Ramillies gates. The lodge cottage, encircled by fluttering plastic tape and with its flower borders trampled, looked forlorn, abandoned now by both the police and the Fourth Estate.

Driving up to the house she could see Adam sitting on one of the white wrought-iron chairs on the terrace overlooking the lake. He was still as a statue, staring straight ahead, and though she waved he gave no sign of having seen her.

When she had parked the car she walked round the side of the house without going in. As she passed the open window of the Green Salon, Jonah was playing a Schubert impromptu, but she went on without looking up.

At her approach Adam looked round and nodded, though he did not speak or smile. The music stopped as Jonah went back to practise a phrase, then began again, light as thistledown floating on the warm air.

Taking her seat beside Adam she too stared out across the lawns, scarred with tyre-marks and defiled with the piles of mud and gravel dredged out of the lake by the police search. The dancing fountains were still, and the flowerbeds were showing the marks even of these few days of neglect. It was a sad metaphor for what their lives here had become.

Without looking at her husband, Penny said, 'Do you want to talk?'

He sighed. 'What is there to say? I've just been sitting here, trying to make some sense out of what happened . . .' His voice trailed into silence.

That meant, naturally, that he was trying to think who could have done it, who could have framed him, didn't it? But he couldn't just say that, ask for her help, instead of expressing himself so ambiguously that doubts could remain. Well, it was his choice. She had work to do.

'Where is everybody?' she said lightly. As she spoke, Jonah brought the piece to its brilliant conclusion and a moment later stepped down on to the terrace from the house door.

'Ah, the wanderer returned!' he greeted her. 'We were all speculating on the reason for your early departure – flight, kidnap – '

'I went to the hospital. Letty Wells, you know.'

She had caught Adam's attention. He turned to look at her as Jonah said, 'Oh, of course, Letty! I'm ashamed to say I'd forgotten all about her. How is she, poor old trout? Shall we send her some flowers?'

Penny grimaced. 'I think it's gone too far for that,' she was saying, when Ben's head appeared from his bedroom window on the attic floor.

'I thought I heard Penny's voice. Decided to come back after all, have you? Is it drinks time, by any happy chance?'

'You'd better ask Maurice,' Jonah called up, then added, 'Having trespassed on his hospitality to this extent I hardly feel I can make inroads into his booze cupboard. In fact,' he looked directly at Penny, 'I phoned Larry, and he's getting distinctly *agitato* about all the things that are piling up, and Larry's bad enough when he isn't agitated. So I've said I'll go back to London. He's coming to pick me up this afternoon.'

'We'll miss you,' Penny said, her tone meticulously casual. 'Still, I'm glad I got back before you went, because – oh good, there are Ben and Maurice now. The thing is, Letty told me some rather startling things that I think you all ought to know.'

It was like pressing the freeze-frame button on a video machine. Ben and Maurice, coming out of the house, stopped as if they had been rehearsing synchronised stopping. Adam and Jonah stared at her as if they had been turned to stone.

She felt remarkably calm, completely composed. Slowly, deliberately, she looked round the four pairs of eyes and knew, as clearly as if they had told her, that there was something, some secret perhaps, that each of them knew, and wondered if she had found out.

18

Unease settled about them like a pall of smoke as the four men sat listening to Penny in unnatural stillness, without the interjections, questions or affirmative grunts of ordinary conversation. Even Ben, his light brown eyes fixed on Penny's face, said nothing.

The account she rendered was as scrupulous as a financial report, every detail disclosed. She stressed that.

Even when Penny finished, the silence persisted until at last Ben, sounding shaken, broke it.

'Have you told the police?'

'Not yet, but I intend to shortly.'

Maurice, who was looking bemused, mumbled something inaudible, abruptly rose and went back into the house.

Jonah was the first to recover himself. 'Well, that's – that's quite a story, I have to say. Fancy dear old Letty keeping all that to herself! I suppose it's quite touching, really, that she was so loyal to her Bert, even if it was all a bit misplaced.

'I wonder what the police will make of it?' He too got up. 'I wish I could stay to discuss it, but I've still got packing to do, and Larry will be here soon.'

He smiled at them and followed Maurice inside.

Ben glanced curiously across at Adam. 'Did you know anything about this?'

Adam shrugged. 'I didn't know anything, no.'

The emphasis on the third word was slight; Penny caught it, though Ben apparently did not. He sat for another moment or two, deep in thought, then jumped to his feet with the air of one putting something firmly out of his mind.

'Well, thrilling as the naughty old thing's reminiscences have been, there's not much to be done, is there? And I've been a bad boy about practising this weekend. If I don't go and make love to my trombone it's going to start to wilt.'

Penny and Adam were left on the terrace alone once more. Penny said quietly, 'Why didn't you tell me what Dominic really was, Adam? You knew, didn't you?' She tried not to sound accusatory.

He raised his shadowed grey eyes to look at her. 'Letty spelled it out, I suppose. I was afraid she had. But actually, you knew too, Penny. You were just determined to blind yourself to the contemptible side of the charm and the brilliance. You'd have killed the messenger, even if that was a role I'd fancied, which it wasn't.'

She bit her lip. '*Touché*,' she said, and another silence fell.

'Will this help, do you think?' Penny asked at last. 'Will it put the police on the track of the person who really did all this?'

Adam rubbed his hand across his brow as if his head were aching. 'I was trying to work it out, but you can't tell how they'll take it.

'Perhaps I'm too tired to think straight, but it seems to me you could make out a case against most of us. We all knew Dominic, we all had reasons for needing the money the picture presumably represented. I needed money to live on till I could make my mark as a conductor. Jonah needed money to go to America and have Rubetskoi turn him from a good performer into a great one. Maurice needed money for an interesting private life that he couldn't ask the Hartingtons to finance. Judy needed a nest egg for her old age. Chris always needs money. Do I have to go on?'

'But did you know about it at the time?'

'Not *know*. You heard me.'

'Adam, if there's anything, anything at all, you must tell me. The police aren't monsters, they're only doing their job. I can tell them – '

He had gone very still again, his jaw clenched. 'Leave it, Penny. There's no point. You must tell them what Letty said, and they'll believe whatever they want to believe. But I want you out of this as soon as possible. All right?'

'No!' she cried, and it was a cry of misery and hurt. But he had turned implacably away and was sitting looking out over the blighted landscape once more.

It was cool and dim in the hall when she went back inside, and the marquetry long-case clock showed half-past two. With a shock, she realised she had eaten nothing since tea the day before, and that she was ravenous. She went into the kitchen and found some bread and cheese to make herself a sandwich.

Through the open window she could hear Ben beginning his scales. The courtyard practice rooms were all soundproofed, so he must have opened that window too. It was very hot this afternoon.

He certainly was a little rusty. She couldn't help smiling, then recollected her promise to do his laundry with Adam's and her own. It would all be lying in the washing-machine getting musty. Still, in this heat if she pegged it out it should dry quickly. She went outside to prospect, with a vague recollection of having seen a washing-line stretched across the courtyard near where the cars were parked.

It wasn't stretched across now. It was there, hanging from one of the iron hooks, but when she picked it up to attach it to the hook at the other end, it wasn't long enough to reach. She looked at it in exasperation. The end was frayed, as if some idiot had hacked a piece off, which was hardly very bright. Still, there was a drain-pipe a bit nearer so she managed to fix it to that, fetched the washing and pegged it out.

She had just finished when she noticed a light showing in Doreen Stone's accommodation across the courtyard. It was such a dismal little house that you would need electric light even on a day like this.

She was very fond of Doreen. She knew she would be worried sick about Gary, and she hadn't seen her since he was arrested. She went over and knocked on the door.

It was a measure of Doreen's distress that she hadn't washed her hair or made up her face. She looked sallow and very worn, and about ten years older than her age. Her eyes were red-rimmed and the skin round about was sore-looking, but she gave a smile her best shot when she saw who it was.

Wordlessly Penny held out her arms and the two women hugged in the double warmth of friendship and fellow-feeling.

Doreen drew her inside, wiping the back of her hand across her eyes. 'Now don't you go setting me off again, for gawd's sake,' she begged. 'Overrated as a sport, crying is. But you're a sight for sore eyes, as you might say.'

There was a vulgar phrase Penny had once heard and relished: 'loosen your corsets and spread out.' As she sat down with the caution of familiarity on Doreen's sofa with the broken spring, that was what she felt like. With Doreen she could stop guarding her tongue; they could admit their fears and share their worries. Doreen, making instant coffee and with a wink tipping in a reprehensible slurp of cheap brandy, was also looking brighter.

'Sooner the better, if you ask me,' was her comment on Penny's intention of going to the police. 'Better safe than sorry and you'll be safer once they know, even if they are a right lot of bastards.'

'I'm sure they'll soon realise they're wrong about Gary,' Penny said comfortingly.

Doreen paused, taking a sip of her coffee. 'Honest to God, I wouldn't say this to anyone but you, Pen. I don't know, I just don't know.'

'But Doreen, surely – '

She shook her head fiercely. 'I can't trust him, you know that? Lies like he breathes, always has. And he's got a temper, same as his dad has, and that sod half killed me more than once.

'And how would I know if he went out on his bike? Sunday morning, sound asleep, I'd be.'

She had bitten her nails to the quick already, but she teased another shred away round the edge of her thumbnail.

'He's my son, Pen, and I can't help but love him whatever he's done. But I can't be sure he hasn't done it.'

And if Gary Stone was guilty, Adam's alibi for Liza Moxon's murder was meaningless. Answering tears sprang into Penny's eyes. 'Oh, Doreen, I can't be sure either. Not absolutely sure.'

'J.D., am I glad to see you!'

Larry Marcini, his bald head gleaming with beads of perspiration, had favoured today white 501s and a purple designer T-shirt, both of which looked as if they had been purchased with some younger, slimmer person in mind. He flung his arms round Jonah, pressed a sweaty cheek to each of his in turn and repeated rhetorically, 'Boy, am I glad to see you?'

'Well, are you?' Jonah, recoiling, spoke sourly. Had Larry really become more unbearable over the weekend, or was his own tolerance breaking down under the strain of the past few days?

With his hairy, muscular forearms rippling, Larry was slinging Jonah's suitcases into the boot of the powder-blue Mercedes coupé with the ease of a navvy wielding a pick-axe. He shut the boot and turned, wounded.

'How can you even ask a question like that, J.D.?' he cried theatrically. 'I tell you, each time the phone rings I about have a heart attack, thinking it's someone calling to tell me you're the next one to have air-conditioning installed in your head.'

'Oh, for heaven's sake, Larry!' Jonah stalked to the car, got in and slammed the door.

After a sharp glance at his client, Larry apologised as he got in and drove off.

'Sorry, J.D., sorry. You know my big mouth. It's the heat. I don't think so good in this weather.

'But you're not looking too sharp yourself, you know that? You'd have got more rest coming back to London, even if they've all been screaming for you. I tell you, these last three days I'm doing nothing but sit at the end of a phone telling the world, sure you're OK, sure your schedule's OK, there's no problem. My ear's red-hot, with Ridley from the Beeb, and Chandos at the Barbican, and Annette Fenton – '

'You'll have to console yourself with the thought that it's just one of the ways you earn your fat percentage,' Jonah said brutally, with calculation.

Larry hated to be reminded that he did this for money – a lot of money, at that – preferring to portray himself as having, in one of his pet phrases, a heart big as all outdoors. He subsided, hurt, but the effectiveness of Jonah's tactic was short-lived.

'Mind you, I have to say you got great coverage, J.D., I have the cuttings for you. "World-famous" was the low end of the scale – '

'Larry, I really don't want to talk about it. In fact, I have a great idea. You've heard of sponsored silences? Well, I'll sponsor you one course at Quaglino's for every quarter of an hour you don't speak, and if you make it all the way I'll buy the drinks as well. Is it a deal?'

Larry agreed with a bad grace and drove on in blessed, if sullen, silence.

Watching the road ribboning away before them, Jonah was frowning. There was much food for serious thought, but somehow the image of Penny Beaumont kept getting in the way. Penny, the free spirit dancing in the moonlight. Penny, the conformable, dutiful wife. Penny, heart-catchingly crushed by the weight of events. Penny today, showing a wholly unexpected composure in a difficult situation . . .

Women often made a play for him. He didn't delude himself that

191

it was for any reason other than his wealth and fame, but sometimes he colluded and it was seldom that there wasn't one somewhere in his life. Most of them were, like Annette Fenton, elegant, experienced and successful in their own careers. There had been, of course, passion – that was more or less obligatory – but where had been the wonder and the wild desire?

Like all musicians, he was in the depths of his soul a romantic. Music was his first mistress; he had wooed her with costly gifts and had never, until now, found a woman who similarly captured his imagination.

He couldn't see, yet, how things would turn out at Ramillies. The crystal ball of the future at the moment remained obstinately cloudy, but one thing was clear.

Whatever happened, he must shield Penny. And if Adam really was out of the picture, he wanted her to come to him as blithely as she had to Dominic. He didn't need someone to be dutiful; if she was his, he would endow her with the freedom to be herself. The song of the wild bird is always the sweetest music.

It was after about half an hour that Penny said goodbye to Doreen with another bear-hug and came back across the courtyard. Ben was still practising, making up for lost time. It sounded wonderful, the notes almost as clear and golden as –

She banished the thought, went over to the clothes-line where everything seemed dry enough. She went inside to fetch a basket, unpegged the washing and left the rope attached in its new position.

Once she had separated everything into four piles – for ironing, her own, Adam's and Ben's (though Ben could do his own ironing; she wasn't his mother, after all) – she folded everything neatly and went upstairs with the three bundles.

Adam's room was empty, with the door open; she put his socks and underwear on the end of the bed, dumped her own in her bedroom next door and went on to Ben's room at the far end of the corridor.

He was presumably still practising. With a perfunctory tap on the door she walked in, planning to leave the clothes on his bed too. The room, however, was in an advanced state of disorder with the bed unmade, and pillows and sheets in a tangle in the middle.

A pair of shorts and a singlet lay abandoned with a bath-towel on the only chair, which stood beside the dressing-table. Penny shook her head maternally and opened the top drawer to find a place to put the clean laundry.

There were socks and handkerchiefs all jumbled untidily together, along with an unopened packet of razor-blades and a hairbrush. And a photograph.

It was in a folder and Penny glanced at it with interest as she began to unload her burden. A girl? she wondered mischievously. Ben had never said anything about a girl. Perhaps it was only one of his own publicity shots, or his mother or something.

Tempted by the serpent of curiosity, she fell. She picked it up, opened it, and found herself looking at Dominic Leigh's bright hair, brilliant eyes and the smile which even now had the power to twist her heart.

She gave an involuntary cry, and the shirts she was still holding fell to the ground. At the same moment she heard footsteps and Ben's voice saying, 'Penny? Penny, is that you?' She swung round with the photo in her hand as Ben came in.

He stopped. 'Ah,' he said.

Penny's face flamed. 'I really didn't come in to snoop.' She gestured helplessly at the shirts. 'I was trying to put things away, and I looked at it. I'm sorry, it was none of my business. But Ben, we've talked about Dom so often – I had no idea you'd ever met him.'

Dom had signed it, and above the familiar, flamboyant scrawl he had written, 'Cheers, Ben! Where there's brass there's muck,' and she remembered that laboured joke too. There was the mark of a drawing-pin at the top of the photograph.

She held it out. He took it from her, closed the folder, gathered up the clothes from the floor and thrust them away all together in the drawer, as if he were playing for time.

'I expect it seems a bit weird that I didn't say I knew him,' he said at last.

'You could say that.'

Instinctively she had moved closer to the door, and Ben snapped, 'Oh, get real, Penny.

'Do you think I keep photographic records of my victims and might bludgeon you to death with my hairbrush? Sit down on the bed and I'll explain.'

He sounded like the Ben she had always known; it was Penny herself who was different, wary, distrustful. She complied, but took her seat at the end of the bed nearest the door.

He went to perch on the chair opposite, oblivious to the pile of clothes he was sitting on.

'Dominic Leigh. Well, he was my "teenage idol", wasn't he,' he said at last, indicating ironic quotation marks round the phrase. 'Other kids had pop stars. I had Dom.

'He came to do a gig at my school, you see, and brilliant as well as cool wasn't something you saw a lot of in a boys' grammar. He did a workshop and heard me play, and he was impressed. It was the first time anyone had singled me out, and when he gave me the address of a teacher I should go to in London he made a slave for life.'

Dom's forte, that. Penny had watched him take pains to dazzle his junior fans; his softer side, she had believed then, though now she saw it cynically as playing for cheap admiration.

Ben read something sceptical in her expression. 'Oh, I know what you think!' he cried defensively. 'I know you've all decided he was a total bastard, but I speak as I find.

'When I came up to London eventually, I contacted him. He didn't remember me, of course, but he pretended he did and he took me out for a drink. And you wouldn't believe how much we had in common. I told him about my father walking out when I was a kid, and his old man had done the same – no one who hasn't been through it knows what that does to you.'

That wasn't what Dominic had told Penny. She struggled to remember the details; his father had been oppressive and impossible to please, surely? Just like her own. She bit her lip but said nothing.

'Then he went off to do the Hartington Festival, and – well, that was it.' Ben's mouth twisted in remembered pain. 'So no more Dominic. Only the memory of someone who was just more vital, more alive than anyone I ever met. You know how he was.'

Penny nodded bleakly. 'Oh yes, I know how he was.' She looked at Ben, and could only think that here at least was one lucky moth who had escaped the flame.

'Obviously getting into the Hartington Phil was a big thing for me, and coming here was a sort of pilgrimage, following in his footsteps. He'd talked about it, described the set-up here – wickedly funny about some of the characters, of course – so that I just had to see it for myself. And then all this happened, and I wanted to find out – I still want to find out – who killed him.

'Why didn't I ever mention him? I don't know, really. It was all a bit complicated to explain, but that's it. Nothing terribly dramatic.'

He smiled, but to Penny it seemed the smile of a stranger, secretive instead of open and cheerful, like the Ben she knew. And just at the moment she was feeling paranoid about secrets.

She got up. 'Have you told the police you knew him? No? Well, I think – '

The telephone ringing downstairs interrupted her. No one seemed to be answering it; Ben ran down and managed to reach it before it stopped. Penny followed him down more slowly.

'For you,' he said, holding out the receiver. 'Detective Sergeant Braithwaite.'

Diane looked round the little tea-room disparagingly. It had been Penny Beaumont's choice when she asked her to suggest neutral ground, and with fitments like ruffled blinds, scalloped table-cloths, flowery china and wall-to-wall affluent matrons conducting caricature conversations ('And I said to her, "But you can't call it a *curtain* if it isn't properly interlined"'), it was just the sort of place she would have expected her to choose.

She was feeling irritated with the woman anyway. She had agonised over the best approach and phrased her request with quite uncharacteristic delicacy, only to have Penny say in her cool, little-girl voice, 'Actually, I was going to get in touch with someone. It might be rather important, I think.'

Well *actually*, darling, if you have important evidence in a murder case you can be charged with obstruction if you don't share it with the police PDQ.

What she said was, 'Good, good,' with as much enthusiasm as she could muster, then arranged the meeting.

And here Penny was now, making her way across the room, gracefully skirting the tables murmuring 'Sorry' to the idiots whose chairs were in the way with a charming apologetic smile which brought an answering smile on each occasion.

Diane's own smile was perfunctory. 'Shall I order coffee?' she said, trying vainly to catch the eye of the Sloane in the floral apron who looked as if she was called Arabella and was being a waitress just for a lark.

'Oh, tea, please. Earl Grey,' Penny said as the girl immediately materialised at her elbow. 'And a toasted tea-cake, please – oh, and a piece of the lemon cake. It's awfully good,' she added to Diane. 'You should try it.'

'Black coffee for me,' Diane said sourly, eyeing Penny's slim figure with resentment. 'Now let's get straight down to business, if you don't mind.'

Penny's story seemed almost suspiciously well ordered. Police are trained to distrust anything which appears rehearsed, but after she had explained the events of the morning Diane was satisfied, taking rapid, competent notes as unobtrusively as she could. She had a good meaty report for Peckham now, with a positive embarrassment of starting-points for further enquiry.

Diane eloquently did not comment on Canning's behaviour. It was inexcusable, from several angles, but all she permitted herself was, 'Well, fortunately we are now broadening the scope of our enquiries. They've got Maurice Hicks in this afternoon. Tell me, did you know he had a passion for Judy Freeman?'

Penny was startled. 'Good gracious, I didn't realise he wasn't still at Ramillies. And I wouldn't have described it as a passion, exactly – '

'She did.'

'She *would*!'

For once in complete accord, the two women laughed, and Penny said, 'I'm sorry, that's really bitchy. It's just that she's the sort of woman who reads those romantic novels which all look the same and have the most extraordinary titles, like *My Purple Passion* or *The Moon in June*. Maurice has been going around looking like a male praying mantis who thinks he's being saved for a late-night snack.'

'I like the thought. Well, thank you, you've been most helpful.' Diane closed her notebook and hesitated. She could leave it at that; it would be more professional, but – 'Penny, has it occurred to you that your husband might have been set up?'

All at once, the other woman's expression became distant, guarded. 'Well, of course,' she said with a touch of the hauteur which Diane always found offensive.

This time she swallowed her annoyance. 'I'm serious. DI Canning isn't ready to accept it yet, but I think both your husband and Gary Stone are innocent.'

What had she expected? Whimperings of joy, tears, gratitude?

Certainly not the gracious inclination of the head, the murmured, 'That's good,' as if she had said it wouldn't rain tomorrow.

Well, stuff you. Be like that. She would just call for the bill and conclude the interview. Just the way she had always walked out on the game if Penny was invited to join in, in fact.

Recognising the reaction, she fought it. It hadn't been constructive then and it wouldn't be now. She looked more closely at the woman, and suddenly understood.

'You think he's guilty, don't you?'

Penny's fair skin flooded with colour. 'No,' she protested weakly. 'Of course not!'

'Look at me,' Diane demanded harshly. 'Do you know something definite that you haven't told me?'

Penny met her eyes squarely. '*No!*' she insisted, and this time Diane believed her. 'No, there's nothing. It's just – it's just I can't be *sure* . . .' Her voice trailed into silence.

Diane was honestly bewildered. 'But you know the evidence against him is weak! You're his wife – surely you must give him the benefit of the doubt! Don't you love him?'

Penny was very pale now and her dark blue eyes were full of pain. 'Oh yes, I love him. I love him very much. But since I also loved Dominic Leigh I don't think you could see that as a worthwhile endorsement of the product.'

She gave a brief meaningless smile, then stood up, scrabbling in her bag and laying some money down on the table. 'That's my share. I – I have to go now. I've got to get some food for whoever's still at Ramillies. Jonah's gone back to London, so it's just the four of us – unless you decide to lock up Maurice this time. It's getting like ten little Indians – then there would be three.'

'Anything's possible but my guess is that it's highly unlikely. Look, are you sure you'll be all right in that house? I wouldn't fancy it myself even at the best of times.'

'Oh, I'll be fine.' Penny was poised for flight. 'Everyone knows all my secrets now, and anyway I've decided that it's just for one more night. Adam can suit himself, but if you people don't stop me I'm going up to London tomorrow to beg a bed from one of my girlfriends.'

Diane nodded and raised a hand in farewell. She would always look at Penny Beaumont across a gulf of incomprehension. She couldn't imagine why Penny, bred to loyalty, would not in traditional fashion be standing by her man.

197

She considered the man in question. Good-looking, in his way, if the effete and cerebral was your bag. Polite, charming even. She would have expected his wife to find it totally impossible to imagine him killing anyone. She found the idea pretty incredible herself.

And she'd always thought the motive was a bit flimsy too. After all, you wouldn't really go and kill somebody just because they'd cancelled a few concerts.

So what was Penny's problem? Well, perhaps like they said, the rich were different.

She failed once more in an attempt to catch Arabella's eye, and had some difficulty in resisting the temptation to put her fingers into her mouth and whistle.

19

The man was practically slavering; like a mad dog, Maurice thought, distaste briefly tempering his alarm. There were flecks of spittle at the corners of his mouth as well as on the harsh ginger bristles of his moustache, and his florid complexion was glistening in the heat of the foetid interview room. The sweat marking his short-sleeved polyester shirt had a rank musky smell, like a fox.

It wasn't at all what Maurice had expected. A chat, the sergeant had said pleasantly on the phone, just to clear up one or two points. He'd had to nerve himself for the encounter even so, but he had imagined at worst a meeting in an office with some searching questions being asked.

Not this. Not the sort of grim interview room all too obviously frequented by common criminals, and certainly not the sort of bullying Maurice hadn't encountered since his earliest days as a solemn, bespectacled Mixed Infant. But then, of course, he hadn't anticipated either that Judy, raging for revenge, would strike so speedily or to such deadly effect.

'So,' Brian Jenks sneered, leaning too close across the laminate surface of the table between them, 'we've established that you've been having it away with your wife's best friend. Charming, really, the two of you at it like rabbits, deceiving the poor lady. When did it get out of hand, Maurice? When did you decide you wanted the penny and the bun – or perhaps crumpet might be a better word?' He sniggered. 'Come on, Maurice, you might as well come clean – when did you decide the only thing to do was bump off your old woman?'

Maurice's chair was bolted to the floor so that he could not move it; all he could do was lean back to avoid the spray of spittle which his interrogator was making no attempt to control.

'I – I didn't,' he stammered, not for the first time looking in entreaty towards Inspector Canning who was standing propped against the wall near the door, a silent spectator.

'Look,' Maurice said, struggling for control, 'if we can discuss this reasonably, I can explain.'

Jenks leaned back folding his arms behind him and committing another olfactory assault. 'He's got an explanation,' he declaimed sarcastically. 'I like that.'

'Judy Freeman,' Maurice persisted desperately, 'was a very sad and lonely woman. At a time when things were very strained in my marriage, I foolishly became involved with her.'

'Started screwing her, do you mean?'

Ignoring Jenks's coarse interruption, Maurice addressed himself to the senior officer. 'I soon discovered that she was bringing to the relationship what I can only describe as unrealistic expectations, and particularly since Anna died I've been at my wits' end to know what to do to escape.'

A faint, sardonic smile twitched Canning's mouth, but Jenks was unimpressed. 'That's not the way the lady tells it. Wouldn't care what you did to get her, she said. And keep the money. Mad for her, she said you were.'

'*Mad* for her?' It was impossible that his blank astonishment could have been feigned. He blinked rapidly behind his spectacles and said, 'Constable – inspector – have you *seen* her?'

Canning was surprised into a brief crack of laughter, which gave Maurice heart.

'Neither Judy nor myself is a romantic figure. I freely admit that I have been foolish – more than foolish. But I swear to you that being free to marry Judy has put me in what I can only term a nightmarish position.'

'Like I said, that's not the way she tells it.' Jenks was leaning forward, poking his face into his victim's once more.

But the shock effect of his aggressive technique and the forbidding surroundings was wearing off and Maurice was regaining his composure. Looking past Jenks he spoke to Canning again.

'Inspector, I came here voluntarily to have what was termed a chat, and I was anxious to give you any assistance in my power to enable you to find my wife's killer. Indeed, I myself felt there were things we might usefully discuss.

'However, if the interview is to proceed along these unpleasant lines, I feel I should have a lawyer present and until I do I shall not be saying anything at all.'

Jenks brought his pale, gingery brows together in a ferocious scowl, but even as he opened his mouth Canning cut in.

'OK, constable, that's enough. Down, boy!' he said casually, then – apparently indifferent to Jenks's outraged humiliation – turned to Maurice.

'Well, Mr Hicks, congratulations. You've convinced me that whatever else we may be dealing with here it certainly isn't a crime of passion. And that being so I daresay we might adjourn to my office.'

But as Maurice, relief writ large on his face, got up, Canning added, 'Not that we've finished, Mr Hicks. In fact, we've hardly begun, but I'm confident we can now rely on you to make absolutely sure that you share every scrap of information you possess.'

One more night, Penny thought, I can stand it this one more night. She looked round the four of them: ten little Indians, she thought again, and I'm the next to leave.

In the dreary kitchen at Ramillies, already showing the sordid evidence of Judy's absence, they were once more sharing a meal of sorts, at least in so much as they were sitting round the same table. But they had all confined themselves within the sterile bubbles of their own concerns and preoccupations, as if afraid that contact might mean contagion.

Ben was on edge this evening, in a sharp-tongued, brittle way. He had not been pleased to learn that Penny had forestalled him by telling Diane Braithwaite that he knew Dominic; he was treating her coolly and almost ignoring Adam, who was listening intently to Maurice, his elbows propped on either side of his untouched plate.

200

Maurice was uncharacteristically garrulous, his spectacles positively glinting with animation. It was perhaps in relief that the Sword of Damocles, having fallen, had apparently missed.

'The thing is,' he was explaining with owlish pedantry, 'in cases of this sort the husband is always what they call the "prime suspect". And in the circumstances of my – er – relationship with Judy, I felt particularly vulnerable. However, they seem to have accepted that nothing was further from my mind than marrying her – even though Judy made suggestions to them which I can only describe as *evil*!' He shuddered.

Ben rolled his eyes and helped himself to another slice of the tired-looking quiche which was all Jackie Vine's bakery counter could supply by the time Penny got there. It was a scrappy meal, eked out by a very British salad of round lettuce, tomato, cucumber and bottled beetroot, with highly-coloured yoghurt for anyone who felt strong enough. Maurice, however, was eating with relish as if he had only newly recovered his appetite.

'Well, now Judy's shot her bolt,' he said between mouthfuls, 'at least it's over. I've never been so taken in by anyone as I was by her. She always seemed such a gentle, harmless creature, but then she just got more and more – '

He did not finish his sentence, but ran one finger round the neck of his shirt, as if the tightening marital noose were still in place.

'You were, of course, the soul of honour yourself. Quite the little *chevalier sans peur et sans reproche*,' Ben said nastily, but when Maurice made no reply beyond a cold look, went on, 'Anyway, what else did they ask you?'

Brightening again, Maurice was happy to elaborate. 'I told Canning what you told us this morning, Penny. I must say, he seemed a little put out that you hadn't told them.'

'Did he mention what happened when I tried?' Penny asked with some asperity. 'In any case, Diane Braithwaite squeezed me till the pips squeaked this afternoon, so they'll have all they need by now.'

'What else?' Ben persisted, and Maurice paused to think.

'Well, they brought up the business with Dominic four years ago – asked me if I had any theories about what happened.'

'And did you?' Adam's interjection was surprisingly sharp.

Behind his spectacles Maurice's expression was hard to read. He said, with a return to his habitual mild manner, 'Oh, I just said that, well, I really couldn't see what was wrong with their original conclusion about Dominic's murder. After all, a casual house-breaker would find a gun and a valuable picture a bonus worth defending.

'And then, where Anna is concerned, I did actually ask them if they had taken into account the fact that young Stone – a convicted criminal, after all – bore Anna a considerable grudge because she had given his mother notice.'

'Gary Stone!' There was surprised respect in Ben's exclamation. 'Now, I must admit that's a wrinkle I hadn't thought of. Yes, I suppose – '

'Oh, it would be very handy, wouldn't it!' Penny lashed out uncharacteristically. 'It doesn't matter, of course, about Doreen, or Gary himself come to that, as long as you can conveniently shift the spotlight away from here and suggest that it is after all just what you would expect from a yobbo.'

'You'd rather it was Adam, would you?' Ben was more than ready to take her on, spoiling for a fight.

Adam said quietly, 'That really doesn't help. Things are difficult enough without us sniping at each other. Maurice, is there anything else they asked you?'

Maurice, who was exuding smug detachment in a manner suggestive of a tree frog exuding venom, thought for a moment. 'Nothing specific, that I can recall. But I tell you when it was that he really pricked up his ears. You know Anna was very tetchy just before the Festival, a bit on edge – '

'Heavens to Betsy, was she? I don't think anyone noticed.'

Ignoring Ben's gadfly remark Maurice went on, 'Oh, she was worried about the Festival and the money and all that. But there was something else she was fussing about, something she had done. She didn't tell me what it was, and I didn't ask her – '

'Anything for a quiet life?' Ben was definitely out to provoke, but again Maurice paid no attention.

'The term she used was that she had, perhaps, Gone Too Far. That was one of Eden's catch-phrases, you know. "Anna, you have Gone Too Far this time!" He used to yell at her, at the top of his voice, and she'd do what she was told.' There was both awe and wistfulness in his tone.

'Whatever did she mean?' Penny wondered.

'Gone too far. She must have done something she thought was unwise – perhaps even dangerous. Sacking Doreen Stone would fit . . .' Ben was thinking aloud.

Adam spoke suddenly. 'She said that, did she? Did she, indeed!' and without explanation got up and walked out.

The other three were left looking at each other blankly. Penny, with a sickening lurch of the stomach, recognised the familiar, terrifying sense of impending disaster which was returning like a homing pigeon to its accustomed perch.

There were three men in the house, and she didn't trust any of them.

Will Canning was standing at the window of the super's office, staring out dismally into the gathering dusk. He was jingling coins irritably in his trouser pockets and with his tie off looked, for him, positively dishevelled. He was showing all the signs of the indigestion which afflicts a man forced very publicly to eat humble pie.

By way of contrast, Jack Peckham was looking fully ten years younger, swivelling his office chair to and fro in half-circles. With pleasure and action making the hours seem short, he had more energy left than he knew what to do with.

Given the flood of information which had come in today, coupled with Will's reluctance to move his feet, there had been no option but to take full control. Now, liberated from the tyranny of his own weakness and aided by an extra dose of pain-killers, he was on a high. He wasn't shirking his responsibility for the mess they had got into; he should never have allowed Will to have his head to such an extent, but guilt, frankly, could wait its turn. Exhilaration didn't often come his way, and he was going to make the most of it.

His general briefing to the officers on the case had been brisk and efficient. They were to start from scratch with the events leading up to Dominic Leigh's murder, he told them, giving no opportunity for 'But sir's' from the floor. He had stated flatly (trying to avoid looking at either Canning or Jenks) that facts must be allowed to speak for themselves and not tailored to fit any existing theory, however appealing that theory might be. He had made effective dispositions for the next day, and finally he had dragged Will and Diane, more or less by the scruff of their necks, up here to try to coax them to kiss and make up. They were both potentially good officers who could usefully work together instead of walking round stiff-legged like dogs, waiting to be able to claim that the other one snarled first.

203

'Right, Will,' he said. 'Just to recap. You'll liaise with the Art boys at the Met and put them on to finding out whether a Poussin was sold at that time, and where. By whom is perhaps more than we can hope for, but who knows? It's not as easy as all that to set up a phoney bank account, and asking for cash is the surest way to draw unwelcome attention to yourself.'

'Yes, sir, of course.' The mutinous line of Canning's mouth belied the correct response. 'If it really was a Poussin, that is. And I still say it would have been fenced – '

'Not necessarily, Will, not necessarily.' Peckham interrupted eagerly. 'Think of our suspects. How many of them would have the first idea how to find a fence? You can't exactly take out an ad in the personal column of *The Times*.'

He laughed, looking to Diane for support, but she, with the air of a rugby forward with hands in the air to escape an off-side decision, did not meet his eye.

'The picture, remember, had no criminal history. Nothing easier than to say that you found it in Granny's attic. You'd certainly get a hell of a lot more money that way.'

Canning shrugged but wouldn't play, and Peckham gave up. 'Diane, you were going to extort permission to see bank accounts, weren't you? They hate doing it; you'll have to be very charming and if that doesn't work put the boot in. Freeman, Hicks, Dancey, Beaumont, Lousada – I need them all. That's where the story of your life is, Diane – your bank account. Apart from your regular superstore, no one knows more about your habits than your bank does. So tomorrow, with any luck . . .' He rubbed his hands.

Canning said stiffly, 'Yes indeed, tomorrow. And since there's nothing more we can usefully do tonight, I think I'll knock off if you've no objection, sir.'

'What about a cup of coffee before you go, Will?' Peckham's patching-up service had not so far shown signs of success: Canning had stood at the window, Braithwaite had sat at the desk, but breathing the same air was as close as they had come to rapprochement.

'No thank you, sir. It's been a long and tiring day and I'm anxious to be fresh for tomorrow.'

'Of course, of course.' He hesitated, then said with blundering sympathy, 'Don't take it to heart, lad. We haven't by any means eliminated Adam Beaumont. You may prove to have been right in the end.'

Canning showed his teeth in what was putatively a smile and without troubling to conceal the irony in his tone said, 'Thank you very much, sir,' and went out.

An uncomfortable silence followed, then Peckham said ruefully, 'Handled that pretty well, didn't I? He didn't actually say "Patronising bastard" as he left, but he'd have been within his rights.'

'He'll be better in the morning, I'm sure. He's just knackered.' Diane tried to smother a yawn herself.

He sighed. 'Very debilitating thing, pride. There's a lesson there, Diane. In this game you owe too much to luck at every turn ever to take it personally – whether you're talking about credit or blame.'

'Yes, sir,' she agreed obediently, trying to smother another yawn with even less success.

'Come on, Diane, you're not going to wimp out on me, are you?' He was dismayed, like a small boy who needs someone to watch him play with his train set. 'It's not an order, but I've a couple of ideas I'd really like to talk through . . . A quick cup of coffee?'

Diane weakened. 'Well – '

'I've got a better idea.' Diving into the bottom drawer of his desk, he produced an almost full half-bottle of whisky. 'Medicinal,' he explained, adding two small glasses from the same source with such an urchin grin she could only laugh and submit.

'The thing is,' he said, taking a sip of the neat spirit then leaning back expansively so that the swivel chair bounced dangerously on its springs, 'that there are two important questions.'

Diane took a more cautious sip. 'What two important questions, sir?' Oh, she could get a job in the clubs as a straight man any time she liked.

'One, who did Dominic Leigh tell about his theft?'

Should she now say, 'And who *did* Dominic Leigh tell about his theft, sir?' But perhaps that would be taking the double-act a little too far. She considered the question.

'Someone he was close to, obviously. But not only that, someone who wouldn't disapprove or shop him.'

'Good. Go on.'

'So, not Penny. She's shocked even now. Not Judy Freeman – she would shock easily, and she's malicious. But then, most people would disapprove, don't you think?'

Peckham took another sip of the whisky. The effect of the painkillers had begun to wear off, and this was helping.

'Ah, that's police-think, Diane. We have to believe that apart from villains the world is full of honest Joes or we'd resign tomorrow.

'But these guys – well, Canning says that Beaumont at least is unhinged where music is concerned, and that probably goes for Dancey and Lousada too.'

Diane stared at him. 'But *murder*?'

'Ah! Murder wouldn't be the original thought. Money would be the root of that particular evil, money to support your genius which is the only "must" you recognise, and which is what sets you apart from the poor benighted sods like us trying to live by a bourgeois code. And Letty didn't really feel that what was stolen was hers in the first place.'

'"A thief who steals from a thief is pardoned for a thousand years," she kept saying, apparently.'

'*The Magnificent Seven!*' Peckham identified the source triumphantly. 'Great film. Right. So, what do we have? Leigh has been boasting about what he did, chummy decides to go one better, is caught in the act and shoots him?'

Perhaps the whisky was actually clearing her mind. 'Not with an unloaded gun, he wouldn't. He'd have had to find the ammunition and load it, wouldn't he? And can we assume Leigh only told one person? Because if so, when he came back and found the picture missing, he'd know exactly who had it – so – '

'So he had to be killed!' Peckham unscrewed the cap of the whisky bottle absent-mindedly and topped up both glasses. 'Right! That's cleared a useful bit of ground. Now, what about the second question?'

Starting on her second whisky, Diane murmured, 'I say, I say, I say. What second question?' and realised what she had said only when Peckham gave her a strange look.

'I think you'd better walk home tonight,' he said reprovingly. 'The question is, in what precise direction did Anna Hartington go too far?'

'The number of ways in which Anna Hartington apparently went too far,' said Diane crisply, 'would make Marco Polo look like a couch potato. She had probably discovered Lord Carswell and HRH had a thing going and was blackmailing them.'

Peckham winced. 'The Chief Constable *really* wouldn't like that. But there are a couple of obvious things – throwing Doreen Stone out on the street, and wrecking Beaumont's career.'

Diane screwed up her nose. 'People are always looking for

resident housekeepers. And Adam Beaumont is surely too good to be held back by Anna Hartington's problems.'

'Ah, but haven't you read the statements from the orchestra?' Under her accusing gaze he stammered, 'Oh – er, yes, well, you – er – probably wouldn't. It was apparently going to be a world-wide musical scandal because she was forcing him to let down some of the most important concert halls and he might simply be written off, whatever his excuse.'

Diane set down her half-full glass on the desk, suddenly conscious of the heavy, metallic after-taste of whisky in her mouth. 'Penny Beaumont thinks he might have done it,' she said. 'I didn't; he just never felt right to me, and the evidence reeked of a stitch-up. But I suppose he could have played the high-risk game and faked evidence against himself, knowing it wouldn't stand up in court – '

It was Peckham's turn to stare. 'Do you really think so? I have to say it would be pretty convenient. Is his alibi for Moxon's murder solid?'

'Unless you can prove he hypnotised his wife, rock solid. Take Beaumont and you have to take Stone.'

'Hmm.' Peckham drained his glass. 'Well, tomorrow is another day. It'll be nice to have a bit of hard evidence to go on instead of gut feeling. But thanks, Diane. That's been very helpful. And now I think we should follow Will's example.'

As he rose stiffly, it was obvious that the pain, so briefly suppressed, was returning.

Diane got up more slowly. 'Do you think she's all right? Penny Beaumont, I mean. She's there in that great sinister house and everyone's gone except Hicks, Lousada and Beaumont. She talked about the ten little Indians in a rather creepy way.'

'Are you still allowed to say that? Shouldn't it be ten size-challenged, ethnically enriched persons?' Peckham was unimpressed. 'We're not dealing with a psychopath here, you know. We're talking about practical and financial motives, and someone who has worked extremely hard to avoid being found out. With these odds you'd have to be crazy to try anything on tonight.'

Diane nodded. He was perfectly right, of course, yet as she preceded him out of the door she shivered.

'Not cold, Diane, surely?'

'No, no,' she said lightly. 'Just a goose walking over my grave.'

*

The flower arrangement in the fireplace beneath Eden Hartington's portrait had begun to die. Like drifts of swan's feathers, white petals had fallen inside the hearth and the sharp green of the foliage was fading as leaves died, shrivelled and drooped. Brown marks like age-spots were disfiguring the bracts of the creamy hydrangeas.

The golden summer evening light was starting to lose its warmth and intensity and the corners of the room were blurring into grey shadow. Penny kept finding her gaze drawn to Eden's pictured face; as with all good portraits, the eyes seemed to follow her even when she changed position. The Maestro, at the height of his powers.

Yet there had always seemed to be something there suggesting failure and self-doubt, neither of which she associated with Eden Hartington. Tonight she could almost believe that what yet survived was the stamp of pain on the strongly marked features, and even despair at the twilight of decay into which his works were vanishing. But then, tonight she was fanciful, her cheeks burning as if she had a fever.

At one side of the fireplace, Maurice was sitting in one of the green brocade wing chairs under a reading-lamp, tranquilly perusing a manuscript. He seemed almost bizarrely relaxed, as if the pool of light about him keeping the shadows at bay had done the same for the problems which must still beset him – the police investigation, the future of Ramillies, the funeral of his wife.

Ben was moodily playing endless games of patience on the coffee table; cheating, Penny observed, watching him idly. She had a magazine on her lap, but the shiny pictures of flawless domestic interiors and their glossy owners grinning plastic grins seemed not merely unconvincing but grotesque.

Adam she had not seen since supper. She had heard the 'ting' of the telephone being used somewhere, so he must have been making a call. Talking to Dunstable, perhaps? He certainly had not chosen to take her into his confidence about what Maurice's remark had suggested to him, and she had reached the stage where she was too worn out to care.

At least her mind, which had for days now run events and problems and speculation like a looped tape, seemed deadened by exhaustion. Her eyelids had started to droop and when the clock in the hall chimed ten she used it as a signal, said her good-nights and went upstairs to the Players' Ghetto.

Was Adam in his room? The door was shut and she couldn't hear anything, but then since he came back he had not, as far as she knew, even turned on the radio she had brought over for him, though until then music had been part of his natural element, something he needed along with the air he breathed.

He had made it impossible for her to open that door, hold her arms out, talk to him ... Resolutely she banished these thoughts, and got herself to bed as quickly as she could before her mind could once again reassert its tyranny over her tired body.

Her pillow was cool and soft. She sighed in deep relief and was instantly asleep.

When she woke again it was still quite dark. She had no idea why, but she was suddenly and completely awake. There had not, it seemed to her, been any loud noise, but her heart was racing and she lay straining her ears for any whisper of sound.

That was what she heard; a whisper. That, she suddenly understood, was what she had heard before too, its very surreptitiousness triggering an alarm in her brain as a normal voice might not have done. Then there were faint creaks in the corridor, the breath of movement outside and then more definite creaks, which could be on the front stairs going down into the main part of the house.

Someone, or more than one person, given the whispering, was moving about in the darkness. She sat up cautiously, trying to make sense of it.

It could be perfectly innocuous. Perhaps Adam and Ben had both been wakeful, and one seeing the light under the other's door had suggested going down to make a cup of tea. Or a sandwich. Jackie's quiche, after all, had hardly been satisfying, and they would be whispering so as not to wake her. That would be entirely reasonable.

Only she didn't believe it. As animals can smell water, she could smell danger on the air.

Oddly, she wasn't afraid. She got out of bed, found slippers and tied her pink bathrobe firmly round her waist, like a soldier buckling on his belt as he dressed for battle. Then she opened the door cautiously.

There was no movement on the dark landing. Adam's door stood open, and when she peeped in it was just light enough to show that the bed was empty.

The night was warm, but she was shivering, though with anticipation more than fear. Her feet made no sound on the stairs as she trod deliberately close to the edges of the risers. From above she could see the faint gleam of the white squares on the floor of the empty hall.

On the landing she paused and for the first time caught the muffled sound of voices from somewhere on the floor below. The uncarpeted wooden stairs of the main flight did creak as she descended, but no one appeared or called out, 'Who's there?' and once she reached the tiles of the hall she could move silently again. There was a light showing under the door of the Green Salon, and it was from there that the sound of men talking came.

She paused. It could be, after all, that she was being melodramatic. Perhaps the other two hadn't gone to bed yet, and Adam had been persuaded to join them. Perhaps.

But she was in the grip of instinct now, and instinct dictated surprise. Feeling the flutters of nerves in her stomach, she seized the handle, turned it swiftly and flung open the door.

Shock transfixed them all. She in the doorway, gaping in stupefaction. Jonah Dancey, his back to the fireplace, eyes widening as he saw her.

And Adam, clad incongruously in bright blue pyjamas was standing near the sofa in the middle of the room. He had turned his head as the door opened, and there in his hand was a small, black, wicked-looking pistol.

20

'Penny, it's not what it seems. I swear it.' That was Adam.

'Penny, don't panic, love, just listen to me, all right?' Jonah's voice was warm, reassuring and very firm. 'Get yourself out of here. Get out, shut that door and keep well away from it. I can handle this, but I don't want anyone else getting hurt. Especially you.'

'Penny darling – '

Both men had their eyes fixed upon her. They were almost holding their breath, and each in his own way was exerting the dominating power of a forceful personality to compel her compliance. It must be something like this for a rabbit between competing stoats.

Only Penny wasn't mesmerised. She felt cool, detached, completely unafraid, as if she had been rehearsing for this, and the butterflies of nerves had disappeared now she had taken the stage. Her voice was perfectly steady as she said, 'What the hell do you both think you're doing?'

'Penny, I can explain – '

'Oh, sure you can, Adam.' Jonah took a step towards him. 'Just hand me the gun, Adam, and you can explain in comfort.'

'Oh no, Jonah. No, I don't think so.' Adam backed away, nearer to Penny, putting the sofa between himself and Jonah. 'I think I'll keep it for the moment.'

Jonah turned to Penny, his voice sharpening. 'Penny, he's too close. Get out – or else come over here behind me, now – '

'Behind you? She doesn't need protection from me, for God's sake! Penny, listen, will you – '

He wasn't actually pointing the gun at her, or, indeed, directly at Jonah. She snapped, 'Shut up, both of you. I'll take the gun.'

She had, perhaps, the advantage of surprise. She made a sudden snatch, and it was in her hand, solid, compact, blunt-nosed and heavy for its size.

Jonah started towards her then, apparently thinking the better of it, stopped.

'Freeze,' she ordered. 'Don't come near me, either of you.'

Penny was no trained shot, but she had handled guns before, had been given a few chances for target-shooting. This wasn't a type of pistol she was familiar with, but the principle was straightforward enough; with a glance she located the safety-catch, which was on, then braced her thumb against it as she covered the two men.

'Sit down, both of you, and let me explain the ground rules,' she said coldly. 'You can stop trying to manipulate me, just for a start. You sit on that chair, Jonah, and you on the end of the sofa there, Adam, where you're both in range. I would prefer to leave the safety-catch down, but I shall raise it if I feel threatened.'

Wordlessly they complied. She did not sit herself, but found a chairback at the right level to brace the pistol. There was no saying how long this might take and, she thought clinically, tired arm muscles would affect her aim. If it came to that.

'Right,' she said. 'I want to know exactly why I seem to have stumbled into the last act of a melodrama, and then, not being a stage heroine, once I'm in possession of the facts I shall simply

211

phone the police. Let's start with you, Jonah. Why aren't you in London?'

'I was, but Adam phoned me earlier this evening.'

Penny had heard him phone someone; she nodded. 'Go on.'

'He sounded – unbalanced, I suppose, is the word, saying really strange, wild things and making bizarre allegations. He wanted to see me tomorrow, and I agreed happily – the sooner we got things straightened out, the better. But then later – well, I couldn't get you out of my head, Penny. If he actually flipped, anything could happen. So I drove down here, broke in at the back door, I'm afraid, then went upstairs and persuaded him to come and talk to me, well away from you. I couldn't bear it if – '

He stopped as if he had said too much, and looking up met Penny's fiercely searching gaze with eyes as clear and tender as they had been the night she looked up at him in the moonlight.

'Penny, you mustn't let him fool you. Jonah's dangerous, seriously dangerous. He's killed three times already – '

'I've warned you both – leave me out of this.' She was icy, implacable. 'Jonah, keep quiet now. You'll get your turn. Adam, you tell your story.'

Jonah, she noticed, sat back in his chair, but Adam, leaning forward with his elbows on his knees and his hands clasped, was almost vibrating with tension, like a violin string too tightly tuned. Instinctively she grasped the pistol more firmly.

'This could take some time. I don't think I've got it wholly straight in my own mind . . .' He paused, as if arranging his thoughts.

'That summer, you spurned the Players' Ghetto and stayed with Dom at his cottage for a night or two, Jonah. And after that, the two of you made jokes about having a secret. Dom didn't tell me what it was – he was always mocking my suburban morality – and to be honest I didn't think it was something I would want to know.

'But Anna did. Anna wanted to know everything that went on, in case it might affect Eden, and she was constantly sniffing around.

'Then Dom was killed, and Jonah somehow suddenly had the money to go to America and study with Rubetskoi – what did you tell me again, Jonah? An uncle had died and left you the money?'

His look at the other man was coldly challenging, but Jonah met his eyes stolidly. 'That's right. Uncle Matthew. Lived in Lowestoft.'

Ignoring him, Adam went on, 'I haven't thought about it since, until I heard what Letty said. And meantime Anna was dead, and

212

somehow I was in the dock with two damning pieces of evidence against me: the pen and the keys.'

'And the picture and the baton,' Penny reminded him.

Adam put his head in his hands. 'Yes, those. God, Penny, you know how angry I was, how despairing. But if you don't know me well enough to know where the limits are for me, there's something badly wrong with our marriage.'

'Perhaps there is. Go on,' she prompted stonily.

'I went over it all in my head a thousand times. I didn't kill Anna, I wasn't in the cottage, I didn't have a pen like that, I didn't have the keys. I have gone almost mad, thinking about it.

'Until tonight. Until Maurice said that about Anna going too far, and suddenly it all fell into place.'

'Oh, please!' Jonah sat back further in the chair and crossed his legs in a pantomime of impatience.

Adam turned to look at him. 'She was blackmailing you, Jonah, wasn't she? She knew something, or guessed it at any rate, and it was a risk you couldn't take.

'We all wondered why on earth you had agreed to come here, with the Ramillies Festival so low in musical esteem. And she was talking about you being a fixture every year, so you'd never be off the hook.'

'It's ingenious, I'll give you that.' Jonah was unruffled.

'So then I thought about the pen. You called me up to London last week, Jonah, insisting on some footling final conditions I had to sign up to. There was a pen on the blotter – a yellow pen, I seem to remember – laid out for me to use; you didn't touch it, nor did Larry. You were planning it all, even then.

'And as for the keys, we stood together in the garden for half an hour. I was carrying my jacket. We stood side by side, you had your arm round me, you had your hand at my side. Not difficult.

'Then, of course, there was that sad, prying child who had hinted in her paper that Anna had passed on her knowledge, and was giving out her home address to anyone who would take it. Nothing easier than to drive round there when you went in to fetch the papers, perhaps, and then let poor weak Gary Stone carry the can.

'But tell me, Jonah, tell me,' and now his voice was rising, with a hard, angry edge to it, 'how did you square it with the way you had just played the *Emperor*?'

Penny had listened silently, never taking steely eyes off his face. She turned to the other man.

213

'All right, Jonah, it's your turn now.'

'It's clever, that's the trouble,' Jonah said ruefully. 'It's all very clever, except of course that he was the person who knew about Dom's theft – they were very close, those two, as you know, Penny – and he needed the money if he was to have his chance as a conductor. Music means more to him than anything – I needn't tell you that.

'Then, of course, he was in love with you. I don't blame him – how could I? – but it was certainly convenient to, shall we say, eliminate the competition.'

Penny bit her lip. Adam was listening with head bent; he did not look up.

'And the reason I came to play at Ramillies was the fact that Anna needed me. I owed a lot to Eden and I was sorry for her. But if she was talking about a permanent fixture, then I can only say it was typical Anna to believe what she wanted to believe.

'As for the pen and the keys, it's so much nonsense. It's the sort of far-fetched story you would have to come up with once you'd made such a catastrophic blunder.

'But leave all that aside, Penny.' The way he spoke her name was a caress. 'What is incontrovertible, what you have seen with your own eyes, is that he had the gun.'

Incredibly, she had managed to forget that. With a leaden feeling about her heart she said, 'Where did you get the gun, Adam?'

She had expected an angry outburst. Instead, he sounded almost puzzled as he said, 'Well, when Jonah and I came into the room, he said to me, "There's something you ought to see. Go over to the sofa and lift up that cushion."

'So I did, and there was the gun. He told me to pick it up – '

'Why?' she said quietly. 'Why would he do that, Adam, if he was the murderer – hand you the gun?'

'I *don't know!*' His voice rose in anger and frustration; again she found herself gripping the gun more tightly.

'Why indeed?' Jonah refused to be perturbed. 'Thank God you got it from him, Penny. Keep him covered while I go and phone the police.'

'No!' cried Adam as Jonah rose and 'No,' said Penny. 'Stay where you are, Jonah. I need to think.'

'Of course, of course.' He sat down again. 'It's tough, isn't it, Penny? You're a loyal person, and because you've loved him you want to believe in him. But then, remember that you loved Dom. It's hardly a guarantee of virtue, is it?'

Again she bit her lip. She looked uncertainly from one to the other, Jonah so solidly reassuring, Adam so febrile and nervous with his grey eyes burning.

Pressing home his advantage, Jonah went on. 'Just go by the things you know about, Penny. You know the police have charged him on that evidence and the motive he demonstrated. You saw him holding the gun. You know, anyway, if you think about it, that I wasn't even here when Anna was killed. I spoke to Judy from London in the morning, and then Larry brought me down after we'd lunched together, remember?'

Of course she did, and through the desolate, icy despair that now seized her Penny recognised at last that she had truly loved Adam, had believed in him in her heart – but then, she had been a fool before. The knot of misery grew until it was a physical pain in the centre of her being.

But whatever would the Colonel say? She had a duty, and she must fulfil it. She was on the point of saying to Jonah, 'All right then, phone the police,' when suddenly a voice came into her head. It was high-pitched, affected, the voice of the woman dripping with diamonds and condescension: 'I always say it seems impossible that Ramillies is only an hour from London.'

Thinking aloud, she said, 'But Jonah, there's no reason why you couldn't have been here at nine thirty, and still back in time to lunch with Larry in London. You told Judy you were phoning from London, but you could have been anywhere. You could just have been checking that Anna would be at the cottage when she said.

'And everything else – well, Dom used to make fun of Adam to me because he was so straight. I let him, because I wasn't seeing straight myself, but I'm seeing straight now.

'So stay there, Jonah. I don't know why you let him have the gun, but I suspect it's part of the same setting up that you did with the pen and the keys. And that's what I'm going to tell the police.'

Jonah's face, as she spoke, changed as disbelief gave way to anger. He got up, moved towards her; Adam too sprang to his feet.

Penny did not waver. 'Don't move, either of you. I'll fire, Jonah. I mean it.' With a flick of her thumb she took off the safety-catch, aimed the gun and braced her wrist. 'I may not be a very good shot, but I can guarantee to do serious damage at this range.'

215

A curious expression that was almost pain crossed Jonah's face. 'And to think I had flattered myself that you had a *tendresse* for me!' The he threw back his head and laughed harshly. 'Oh, Penny, what a naïve child! You don't imagine it's loaded, do you?'

Without a second's hesitation she pulled the trigger. There was a click, and the next moment Jonah had it in his hand with the magazine lever pulled down. He deftly produced a small brass case from his pocket, snapped it into the receiver and flipped the lever back, locking it in place.

'Of course, it is now,' he drawled, then he took her hand, still limp from shock. 'You'd have killed me, though, wouldn't you, without compunction. My admiration for your aplomb knows no bounds.' He raised her hand to his lips and she snatched it away and wiped it on her robe, like a child.

He sighed. 'Penny, Penny! So very sad. We could have made sweet music together, you and I.'

His eyes were hard and cold and inhuman, and then she was afraid, she was dreadfully, horribly afraid, flying across the room to Adam, to stand in front of him

He put her firmly to one side. 'Don't get in the way, Pen. This is between us.'

'Well, it should have been.' Jonah sounded regretful, almost normal. 'That was what I had intended, until you came in doing your SAS impersonation, Penny. I had got Adam's prints nicely on the gun so when I took it from him and shot him it would have been in a struggle.

'But I wanted you, Penny, and if only you had trusted me you would have been free to dance in the moonlight whenever you wanted, and Adam would have been on his way to a nice safe prison sentence.

'But you've really left me no option. It grieves me, you know, it grieves me more than I can say. Such a wonderful talent lost to music, Adam – and we were such a perfect partnership. Will I ever, I wonder, play quite as well as that again? But you must be first, I think Adam, then Penny – '

He raised the pistol. Penny thought wildly of charging it, throwing herself in the way, but Adam had her in an iron grip.

He tried to play for time. 'Jonah, let's talk – '

Jonah shook his head. 'No talk, Adam,' he said, steadied his aim and fired.

Penny had shut her eyes, waiting for the explosion that would

216

blow her world apart. At the sullen, futile click, she opened them again, uncomprehending, but already Adam had catapulted himself across the room, chopping down on Jonah's wrist and sending the gun spinning across the parquet to land on the Aubusson carpet before Jonah had recovered from the shock of failure.

Penny dived towards it but Adam yelled, 'No! It could go off! Help me here!'

It was hard to separate the two men as they fell to the floor, rolling and wrestling, but she flung herself into the mêlée, grabbing at Jonah's arms, scratching his face, kicking, punching, biting. His powerful musician's hands were strong, though, as he grappled for Adam's throat, ignoring the injuries she was managing to inflict. He was a bigger man than Adam, heavier by more than a stone.

She heard the door open, and without loosing her hold on Jonah's wrist looked up to see Ben standing, astonished, above them.

'What the – '

'Ben, help – help us!' she found breath to scream. 'Jonah's the killer – '

'They're – they're in this together!' Jonah's breathing, too, was laboured; where Penny's nails had torn his cheek, blood welled up in the scratches. 'Trust me, Ben – '

Ben's brilliant dark eyes surveyed the tableau. 'I always thought you were a two-faced bastard, Jonah,' he said, almost conversationally.

There was a Victorian mahogany music stand beside the piano, a solid piece. Seizing it like a club, Ben said, 'This is for Dominic Leigh,' and brought it down hard on Jonah's head.

21

'Told you before he was lucky it went off at all, didn't I?' Ron, the ballistics expert, was overweight, middle-aged and balding, but he was cradling the pistol in his huge hands with all the tenderness of a small girl fondling a hamster. He was also looking smug. 'Told you he was lucky last time he could do more than just shout *Bang!* What happened this time – he forgot to shout?' He laughed merrily.

Peckham and Canning looked at him sourly. It had been a trying morning. On hearing of Jonah Dancey's arrest, the reaction of the

Chief Constable's wife had been, apparently, theatrical to say the very least, which had put him in no very receptive frame of mind for their explanations as to why only an accident of chemistry had prevented two more murders on his patch.

'Little beauty, isn't she?' Ron crooned. 'Beretta 9mm, Modello 1934. That was pretty much what I reckoned, remember? Neat, compact, accurate enough at close quarters, slip it in your jacket pocket and it wouldn't even spoil the line of your natty gents' suiting.'

'Reasonable that it could have been a war souvenir?' Peckham asked.

'Spot on. Our lads half-inched every one they could get their hands on – North Africa, usually. Tank regiment, maybe?'

Peckham looked enquiringly at Canning, who nodded. 'We checked. Bert Wells was with the Hussars – Prince Albert's Own.'

'That would be right – they were there. New design, this was. British Army issue was a revolver – an Enfield or a Webley or something like that, bigger and heavier. A Lamborghini, this was, compared to a Rover. Self-loading; nifty little magazine, seven bullets.' He released the small brass case, still smeary from finger-print powder. 'But not one of these cartridges detonated; gunpowder was damp, see? So he was lucky before, like I said.'

'It depends,' said Canning tartly, 'what you define as lucky. But the original bullets were definitely fired from this gun?'

'Pistol. That's right, not a doubt. We fired some off for comparison and I can show you the striations under the microscope, if you like,' Ron offered eagerly, and his face fell when the two officers declined the treat.

They weren't looking for ways to pass the time. Dancey, in custody with the air of one who, despite being battered, bitten, scratched and bruised, is indulgently taking part in some ludicrous charade, had Dunstable primed at his elbow. He had readily admitted to selling a Poussin at Sotheby's, the property of his bachelor uncle Matthew Dancey, deceased, of Lowestoft. With Dunstable's approval, he pointed out that as Matthew Dancey's estate – willed, of course, to his nephew – had been valued only at some £2000, the tax authorities should have got their cut, but since it was some three years before he realised the value of the painting it simply had not occurred to him. He would now, of course, be happy to make restitution.

'You bet he would,' Canning said bitterly as they discussed this on the way back to headquarters. 'Nothing he'd like better than to get off with a fine and a slap on the wrist. And we can't prove where the bloody thing came from – the old bird's not going to be around to identify it, is she?'

'By all accounts, no. Diane's been keeping in touch, but they're pretty gloomy.'

There was a long silence. Then Peckham said, struggling to take the positive view, 'Still, even if we do have a problem on the motive there's the gun evidence linking him to the first two murders.'

'Depends how convincing the Beaumonts are when they put them on the stand. I can just see some smartass like Dunstable' – there was particular savagery in the description – 'tying her in knots about choosing to believe her husband instead of Dancey. You know as well as I do that he's claimed already he was obliged to defend himself because she got it wrong.'

There are few things more exasperating, when you have pointed out a silver lining, than to encounter determination to find the black cloud outside. With an irritable glance at his colleague, Peckham tried again.

'Fingerprints on the magazine of the pistol,' he suggested. 'Nice ones, they show up well on brass. They've taken some pretty pictures.'

Canning sniffed. 'He'll find some excuse – it fell out in the struggle and he picked it up, or something. He'll make it sound good too. When he looked me in the eye, even with Penny Beaumont's claw marks on his face and a black eye, I almost believed him myself. And I can't see that we can even charge him with Moxon's murder. We've got the rope but no evidence that he cut it, and there's nothing to place him at the crime scene.'

If you could graduate in gloom, Canning would come out *summa cum laude*, and Peckham was no match for him. If you can't beat them, join them.

He sighed heavily. 'No. And now we've released Stone there'll be another compensation claim out of next year's budget.'

He sighed again. 'Maybe we'll have to get in the psychics after all,' he muttered elliptically and sank into morose silence.

Outside they were rounding up the peacocks. Maurice Hicks had given orders for them to be taken away, and the air quivered with the almost human screams of outrage and terror as they were

219

bundled into the van that would take them to a local wildfowl park.

In the Green Salon the flowers in the vase in the fireplace were in serious decay now, the fallen petals browning into a messy sludge, the water slimy and stinking.

Diane Braithwaite, shifting uncomfortably in the chair beside the fireplace, had mentioned the smell, but beyond murmuring something bizarre about festering lilies and weeds, Penny Beaumont had seemed unconcerned.

The face of the girl – no, Diane corrected herself, the *woman* opposite, showed the marks of last night's shocking events. Her eyelids were heavy and swollen, and under the dark blue eyes delicate blue circles showed through the flawless skin, pale almost to translucency this morning. The cotton shirt she was wearing was a soft blue-grey and she looked, as always, quite perfect for the situation in which she found herself; if you had employed Central Casting they couldn't have done better.

Adam Beaumont had gone in to HQ to get things sorted out, but Diane, still trapped in this irritating fiction of her friendship with Penny, had been sent out here.

Penny had given her statement with a military precision which sat oddly with her fragile appearance. Diane recorded it, almost without comment, then stowed notebook and pen in her bag and slung it over her shoulder.

'Thanks, Penny. That's very clear. Look in and sign it at headquarters tomorrow, will you?' She rose to go.

'Sure.' Penny too stood up and, a little self-consciously, they shook hands. The light and the dark blue eyes met, and after a second Penny smiled wryly.

'You really don't like me, do you, Diane?'

This was where, as a policewoman, Diane should have murmured some soothing platitude, but then platitudes had never been her style.

'I'm uneasy with you,' she said with her customary directness. 'You always look the part so bloody perfectly, and I can't work out what's going on underneath. I'm not keen on sugared almonds either – all sweet pastel shades on the outside then tough and bitter when you get below the shell.'

Penny winced. 'I should have known better than to put myself at your mercy. Mercy's for wimps as far as you're concerned, isn't it?'

A slow flush mottled Diane's cheeks. It was surprising, given how straightforward she was with other people, how seldom plain-speaking came her way, and now the ancient and beautiful phrase, 'to do justly and to love mercy', was ringing in her ears like a reproach.

'I'm – I'm sorry about that interview,' she said uncomfortably. 'I was unnecessarily brutal, and if it's any consolation, I've really regretted it – along with one or two other recent blunders I've made.'

The other woman made an impatient gesture. 'Oh, let's not start listing all the things we regret. I daresay they're expecting you back at the police station before the middle of next week.

'I accept the criticism. I've surprised myself over the last couple of days. Up till then, I was always trying to be what someone else wanted me to be, to the point where even I don't know who I really am. I thought with Dominic that I was a free spirit, but probably that was an illusion too.

'So what I do admire about you is that you are emphatically your own person.'

'Yes, I suppose I am,' Diane said slowly. 'For what it's worth. But everybody likes you.'

Their eyes met again, and almost reluctantly they smiled.

'Well, as my least favourite workmate likes to say, you can't have the penny and the bun,' Diane said, and this time they laughed. They would never truly understand each other; they would never be friends, but for her at least a ghost had been laid.

They were in the hall when the phone rang, and Penny answered it. In the course of a brief conversation her face brightened; she was smiling as she put down the receiver.

'That's very good news. Dear Letty Wells is responding to treatment at last, and they think she might be well enough for a visit in a day or two.'

Diane, who had turned to go, spun round at her words. 'Letty Wells? I can tell you, that will be the best news my super has had since England won the World Cup.

'And your little chat will have to wait. We're on the trail of the Poussin and once we get hold of it we'll be camped outside her door to have her swear an affidavit identifying it the minute she's strong enough.'

*

221

As the door closed behind Penny Beaumont, Letty Wells settled back into her pillows and shut her eyes thankfully.

She had done well, these last few days. 'You're doing well, Letty,' they kept telling her, topping up the bottle for the drip that was strapped into her poor old bruised arm. They felt positively proprietorial about her, because they'd brought her back, after all, hadn't they?

Yesterday she'd been able to talk to the police and identify the little picture she'd never expected to see again. It was nice enough, but she felt sick looking at it, as if Death himself were peering over the shepherdess's shoulder. Still, the police had got what they needed from her now – just in case, they had said, but never finished the sentence.

Today she'd seen lovely Penny, poor lamb, struggling to 'find herself', whatever that might mean, like someone peeling an onion looking for its core. She was haunted by guilt and the spectre of her lack of judgement, ashamed to go back to darling Adam because she hadn't trusted him as she should. Well, no one could do her learning for her, and at least she'd got over Dominic, poor, beautiful Dominic with his desperate greed for every sensation life could offer, as if he had always known the brevity of his allotted span.

She understood Penny's problem, because Eden Hartington had had something of that same unscrupulous charm, and in the days when she had been a wild young thing herself their affair had been just as impossibly romantic. When Eden had thrown her over she had wanted to die; her darling Bert had needed to be patient for a long time until she learned that, after all, their love was not only different from that glamour and excitement but much more wonderful. That was what she had been determined to explain to Penny; she wasn't sure that she was quite ready to hear it yet, but Letty could see with the clarity which was a recent gift that sooner or later she would understand.

And the last thing was Bert, Bert whose thoughtless wrong-doing had given occasion for all these mortal sins, Bert, without whom whatever hereafter there might be would be meaningless and empty. Would it count, that she had tried so hard to atone? Under her closed eyelids, tears spilled slowly down her wrinkled, wasted cheeks.

The darkness was there again, a whole ocean of darkness, deeper and more velvety and more enticing than ever, and this time she had no duty to struggle. She drifted on wave after wave, further and further out.

Was it no more than a sunset-touch, that she thought she heard somewhere a trumpet sounding for her, and notions of Dominic, and Bert, and forgiveness flickered together in her tiring brain?